# THE B[illegible]E SAND AND THE FLOWER

# THE BOY, THE SAND AND THE FLOWER

Clare Linda Roberts

The Book Guild

First published in Great Britain in 2025 by
The Book Guild Ltd
Unit E2 Airfield Business Park,
Harrison Road, Market Harborough,
Leicestershire. LE16 7UL
Tel: 0116 2792299
www.bookguild.co.uk
Email: info@bookguild.co.uk
X: @bookguild



Typeset in 11pt Minion Pro

Printed and bound in Great Britain by 4edge Limited

ISBN 978 1835741 382

British Library Cataloguing in Publication Data.
A catalogue record for this book is available from the British Library.

*To all who lost their lives at sea*
*inspired by their belief in democracy.*

# Outskirts of Agordat, Eritrea, August 2014

Osman watched Sebhat's face as he examined his shallow basket; heavy eyes touring its circumference examining the smoothness of weave, precision of the blue wave curling up from the bottom towards sharp yellow triangles above. Behind his greying moustache and beard, Sebhat's soft red lips moved, 'Sun and sea, umm.'

He put it down, Osman's heart sank. *It's not good enough.* The sound of rain pounding the tin roof and gushing onto the dirt outside returned.

'Nice idea: a wave; not easy.' Sebhat looked at the inside. 'Smooth and tidy, well done.'

Osman relaxed. 'Thank you.'

'Better to take your time and do things properly.'

It had taken three days.

When they sat side by side in the middle of the workshop, Sebhat's hands were never still. There was no hesitation about which tool to pick up. Thin strands of doum palm flowed from his fingers coiling around the dry grass. He circled the basket in one sinuous movement building the chequered rope into triangles or spirals of vivid colours. Osman longed to be able to do that.

'Okay, you can go higher but no bigger; build a circular basket with a lid, like that.' Sebhat pointed to a basket as big as a cauldron then folded his hands across his grey and white striped belly.

'Lunch time,' he said and disappeared through a side door to join his wife in their house leaving Osman in the lean-to that served as a workshop.

Osman was glad to have the place to himself. It had been a good morning. He lifted the flap of his canvas bag and smelt his mother's flatbread and its spicy vegetable filling. There were a couple of little bananas and some dates. He was hungry. Osman was as thin as a reed and still growing. He went to the front of the workshop and pushed his beaker out from under the shelter of the corrugated roof. It filled in minutes. He settled back on his leather pouffe snug under the comforting sound of August's rain watering his mother's tomatoes, swelling seeds and stems to reach for the sun and make fruit. It drowned all other noise and reduced traffic to camels and donkeys as roads became streams. Few wanted to venture out or expose their goods to the downpour.

He thought of Sebhat and Faven huddled in their back parlour instead of enjoying the arbour in their garden. He wondered if Sebhat was telling her about his basket. It was only a few months ago that Sebhat had asked Osman's father if he could help when his second daughter joined her sister in Keren with her husband abandoning the business. Basket making was women's work but Osman's father and Sebhat had been friends since childhood and Sebhat had watched Osman grow, seen his artwork, his nimble fingers and how restless he was when he first left school.

Osman liked the workshop with its bunches of dried leaves, bark and berries where Faven made dyes and prepared the fibres. Mysterious bottles and little bowls sat on a shelf above an old gas burner that was surrounded by pans. In the other corner, palm leaves, papyrus and dried grasses were stacked in bundles beside a tin bath of water.

Throughout the day, Sebhat and Osman sat among bases, half-finished bowls and lids waiting for materials or inspiration.

Pliers, secateurs, hooks and large needles were set out on a low table for Sebhat. They didn't share tools, Sebhat didn't want his flow to be interrupted so he presented Osman with his own set when he started. It sat on the floor by his side, full of promise. Osman traced the fat curve of the basket Sebhat had told him to copy. He liked to feel its generous swell in his hands and he understood why it was the most popular shape.

Baskets for sale were hung around the entrance or set out on tables and shelves at the sides, a treasure trove of colour and design. Osman's favourite had a deep fuchsia lid cut by a perfectly executed spiral of jet black and, curling up from its base, pink flames outlined in black. Baskets of every shape and size were decorated with triangles, circles and stripes in vivid primary colours. Every design precisely executed, every curve balanced; works of art sought by galleries and museums all over the world. Each one was immaculate and unique. Their bold patterns adapted to the contours they followed. Osman wanted to make something as perfect as they were, something beautiful and useful, something to be proud of.

Sebhat was a good teacher. Osman knew he could experiment, create his own design. When they returned Faven brought him half a latticed mango.

'For you,' she said happy to see his face light up.

'Thank you.'

He looked guiltily at Sebhat who was settling down to work ignoring them. He bent back the skin and bit off cube after cube of the sweet spicy treat, held his fingers out under the rain and dried them on his baggy red shorts before picking up a length of palm.

'Any ideas?' asked Sebhat.

Osman looked at Faven. 'I'm thinking of gerberas, can I have pink, purple and yellow?'

She smiled. 'That will be bright and cheerful, a bit of a challenge for me. What have I got here?' She lifted down jars of dried petals, buds and leaves.

‘Think about developing your own style; your signature,’ said Sebhat.

Osman picked through bundles of papyrus and palm. He chose the most pliable palm strands and started on his base. Sebhat was creating a high round table. Osman’s head filled with gerberas, swathes of brilliant colour in the foothills of the mountains where Mariam, his elder sister, took him exploring or dotted around the edges of fields or plots of land they passed – orange, yellow, red, purple – their cheerful faces open to the sun. He pictured their petals and big frilly hearts and no longer heard the rain thundering on the roof as his fingers spun strong threads around long thin bundles of dry grass.

A land rover stopped outside and a man in a suit jumped down and ran for cover holding a newspaper over his head. He was followed by a boy in jeans and sweatshirt sheltering under a magazine.

Sebhat beamed and spread his arms, smiling. ‘Welcome, welcome,’ he said.

The man stamped his feet on the dry floor. ‘Selam, good to be back,’ he said.

‘So, this is your son?’ asked Sebhat looking at the boy’s halo of bushy hair.

The man put a hand on his son’s back and ushered him forward. ‘This is Mike, Mister Solomon.’

The boy took Sebhat’s hand and murmured, ‘Selam.’

Faven was hovering inside the workshop in a long lavender robe with a panel of white embroidery down the front.

‘Greetings, how are you?’ asked the newcomer delighted to see her.

Faven smiled. ‘We are all well, thank you.’

‘Please sit with us to refresh yourselves my friends, it has been a long time,’ said Sebhat.

‘Too long, too long. Never mind, we’re here now with an empty car and a full wallet.’

Sebhat inclined his head with a gentle smile and waved them to the back of the workshop where a tray of tea and little pastries waited. They settled around Sebhat's table. The boy sipped his cordial and took some bani before leaving the men to talk. He wandered desultorily around the workshop occasionally poking something as if he were in a laboratory. Osman watched the boy's simulated interest, his attempt to muster enthusiasm and wondered what would excite him. They were probably the same age, perhaps the boy was a bit younger.

He stopped in front of Osman.

'Hello,' he said.

'Hello.' Osman looked up from the boy's black and white leather trainers to his pale detached face. His own bare feet, washed out T-shirt and shorts set them worlds apart but it did not bother either of them.

'How long have you worked here?' asked the boy in Arabic.

'Five months.'

'My father says you make the best baskets here.'

'Check them out,' said Osman nodding his head towards the display at the entrance. 'You can take them down if you want.'

'Thanks.'

He went to the front and Osman watched him pick up the fuschia coloured basket and turn it round in his hands then put it very carefully down. He looked at the others, animated for the first time, picking up one after another for closer scrutiny, too involved to notice that the two men were on their feet. His father looked over his shoulder at the blue waves and yellow triangles of the basket in his son's hands.

'Not bad, eh?'

'I like them.'

'Want to help me choose?'

'Sure.'

He chose bold, different designs that Osman liked too, including the fuschia basket with the black spiral lid, so, it would be crossing the sea to England with all the other baskets, a different world, what would it do there? Father and son chose basket after basket, reluctant to pass any over. Sebhat stacked and wrapped their treasures.

The workshop, Africa, was an unreal world to the boy and he and his father represented the same to Osman. Their fine clothes and hired car served no purpose in Osman's world. Like Sebhat, he simply wanted them to buy their baskets and show the world the beauty of Eritrea. Once the deal was done and the baskets were loaded into the car, Osman and Faven manned umbrellas to keep their customers dry while they returned to the car.

'Until the next time,' called their happy customer through the car window and they were surfing down the street leaving their paper and magazine behind.

Osman tucked them under his pouffe and spent his lunch times engrossed in their dynamic, expansive worlds, grateful for his bit of English and Mariam's help with it. There were photos of concerts with thousands of eager white faces turned up to hidden stages and pictures of parties but not the kind of parties Osman knew – birthdays, wedding, or child naming ceremonies – family affairs run by parents. He sometimes met his friends for a drink in the local café but there were no clubs or bars and girls wouldn't be allowed out unsupervised anyway. His only music came from the local radio.

There were film reviews as well. Films he would like to see but the cinema in Keren was eighty-two kilometres away and he didn't know if those films would be allowed. There were articles on cheap travel; hostels, camping, hitch-hiking. You could go anywhere the world beckoned, anything was possible. But in the end, it seemed a frenetic world where speed reigned. People cycled without going anywhere or travelled in cars too fast to enjoy the crops in the fields or see the wildlife. There were boats shooting spray; they weren't going to catch fish or see the coastline or beaches. The one trip Osman had to the sea with a friend of his father's, he brought home fish enough for the whole family and felt like a king.

Everything looked artificial to Osman especially the expressions on people's faces. They weren't smiling at each other or anyone in particular and the fashion photos with their white cellophane faces cut by thin red smiles wouldn't convince him to buy their goods even if he could. Someone was complaining about bullying on Facebook, Osman was glad he didn't have to worry about that, he had seen very little bullying; teasing, pranks, but nothing consistent. His school mates and friends all got along okay. Around Agordat, the land supplied their needs, the sun shone, the rain came, the rivers and mountains were full of life, there was nothing to be angry about. He was curious about Facebook though. He'd heard of people making friends miles away, sending photos, talking to each other. They didn't have a television or a camera at home. Osman shrugged his shoulders, he didn't really need photos, they were all together anyway, apart from Mariam. Yes, it would be good to have her photo but he'd rather have the real thing. He turned a page, there was a picture of students carrying banners protesting about racial prejudice. Osman was glad that he was not prejudiced or his friends and family.

The father's paper was more serious, articles about leaders of state, their meetings, ideas, it was all up for debate. It spoke of countries all over the world, not just Asmara, from what he could make out change was possible in this world. The paper gave a glimpse of a different world, the variety of mankind around the globe but it spoke of policies that had nothing to do with life in Eritrea. Osman's ideas of Europe came from hearsay, stories from visitors, friends and family. No one travelled far or heard very much about the world outside Eritrea. They lived an open, shared life, every home was their home and the village was friend and family. There was little need for anything more.

He didn't know whether he envied their life or not; the trainers not, cool though they were. It was more the feeling behind it all, what it amounted to, that he couldn't put his finger on – the feeling that anything goes, everything is possible, that young people could, should go beyond their neighbourhoods but Osman didn't know whether he wanted that much choice.

At the end of the week, after wishing Sebhat and Faven 'selamat,'[1] he wrapped the magazines in plastic to keep them dry and took them home. His T-shirt clung to his ribs and his shorts were soaked in minutes but it was not cold and the air was fresher. He did not mind the long walk home; it gave him time to adjust. At least he didn't have to water his mother's vegetables. His little brother ran out to meet him.

'Wani!'

'Osman!'

Osman swept him up and swung him round.

'What are you doing out in the rain?' asked Osman dumping him down.

Wani's thick dark hair was already soggy.

'I like it.'

Wani stamped his rubber sandal in the water streaming past their house. Osman dodged the splashes. He knew why Wani was there. He started a pretend boxing match, poking him in the ribs then the shoulder. Wani wriggled away and leapt up his back. Osman supported his bottom and piggy-backed him through the door. The floor was covered in fresh palm leaves, cool and clean and their mother was folding a kaftan by her sewing machine.

'Another one done.'

She sewed for a shop as well as growing fruit and vegetables to sell at the market.

'Wani, what do you think you're doing running out in the

---

1 Goodbye.

rain? Osman!' She opened her arms then thought better of it at the sight of his soaking T-shirt.

'Hi, Ma.' Osman looked apologetically down at his sodden clothes.

'Go get out of those wet things, both of you.' She looked exasperatedly at Wani. 'Dinner's nearly ready.'

Osman could smell it; rich and savoury, it was tsebbi.[2] He was ready for that.

'Hi, Dad.' His father was carefully loading a log onto the fire under the pot.

'Good week? How's Sebhat?'

'I finished my basket, he liked it.'

His mother looked up from mixing dough. 'Your sea and sun?' she laughed. 'You'll have to do moon and stars next.'

Osman shuffled off his clothes and hung them on a rail by his mattress. He rubbed himself down and pulled on a T-shirt and sweat suit bottoms.

His mother poked her head out of the door.

'Delina,' she shouted.

'Coming, five minutes.'

They all had their jobs. Osman's younger sister, Delina looked after the goats. Genet and Lemlem were gentle creatures who got along quite well and were no trouble apart from when their curiosity got the better of them. They kept the family in milk and yoghurt. His mother dropped spoonfuls of dough onto a griddle, let them spread then flipped them over and stacked them on a plate. She arranged thin slices of cucumber, tomato and pepper on a wide flat basket around a bowl of minted yoghurt. Delina came in and rubbed her face and hair with a towel.

'Hi,' she said to Osman and settled on a cushion.

'No market tomorrow, Salma?' Osman's father asked his wife.

---

2 Beef stew.

'I'm not sure, it depends on the rain. We'll see what it's like in the morning.' She filled an injera with stew for him. They helped themselves to salad and pickles and ate in silence by the light of the fire.

The sound of the rain on the thatched roof was softer, more like a sigh then a shout.

'Have you heard from Mariam?' Osman asked.

Their meals were more subdued since Mariam left. They all missed her. Delina looked hopefully from her mother to her father's face.

'Nothing, not a word,' said her father bitterly.

'It's not like her,' said her mother.

'It's final year, I suppose she's working for the exams.' Osman excused her although he was even more disappointed than his parents.

Salma scraped out the last of the meat.

'Osman?' she asked. He shook his head.

'Dawit?'

'Delina needs it more than I do,' said their father. 'Give it to her.'

Delina bowed her head embarrassed by her father's acknowledgement of her womanhood. Salma filled a flatbread and handed it to her daughter with a smile. Delina was glad to sink her teeth into it. She had run all the way home from school pushing through the rain, feeling its force wash her ready for her other life, home and family, their smallholding. After the meal they sat round the fire, more to share its glow, friendly crackle and shift as it settled into ashes, than for warmth.

The sound of the rain on the roof diminished to a whisper and finally stopped. Osman went out to savour the peace that these little lulls brought. Lemlem bleated from the bottom of the garden. Her pale coat shone through the gloom. He took a twisted cassava from the reject bin and passed young tomato plants, peppers, chillies and corn, that he had helped to plant, on the other side of his father's low stone wall. He held the root while Lemlem bit into it. Genet butted his backside until he gave her what was left.

Over the wall at the end of the garden, a full moon shone on the familiar pleats and folds of the Beni Amer mountains. Their outline softened by the burgeoning green of another baptism. He and Mariam had discovered protected corners hidden between high outcrops in those green foothills and springs that trickled until the end of October falling into rocky basins surrounded by clover, poppies and swaying grasses for just three-four months. They had so many adventures together. Mariam would stuff paper, matches, a tripod and a tin into her 'sack of surprises,' – a cotton bag gathered at the top with red cord, trellised by bright pink, purple, yellow, red, and green diamonds. They would eat left over breakfast of fava beans mashed with onion, tomato, lemon juice and chilli spread on injera and topped with yoghurt. But it wasn't the food or even the fire or the hot tin mug to burn away the night cold, it was the places they found that made those trips special; the crevice where they sheltered from a sandstorm and disturbed a snake that came out hissing. Mariam had picked up a handful of gravel and pelted it. The snake scurried away followed by a bombardment of stones.

Osman had shouted, 'Don't do that!'

'That's a saw-scaled viper, you'd be dead in minutes if it took its spite out on you. Then where would we be?' She had rubbed the top of his head, pulled his face up to hers and kissed his forehead.

'Precious, beautiful boy.'

She always made him feel special. She made everyone feel special.

He had replied, 'You're the special one, Mariam.' It was true, Mariam was clever. She could do anything, nothing ever phased her. She made everything seem easy.

Osman turned and looked at their hut, huddled in the dark;

damp and miserable as if it were in mourning for Mariam, the lost one. Inside, his parents were already in bed and Delina was sitting on her mattress hugging her knees.

'You all right, Delina?' he whispered.

'Lonely,' she said rocking.

'Mariam?'

'Ummm.' she nodded too close to tears to speak.

'She'll be home soon, don't worry.'

'But it won't be the same. She won't be coming to school with me.'

'No, she's growing up, doing her exams. She's clever, she'll do well and have lots to share with us.'

'She won't stay.'

'Maybe not for long. Things change but people don't change. She'll always be our sister, the same old Mariam to us.'

'I want her here with me, like we were.'

'We can't go back, we've got to move on. You're growing up too, next thing I'll be losing you.'

'No, you won't, never.'

'You wait, some fellow's going to come begging.'

'Rubbish.' She swept her cushion into Osman's chest and they giggled quietly.

In the middle of the night, Osman heard Wani creep across the floor to climb into bed with his mama and papa.

***

When he was at school, Osman used to play football with his friends on Saturday evenings. This had graduated into meeting at the café with Robel and Ariam, who carried on at school for another year after Osman and their other friend, Daniel, left. Daniel could not wait to help his father in their garage.

The rain had stopped but his mother insisted that he take her bright striped market umbrella.

'I'm not having you sitting in wet jeans all afternoon,' she said, 'and that's final.' She poked his belly with the handle and he took it. Osman didn't care what they said, he was looking forward to seeing them.

He passed another couple of round, thatched houses like theirs. Then lines of low houses one after another, with the odd patch of rubble and grass between, until he came to the square – a patch of beaten earth with a couple of doum palms surrounded by houses, a ramshackle garage, a leather shop, butcher, grocer and the café.

He could see them sitting round a little table, long legs sticking out, filling the space under the faded awning of Zaid's café, the only meeting place in their small village.

'Osman!' called Robel, swinging back on his chair, arm across Ariam's shoulder. Ariam stayed on at school because he was clever, Robel because he didn't know what else he wanted to do. Osman shook his umbrella. 'Hi,' he said.

'Are you going to market, man? Setting up stall?' Daniel laughed. 'Going to sell your baskets with the rest of the women?'

'Enough, Daniel, Sebhat needed help. The pay is okay, anyway, weaving a basket is better than lying on your back under a car,' said Osman. He propped the umbrella against the wall next to a motor bike.

'That is Ibrahim's motor bike! You will get grief for that.'

'Not anymore.' Daniel shook his head sadly. 'Not since he's been in the army.'

'I thought his training ended long ago?'

Daniel shrugged. 'So did he but without discharge, there is no leaving.'

'They can't keep people on.'

'Oh yes they can. They send you off on 'voluntary' work; rebuilding the country after the war, except that Ibrahim did not volunteer.'

'Bring your chair over here,' called a man in full combat

gear. Osman hadn't seen Jamil in the corner behind a stack of chairs. He hadn't seen his best friend since he started military service. Jamil was in the year above them at school. A big grin split Osman's face.

They hugged. 'Salem aleykum, salem, welcome home,' said Osman.

'Salem, dear friend. I have missed you.' He stepped back holding Osman's bony shoulders. 'Look at you, no change, still thin as a reed.'

Osman laughed. 'Centimetre taller.' He straightened up, 'And you…?' He stared into his friend's stubbly black face. 'Are you growing a beard?' Jamil looked different in his soldier's uniform. It set him apart.

'Shaving is a waste of time.' He stroked his stubble fondly. 'The new me, do you like it?'

'As long as you haven't changed inside, you can have a beard a metre long and walk with crutches.'

'Like a wise old man.' He collapsed back onto his chair and patted the seat beside him.

'What's it like?' asked Osman.

'Great, I'm in the top squad; crack shot with an M16. Learnt to handle a DShk.[3] That thing can turn a tank into a vegetable drainer in a couple o' minutes; magic.'

'It's okay then?' asked Osman.

Jamil raised his shoulders. 'Some don't come up to scratch. They whine and mutter but they soon get sorted.'

Osman took the magazine and newspaper from the waist band of his jeans.

'What you got there?' asked Jamil picking up the magazine.

'Customers from Asmara left them.'

'City gents, look at these,' Jamil said turning over pages of fashion and pop stars.

---

3 Heavy machine gun.

Robel looked over his shoulder. 'White babes, all teeth and eyes,' he said.

'And long fair hair,' said Jamil.

'Check out the gear,' said Daniel, pointing to a lilac sequined mini dress accompanied by silver stilettos and tights. 'Cool.'

'Turn over, turn over,' said Robel.

There was a model in a leather bikini, sitting on a motor bike, long fair hair lifted from her face by pink goggles resting on her forehead.

'How cool is that?' asked Daniel.

The model stared impassively into the distance. Osman and Ariam exchanged a look.

When they turned the last page, Ariam picked it up and flicked through. 'An iPhone, now that's what you call cool. It's got everything you need,' he said.

'Like what?' asked Daniel.

'Safari, email, message, WhatsApp, Facebook, videos, games, music, books, films, you name it, it's got it.'

'All in English,' said Jamil. 'Not much use to me.'

'You can change languages,' said Ariam.

'Really?' Jamil looked at the picture.

'The whole world in your pocket.' Daniel shrugged.

'You've got a mobile, haven't you?' said Robel.

'Not like that,' replied Ariam.

'I'd like one,' said Robel.

'Not much use here,' said Daniel. 'Where's the internet?' He looked around dramatically.

'True, connection's useless, no internet. Dad pays a fortune and it doesn't always work. All I can do is make calls and get music and games,' said Ariam.

'How did you get it?' Osman asked.

'Our maths teacher at school showed me his laptop and all the things you can do if you're connected, wow! It was so quick, with so much information. There was no fooling it, it had all the answers,

I loved it. He gave me lessons and said I could do well with IT. My mother thought it was a good idea, persuaded Dad to get it for me. We need more lines, more connection. I want to do that.'

'They'll never let you, my dad says it's deliberate. They don't want us to get ideas,' said Daniel.

'Missed you last week,' said Robel to Osman. 'How was Keren? Busy? Wet?'

Osman laughed. 'Both,' he said.

'Tell us about the girls,' said Jamil.

'No girls.' Osman pulled a sad face.

'No girls in Keren? Has the town been bombed?'

'I didn't see any, apart from a six-year-old eating candied nuts.'

'You're hopeless. You don't know where to look. You should have taken me with you,' said Jamil.

'Watch out for Jamil's divining rod!' Robel roared.

'It's the girls who have to watch out for that,' sputtered Osman.

'I know what girls like. Where they're going to hang out,' said Jamil.

Robel looked down the street and across the square. Not a bright kaftan, dress or sarong was in sight. 'So tell me, where are they now?'

'Too early,' replied Jamil.

'What are you drinking?' asked Osman.

'Orange,' said Jamil.

'Lime soda,' said Robel.

Ariam stood up. 'I'll get these.'

'It's okay,' said Osman.

Ariam sat down. 'Thanks, I'll have lemon.'

'Same for me.' Daniel pushed his glass forward.

When Osman opened the door into the café. The radio was playing dance music. He started to sway, tap his feet, bend and stretch to the rhythm, waving his arms in the air.

'Check him,' Jamil pretended to yawn. 'We have heard that so many times, we need something with a bit more energy.'

'It's better when we play for ourselves,' said Daniel. 'In the village.'

'Don't you like to dance? It's great to dance to,' said Osman swinging round.

Ariam pulled out his mobile phone.

'Here, listen to this.'

Pharell Williams's, 'Happy' sang out.

'That's great,' said Daniel.

'You not heard it?'

Daniel shook his head. 'There's nothing like that on the radio. You know they don't think we need a change.'

'Or more choice,' said Robel.

'It's the future,' said Ariam.

'And we're stuck in the past,' said Daniel. 'We can't even get parts for the cars sometimes.'

'There aren't that many cars,' said Osman. 'Donkeys are cheaper to run.' His mother took her produce to market on their donkey.

Jamil sighed. 'Mobile phones are not allowed in the army.'

Daniel leant forward. 'You sure?'

Jamil shrugged. 'One girl had one and they took it off her.'

'Probably kept it for themselves,' said Ariam.

'You guys going into Agordat for 1*st* September?[4] asked Robel.

'Allah knows where I'll be,' said Jamil. 'Probably marching somewhere.'

'Watched by all the girls,' said Osman. He felt a pang of disappointment. He realised that he had been counting on seeing Mariam but of course she would be on display somewhere. Sawa probably, her military training centre.

---

4 Celebration of the beginning of the war of independence from Ethiopia.

Ariam said, 'We'll be there, the whole family.'

'What about you Osman?' asked Robel.

'We're having lunch with my father's friend, Yusef Mohamed. Do you remember the family? We used to play with their children at school, Aaron and Hanna? They've just got back from Germany.'

'What were they like?'

'Hanna was cute. Aaron was a bit full of himself. Cool T-shirts and trainers.'

'Didn't their dad have a chevy?' asked Daniel.

'He did, trust you to remember that.'

Daniel shook his head smiling. 'That was a long time ago.'

'Seven years,' said Osman, 'and they're back.'

'All change for us on 1st September,' said Ariam looking at Robel.

'Yes, end of school for you two,' said Osman. 'You'll be following Mariam to Sawa.'

For the first time he felt sad that he hadn't stayed on at school and gone on to board at Sawa.

'You will join us won't you, Daniel?' asked Robel.

'Sure thing,' said Daniel.

'What's Sawa like, Jamil?'

'Depends on how you get on with the officers. They can be a mean lot or pretty cool.'

***

September was Osman's favourite month; a virgin sun restored life to Agordat. Rain beaten plants reached for its warmth and grew – white lilies, blue scabious, red and orange poppies and in sheltered corners, the vibrant yellow, pinks, orange and purple of gerberas. Tomatoes and watermelons swelled, bananas plumped and orange and lemon trees spilt perfume. Rivers receded to pleasant flows and warmed their waters under its light. Sitting by the entrance to their hut, Osman watched a weaver bird carefully construct his nest under the sharp eye of his targeted bride, a bird almost twice his size. When the last strand was woven into place, she started to demolish it. He had to build bigger, better. Osman smiled at her outrageous behaviour and pitied the little nest pecked male as he started all over again.

They all dressed up and wore shoes for the celebration. Osman wore blue plaid shorts and a white T-shirt with, 'If you want to travel fast go alone, if you want to travel far, go together,' written in blue across the chest. He searched the crowd for his friends but there were too many people. The ceremony raised conflicting emotions. The hoisting of the flag never failed to raise spirits. Invasion after invasion from the Ottoman Empire, Italy, Britain, Sudan, Djibouti and Ethiopia had been repelled by the group of people who called the land between the mountains and the Red Sea home. During the minute's silence, Osman felt even more deeply what those brave men and woman had sacrificed because he knew the joy of September in Eritrea.

The National Anthem was a happy chant, full of energy and strength, he loved it. If a national anthem was meant to capture the spirit of a nation, his did; positive, determined, full of love for the land. The cradle of human civilisation, a land that had natural wealth beyond measure under its soil, in its scenery, trees, plants, fruit and fish, animals and birds. There was no more beautiful or generous land on earth. He watched boys and girls in their smart uniforms marching to the beat of their military bands. He thought how smart Mariam would look in her uniform. She was always neat and tidy.

After the ceremony, they walked to Yusef's house in a select part of Agordat. Osman had seen houses like theirs but never been inside. He could see the tops of palm and banana trees above the terracotta topping of the high white wall. The courtyard had aloe and cacti set in gravel.

They stood nervously at the front door and his father rang the bell. His mother was carrying a basket of fruit and vegetables and a packet of fresh goat's cheese and his father had a bag of green coffee beans and a bottle of lemon and honey cordial.

The door was wrenched open almost immediately. Yusef hugged Dawit and ushered them all inside.

'Welcome, come in, come in… and this is Wani?' He put a finger under Wani's chin. 'You were a bump in your mummy's belly when we left. Osman, what a handsome young man you've become and Delina, prettier than ever.'

He shook their hands pulling them over the threshold. Dawit gave him the cordial.

'Thank you, where's Mariam?'

'Sawa, military service.'

'Time passes, they grow and go,' commiserated his friend.

They were in a long corridor with arches on either side and double door at the end.

'You didn't carry that all this way, did you?' said Yusef, taking the basket from Salma.

'A few things from the garden.'

'Come through. Come and see the family.'

He led them down the corridor. Through a half open door Osman saw big soft chairs and a sofa in front of a television. The room at the end had arches onto the garden and a high, glass-topped table surrounded by white cane chairs that seemed to emphasise the room's emptiness. It felt solemn, attentive. Osman missed signs of family life, mementos, everyday clutter. They stood awkwardly in the space around it. Osman heard a trickle of water. There was a fountain at the end of the garden pouring into a runnel that reached almost to the house. It was on the shady side of the garden, protected by a grand mango tree, a banana, and a palm. Birds were splashing, shaking their wings, and drinking from it. On the other side, closer to the house, a jacaranda spread branches of purple flowers towards a trellis of deep pink bougainvillea. On the other side of the garden rocks were piled high to display giant aloes, cacti, and succulents. Osman absorbed every detail of the artistry.

'You haven't seen Hanna for a while have you Osman?' His mother called.

He turned, Hanna was framed by an arch; taller, slimmer, in a short, yellow and white patterned dress. She pulled her hair from her face and it sprang back in thick shiny waves. Her face was more sculpted. Osman had forgotten how alive her eyes were. He didn't know what to say.

'Selam Aleykum,' he muttered, his voice unusually thick.

'Selam Aleykum,' she flicked back mischievously. 'Good to see you.'

'Long time,' they both spoke at once and laughed.

Her mother handed her a glass of orange juice. 'Give this to Wani,' she said.

Standing at the table holding a bottle of champagne, their host looked fondly around the table and declared, '1st September, we must celebrate the fight for freedom!'

He pushed up the cork. 'Pop!' They all laughed. Fizzy liquid was poured into tall glasses – Osman and Hanna included. Delina was given a sip but preferred orange juice. Osman liked it. Not so tasty as his usual lemon or orange but it was light and refreshing, he thought. He was thirsty.

'Sit down everyone,' said his wife and swept her arm over the table. Osman sat between his mother and father facing the garden. Hanna sat opposite with Delina at her side and Yusef sat at the head of the table next to his old friend.

'Where is Aaron?' asked Dawit. 'I was expecting to see him.'

'Stuttgart.'

'What's he doing there?'

'He's at the University studying infrastructure planning – engineering, architecture, town planning.'

'When will he be back?'

Yusef shook his head. 'Allah knows.'

'You came back without him?'

'We had to come back, our parents are old, our brothers and sisters poor. We must help but Aaron is free, he can have a better life there.'

'What kind of life without his family, his home?'

'There are opportunities there, Dawit, you wouldn't dream of. A clever boy who works hard can do anything. He'll have a comfortable life and be secure.'

'Family is all we have. You have made a big sacrifice, Yusef, you are very brave.'

'Or foolish,' laughed Yusef. 'That is what you are thinking, Dawit. How is life at the mine?'

'Not bad, not bad old friend. Nothing changes.'

'No.' Yusef lowered his head. 'It doesn't seem to. There are too few opportunities for our young men. Osman is not working at the mine with you?'

'No, Osman is happy helping Sebhat.'

'Making baskets? That is women's work. There has to be more for a man than that?'

'Sebhat's baskets tour the world.'

'True, true, they are works of art. I am glad Osman found his path with Sebhat but for boys like Aaron there is very little to offer here.'

'Eritrea is rich, you can have a decent enough life here.'

'Allah knows I agree. Our country is beautiful. We are good people but there is so much happening in Europe and nobody here knows. Our people are kept ignorant and dependent.'

'We don't see protesters on our streets like other countries.'

'Because people are afraid. Millions don't have electricity or water, never mind phones or TV. Computers and internet are almost unheard of.'

'We have more clinics and better schools since the war ended.'

‘To prepare the young for what?’

The maid set a bowl of fluffy rice, a plate of injera and a dish of collard greens on the table then a pot of lamb zigini and an assortment of sweet and sour pickles.

In front of Osman were two plates, one large and one small, a napkin and a knife and fork as well as a spoon. He froze, he couldn’t look at Hanna. Salma rose with an injera in her hand, filled it with stew and handed it to Wani. Osman wished he were seven.

‘I’ll have the same,’ said Dawit.

Osman sipped his champagne watching Hanna spoon rice onto her plate followed by collard greens and pickles.

‘Can I help you?’ she asked.

He nodded. ‘Thank you.’

‘What would you like?’

‘Same as you.’

‘No zigini?’

‘A little, please.’

She handed him a generous plate full.

‘Thank you.’

He watched her chop her chard and spear it with her fork then push a little pickle onto it with her knife. The plates were cold and slippy, his chair seemed like an island and the table cut them off from each other and the food. There was nothing warm and close, no sharing, nothing intimate in this meal. Yet he remembered the family as warm loving people before they left. He emptied his glass and the sharp edge of his anxiety softened and began to melt. He pushed a forkful of rice and stew into his mouth and mellowed to the company.

‘You’ve started work?’ Hanna said.

He had missed some of the conversation.

‘I’m with Sebhat Solomon.’

He saw Hanna’s blank face.

‘Basket maker,’ he explained.

'Ah,' she said. 'All those tightly woven patterns and colours, that takes patience.'

Osman looked down.

'And skill,' she said.

He smiled and silently vowed to make a basket for her.

'What are you going to do?'

'I've got a year before I need to think of that. Maybe fashion designer or dress maker.' She laughed. 'It was your mum who got me interested in sewing.' She turned to Delina. 'Do you remember when she gave us scraps of material to make something?'

'I made a draw string bag,' said Delina.

'And I made a purse with a press stud. I was so proud of that. I don't know what happened to it.'

'You gave it to me, I still have it,' said Osman, remembering how far back their history went and how special she seemed to him.

After the meal Hanna, Delina and Osman went out to sit in the garden while the adults stayed round the table.

'What's it like in Germany?' Osman asked.

'The countryside is different, less space, more trees, greener, darker. The sky is grey but the sun goes down slower. That is beautiful but there aren't the same stars.'

'Can you tell me about the shops? What do they have?' asked Delina.

'They were so big. You have never seen anything like it, honestly. I could not believe it when we went into the city. You could buy anything there.'

'If you had the money,' said Osman.

'There was hardly any money, it was all credit cards.'

'Mother isn't going to sell a pumpkin for a credit card.'

'It's all machines there. Machines to wash cars, dishes, floors. But they are expensive. There's a machine for everything and computers – you can buy tickets for planes, boats, trains, hotels, buy books, make-up, clothes. Any question and it gives you the answer. You can visit places, see shows or call a friend anywhere in the world for free.'

'Wasn't that all a bit too much to cope with?'

'The more I saw, the more I wanted to find out. Then you take it all for granted.'

'What was school like?'

'The language was difficult at first but we had home tutors and that helped. The school had everything. There were long rooms full of computers and classrooms with white boards. We had films of the world and went on trips to concerts, theatres, hiking and camping but it was so big. Some people shunned me and called me names.'

'Why?' asked Delina, in awe of her beautiful friend.

'Because my skin is black.'

Osman was shocked. Her skin shone like satin over her high cheek bones and delicate nose – warm, beautiful, welcoming. All those anaemic faces seemed suddenly cold and cruel.

'I'm glad I'm back,' said Hanna.

'So am I,' Osman and Delina chimed back. Delina hugged her and Osman felt a bubble of joy stop his chest. She was looking at him.

'Do you remember when you and Aaron made a go cart at your place and pulled Delina and I around on it?'

'And you wouldn't do the same for us!' replied Osman.

'You were older and bigger!'

'Mariam pinched one of mum's watermelons to make it up to us,' said Osman.

'And you put it in the cart and dragged it to the creek and let it cool in the water,' said Delina.

'And I fell in getting it out,' laughed Osman.

'We joined you and dried off eating watermelon.'

It didn't seem long ago at that moment but it was. Osman didn't want anything to change but Aaron was in Germany and Mariam had disappeared.

Osman felt anything was possible when he was with Hanna. They could have a full and happy life together but as soon as he left their oasis of luxury, he realised how far away she was. He could never win her. She was destined for greater things.

***

Life settled back into its familiar routine; helping his mother load the donkey in the morning and irrigating their vegetables in the evening. In between, he made bigger and better baskets. Sebhat was proud of him and took pleasure in recommending his work to the buyers. Sebhat and Faven had a wide network of contacts. He told them that they hadn't heard from Mariam and hoped for news but there was no information about the internal running of Sawa or any of the other training centres.

One evening when he returned, the whole family were waiting for him with a cold stuffed injera for him to eat on foot. Someone at the market had told Salma that a friend had news of Mariam. They walked for an hour along the valley and stopped to picnic by the river where ruddy shelduck and Eurasian wigeon dabbled circling in front of them. Green-winged teal and northern pintails paddled smoothly upstream. A ringed plover stalked the shallows by the banks where they drank before carrying on to the settlement.

The sound of children's voices drew them towards a group of huts and houses stretching along an old riverbed.

'She said her house was at the beginning of the village; round houses with thatched roofs like ours.'

Five houses formed a little community nestling under a hill on the outskirts. Wani ran and dodged between the cacti, kicking up stones.

'There'll be snakes and lizards there, leave them alone. Here, have some basbousa.' Salma offered him a piece of coconut cake and Wani was happy. A woman in a deep ochre kemis,[5] emerged from the shadows of the second hut.

'Selam Aleykum.'

They returned the greeting.

'You have word of our daughter?'

'Mariam?'

'Yes, yes.' Dawit sounded brusque, impatient to hear her news.

'We haven't heard from her for months,' explained Salma.

The woman shook her head. 'It wasn't permitted.'

'Why should they stop her from seeing her parents?'

'The military have their own rules. I am sorry, I heard she wasn't well.'

'Mariam? She's as strong as an ox. What has she caught?'

'One of the sons in the village said he'd seen her; she was thin and looked unhappy. That's all I can say I'm afraid. She wants to see you; she'll try but it's difficult.'

'I shall go to Sawa and demand to see her,' said Dawit.

'Don't do that. The boy says to be careful, they will only take it out on her if you complain. She is trying to get leave; she will send word when she can.'

The return was hard. Each in their own separate misery with no words of comfort for each other. The next day Salma baked Mariam's favourite biscuits and put oranges and dates into a bag with them. Osman bought her a bar of chocolate and Delina added a bracelet she had woven. Wani sent a card of them all waving to her. Salma packed it up and they retraced their steps to the hut under the hill. She gave the woman fresh vegetables for her trouble and begged her to see the parcel delivered.

People came from all around to their village market every Saturday, some had babies on their backs, others had children at their side. It was a great meeting place. Older friends and

---

5 An ankle length dress typically worn by Eritrean women.

grandmothers chatted, swapping stories and Salma listened. Faithful customers enquired after Mariam and Salma confided in them. Questions were asked about Sawa and the vegetable seller's daughter, but nothing came back. Dawit vowed to take time off work and go to Sawa.

Finally they were given a letter; bright and cheerful, talking of exercises, drills, awards; the great future they were building for their country. There was no mention of their parcel. No familiar family chat or jokes. No promise of her return. It was as if they had lost her, she seemed so distant. Salma was weighed down with grief and confusion when she sat to reply. The letter irritated Dawit rather than reassuring him. He wanted to see her in Sawa. Even more to find out if they had really lost their daughter. Osman rejected this Mariam who was happy away from them, who loved being regimented. It wasn't the spontaneous, gentle sister he knew; there was something brittle about it, too shiny. He wanted his real sister back. He had friends in Sawa, one in the army. He couldn't wait to see them. They all knew Mariam; Jamil once had a crush on her.

October passed to November; the shop was quieter with fewer tourists browsing. There were orders to fill for customers in Asmara and stock to replenish after a busy summer, so they were kept busy. The few foreigners who made it to the workshop complained of lack of internet. Osman wondered why they didn't take the opportunity to look around, see tall sorghum plants in the fields, the trees, birds and camels, instead of mourning the loss of a tiny screen. Osman made bigger baskets, with lively patterns inspired by nature. His subjects changed – cacti in the mountain passes, their exotic flowers, the bright green crests and red eyes of turaco birds, the elegant shape of gazelles, their ears and horns, hyena stripes and the vivid blue and red of the agama lizard.

Saturdays were quieter with only Daniel at the café. It was not until December that Osman saw three figures stretched out in the shade of the awning instead of one; Ariam and Jamil were back. Jamil jumped up and hugged his friend. Osman was glad Jamil wasn't in uniform. He looked more like the old Jamil in his T-shirt and shorts. Daniel watched the reunion grinning and muttering, 'salem' and Ariam stood repeating, 'salem, salem' until he and Osman slapped palms. They stood awkwardly in a circle before sitting down. Osman's smile had evaporated with his moment of joy, the weight of Mariam's absence dragged him down.

'I thought you were glad to see us.'

Osman tried to pull himself together. 'Oh I am, I am…' he protested.

'What's wrong?'

'We haven't heard from Mariam. She's at Sawa. Have you seen her?'

Ariam shook his head. 'I am sorry, Mariam is a year ahead of me. She will have moved on with her group.'

Osman tried to hide his disappointment. 'What is Sawa like?' he asked.

Daniel answered for him, 'He says the food is awful, the barracks are overcrowded and it's all the same thing.'

'It's education with military drills as a bonus,' Ariam explained.

Osman laughed, 'You had it too good. You've got to toughen up for all those nights under the stars.'

'I'd rather be under the stars than in that barracks with all those farting masturbators.'

'Wait until you're out on the road. That's when it gets tough,' said Jamil.

'What do you mean?' asked Ariam.

'You think that Sawa is bad? When it's over you'll work twelve hours a day and sleep in cold corners of old ruins on rations that wouldn't feed a bird and you'll be at the mercy of any officer they deal out to you. If he doesn't like your face you're done for,' replied Jamil.

'Mariam was at Sawa last year; did you hear anything about her?'

Ariam shook his head. 'Sorry. The girls don't always get a good deal in the camps.'

Jamil looked at the floor and mumbled, 'I heard things…'

Osman swung round. 'What did you hear?'

'She's not had a good time there.'

'We had a letter saying she was doing well,' said Osman defensively.

Jamil looked doubtful, then shrugged.

Osman asked, 'When did you see her?'

Jamil nodded. 'A while ago, only in the distance.'

'How did she look?'

'Thinner, head down, not like the girl we knew,'

He saw Osman stiffen. He sat back saying, 'I don't know, those uniforms change everyone.'

Osman couldn't talk. He tried to picture her, but he couldn't. His elder sister wore fluid kaftans in pink, green, yellow or blue. She was tied up with home, the fields, river, mountains, their life as a family. Not drills, deadlines and barracks.

Where's Robel?' he asked.

Ariam's face changed. 'He's back in camp.'

'Until when?'

Ariam shrugged bitterly. 'Who knows?'

'What do you mean? He can't stay through the holiday.'

'There is no way of knowing what they will do; it's up to them when you come and go.'

'Robel likes his mother's cooking and his father spoiling him. Why is he staying on?'

'You don't think he wants to, do you?'

Osman shrugged. 'Depends on the incentive, but we know our brother. It would have to be something very special to keep him away. So, who is she?'

'There are no girls involved. Robel likes the easy life so he was a bit slow and his officer could smell 'rich boy' written all over him. He picked on him and to give him his due, Robel wasn't taking it. He kicked up. He was whipped in front of us all. I thought he'd fold but he took it. I cleaned up his back. It was a mess. He cried and tried to toe the line but he only had to blink and the man jumped on him. Next time, they took him to 'the shed' and beat his soles raw. The more he told them that they'd answer for it, the worse it got. He was staked out in the sun for a day and finally, he was dropped into 'the pit' and left without food or water. He was delirious when they dragged him out. It took days to get enough water into him,' said Ariam.

'Have you told his father?'

Ariam nodded. 'He was beside himself, went straight to Sawa. He was given an official report of Robel's 'crimes.' They insist he completes his 'sentence.''

'He'll go higher then?' asked Osman.

'Who to? Nobody's going to listen. They stick together. They can do what they want,' said Ariam.

Robel's rich, influential father being defeated by men he would normally command was unthinkable to Osman.

He asked Jamil, 'You don't want to stay in that do you?'

'No way. I've seen enough, had enough,' he replied.

'You don't think they're going to let you out do you?' asked Daniel.

'Let them try to stop me.'

'They will,' said Daniel. 'Ibrahim's service finished in September and they wouldn't let him go. He's taking down ruins stone by stone and rebuilding them. He's on army pay – just about fag money. He sleeps on-site with his unit on starvation rations – they catch vermin and eat cactus. Their gang leader has been on forced labour for a decade. The others, two or three years; it's slavery.'

'Why doesn't he run?'

'They shoot deserters.'

'My eighteen months service is up at the end of March and I'm walking free,' said Jamil.

'I'm going abroad to study IT when I've finished Highers,' said Ariam.

'You'll have to do service; they won't let you out of the country.'

'Our country? It sounds more like a concentration camp,' replied Ariam.

'The only way out is escape. I'm going to run for it,' said Jamil.

'Where can you go?' asked Osman.

Ariam answered, 'I've heard of people making it across the Mediterranean to Italy and Greece. You can have a good life there.'

Jamil nodded. 'It's true. There's a bloke in my platoon whose father is a lecturer at the University. He says there's decent pay over in Europe and plenty of work, mobile phones and internet everywhere. You're free to live as you please.'

'Not stifled by censorship and lack of infrastructure. There's choice, hundreds of different TV channels as well as radio and shops loaded with luxuries,' added Ariam.

'I don't know that I need all that,' said Osman, 'we're okay without it.'

Daniel whipped round, surprised. 'What do you want?'

'To make good baskets, get married, have a family and friends.'

Ariam said, 'Sounds simple but if the government has other ideas, you're stuffed.'

Daniel looked at Osman. 'You'll find out. When you're eighteen and you're no longer a free man, they will take you for conscription then labour – rebuilding the country. I'm getting worried. After losing Ibrahim to the system, Dad wants me to get away. When is your eighteenth?'

'24th March.'

'Time to think about it. Mine's beginning of February. With Christmas in between, it'll soon be here.'

Osman felt the ground under him less stable. Mariam's absence – that was their doing, he was sure of that. Mariam would never forget her family.

'What are you guys doing for Christmas?' asked Ariam.

'We'll do the usual round of visits to friends,' he said. Christmas without Mariam was unthinkable. Osman didn't care what they did, it would be empty without her.

'It's non-stop family for us. They all come and stay. Some for the foreign Christmas but most for the 7th January. It goes on and on – food, kids, dancing.' Daniel grinned at the thought of it.

'I'm off to the sea. Dad's taking us to Gurgusum beach,' said Ariam.

When they parted the rain had stopped. Osman stood in the square letting the warm sun dissolve the cold grey walls he had felt closing in on him. On the other side, a camel's sad, wise eyes brought him back to the perfect, easy reality of his everyday world. A man in a dashiki and leggings was talking to another in jeans, leaning against a wall smoking. Great bunches of red brown dates hung from golden fronds around the tops of the palm trees; nature was undisturbed. The men seemed oblivious. Perhaps the threat was imagined but the victims were real enough; the stories too awful to be made up. He strode out purposefully, but the conversation hung over him. Men he had known all his life. Men, that was the point; they had grown up together; children in paradise, never alone, loved, and happy. Growing up was hard; time to take control but he had no control over the gaps in his life – Mariam and Robel – unquestionable, real. He felt confused; something dark, cold, and cruel lay under the surface of his everyday life. One by one they would all be sucked into the government machine. They would lose each other, their freedom, families, dreams. His pace quickened as he tried to run away from unformed thoughts and fears.

He drank in the balmy air, clean earth and the greenery around. His chest expanded as he looked up at birds cruising the sky. The sight of home with his father's motor bike by the front door. His mother's stretch of corn, tomatoes, courgettes, okra, beans and onions was a relief. Their dear old donkey pushed his nose into Osman's hand when he had finished scratching behind his ears. He took a carrot from the bin.

Delina ran to him. 'Mariam's coming. We're going to see Mariam!'

Dark clouds gone; he was surprised by a flood of relief so powerful it made his knees weak.

Inside the hut was cool and quiet.

His father looked up. 'You heard the news then?'

Osman's smile said it all. 'Where's ma?'

'Where do you think? Out in the garden washing clothes to take.'

'Take where?'

'Didn't she tell you?' Dawit looked at Delina.

Osman shook his head.

'Keren. We're meeting her at Lydia's place.'

'When?'

'Next Thursday, I'll have to get the day off work.'

'You can get your Christmas present,' said his mother from the entrance.

'What about me?' asked Delina.

'I'm making yours; you know I am.'

'Can I have a satchel?' Wani added.

'Ask your father.'

The bus left early and once out of the village it headed for the mountains. Osman stared blindly through the window at a world of stone, stunted trees and dust. He saw a bird of prey hovering above them but missed its swoop as the bus wound its way round to the other side of the mountain and down into a valley with channels of mud surrounding fields of sorghum and maize. Golden sparrows chattered among the branches of low trees at the corners of the fields and beneath them, three or four ravens stalked the edge of a field. A troupe of monkeys crossed the road behind them. When Osman turned his head to follow them, his mother smiled. They were all looking forward to seeing Mariam but she could not get to Lydia's until the afternoon so they all had precious time in town.

The sun had risen higher and hotter. Most people stayed indoors or sheltered under parasols. Osman was uncomfortable in his jeans, trainers and T-shirt but he was determined to make the most of shopping for his present. He kept to shops under the cool Italian arcades where he could but found what he wanted in a small, young fashion shop: a black T-shirt, jacket and white trainers. Job done, he stepped out into the midday sun holding a large, black, paper carrier bag. He had time to kill and he was thirsty. He turned towards the bus station and spotted a narrow café with tables inside as well as out.

When he stepped into the café's dark interior, his eyes flared red then black. He heard angry voices competing to his left and a woman whispering behind. A paper rustled and the coffee machine hissed before his eyes had adjusted enough for shadowy tables and chairs to emerge from the gloom. He peeled off his cap and ran the back of his hand across his wet forehead.

'Tea please,' he said to the elderly woman behind the counter.

'Sit yourself down,' she replied, transferring biscuits onto two plates without looking up. *They look good.*

Osman looked around; three men in shorts and boots were drinking beer on his left and in front of them, a man in a shirt and trousers was smoking a cigarette over his coffee. Someone in full combat fatigues was hidden behind a newspaper in the far corner. *He must be hot.*

The waitress carried the peanut cookies to a mother and daughter at the front. Osman chose to sit behind them even though it meant seeing the biscuits go down. He propped his paper carrier bag against a chair and dropped his hat on the table.

As he took his glass of tea from the waitress the newspaper at the table in the corner edged down. A young man with a beard was watching him. His hands on the paper looked hard, strong. Spirals of hair dropped onto his forehead from a halo of black curls. Osman could not avoid his eyes, inspecting, questioning. It made him feel uncomfortable. *What does he want?* He gave a wan smile and the young man relaxed back, his big, muscular frame overlapping the chair to watch Osman settle over his tea with studied concentration. He heard the newspaper being shaken. The scrape of a glass as he pushed it aside. Osman watched spellbound as the man stood and slung a large canvas rucksack over his shoulder. He stopped by Osman's table.

'Hi,' he said.

'Hello,' said Osman looking up.

The man smiled a slow, gentle smile. 'Not seen you around before. Not local?'

'Not that far, Ad Ali Bachat but I bet you've never heard of it.'

'Don't you believe it, may I?' He indicated the other chair.

Osman moved his paper bag. 'Sure, please do.'

The rucksack thudded down and Osman wondered what was in it.

'Camped in the foothills near there, peaceful, lush – you're lucky. Farmers?'

'Nah, father works at Bisha Mine.'

'For the Canadians, lucky man. You at University?'

Osman was surprised. 'No, no chance, not me.'

The man assessed him doubtfully. 'Not still at school?'

Osman shook his head, smiling. 'Nah, left last year. I'm learning basket making.'

His companion looked surprised. 'That's for girls.'

Osman smiled. 'More masters at the top than mistresses.'

His interlocutor thought for a moment then said, 'Like most things, women get a raw deal.'

'So my sister keeps telling me.'

'What does she do?'

'She's at Sawa. Last year of school.'

'What does she think of it?'

'Don't know, we haven't heard. We came here to meet her.'

The young man clicked his tongue sadly. 'Fifteen years since the war ended. What is the point of all this military training?'

Osman shrugged. 'It's the way it goes.'

'Sawa's not a school – final year boarding at a military academy? Why? To get you away from your family. Make sure they've got you so you can be used for whatever work they decide you're fitted for.'

'Mariam's clever. She got top grades for Highers in the summer.'

'If she's bright, she may be sent into schools to teach but the government employs you and they call it "service" so they don't have to pay you any more than subsistence. She'll get minimal pay, no papers to set her free and no choice as to where she's sent.'

'She seemed okay with the set up in her letter. We haven't seen her for a while, she's not been well.'

'Girls don't always have it easy with the military.'

'No one will get the better of Mariam.'

'Hope not.'

'We're meeting her here in Keren for a meal together and a big catch up.'

Nothing could prick the bubble of anticipation for Osman. He looked at his strange new friend. 'Where are you from?'

'Nakfa.'

Osman whistled. 'That's something to be proud of.'

'And live up to.'

'I suppose. Did your father fight for freedom?'

'He did, uncles and cousins too. Everyone who could.'

'My father fought in Keren but they couldn't hold it.'

'Against Russian napalm and cluster bombs? No wonder.'

'But Nakfa held on.'

'At a cost. Holed up in the mountains without supplies, while their houses were destroyed but we don't stay down.'

'It's not the number of times you're knocked down that matters, it's the number of times you get up...' Osman recited.

'You learnt the history.'

'Of Nakfa, what Eritrean didn't? You won the war for us.'

'Some empty victory.'

'Empty?'

'We swapped Ethiopian domination for Eritrean tyranny.

'Afwerki?'

He nodded grimly. 'Our victorious general.'

'I didn't think things changed much apart from being free from foreigners.'

His earnest brown eyes studied Osman's innocent face, then he shrugged.

'Ali Bachat, father at Bisha, I can see where you're coming from. Bit of a bubble but it'll burst the moment you're eighteen.'

'Eighteen?'

'National service.'

'Oh that, yes I know. Eighteen months, I can put up with that.'

'Sure, not that it's necessary with peace monitored by UNMEE[6] anyway. But it won't end there, there's no end, you'll work for the government as long as you're useful – where they say, what they say.'

'Is that what you're doing?' Osman looked at the camouflage gear.

The man shook his head emphatically.

---

6 United Nations Mission in Ethiopia and Eritrea.

'Afwerki's army is not the army I want to fight for.'

'How did you get out?'

'I never got in. I slip through their nets, never stay in one place for long.'

'How long can you keep that up?'

'As long as it takes to get out.'

'Get out? Where to?'

'The Mediterranean, Europe.'

Osman was stunned. 'That's a long way.'

'And a lot of money but I'm almost there.'

'How will you get there?'

'Sudan, Libya, boat. Your T-shirt, 'ITAOIL' where did it come from?'

'My uncle in Libya. He works for the company.'

'You've got a contact in Libya?'

'My mother's elder brother.'

'What's he like?'

'Uncle Birhane? Great; good Muslim, family man, wheeler dealer selling oil.'

'I've got contacts in Sudan, just need someone in Libya.'

'You're serious.'

'Eight thousand American dollars serious. That covers desert and sea.'

He sounded so matter of fact, as if he'd been living with the plan for a long time, groundwork well under way but it was earth shattering to Osman. Even though Jamil and the others had talked about it, he hadn't taken them seriously. Now he began to think that it wasn't all escapist dreams, perhaps it was possible. Refugee, he'd heard that word. Families running from bombs, rubble, protecting their children by escaping but young men escaping tyranny within, running for freedom… He wasn't sure. It seemed an exciting adventure but not real enough to believe; such a massive upheaval of lives, nothing could be worth leaving family, friends, homeland. The young man could see Osman's doubt.

'How old are you?'

'Seventeen.'

'One more year of freedom and you'll be called up, registered and delivered into the system.'

'Four months, not a year, my birthday's in March.'

The man looked troubled. 'Think about it, don't bury your head in the sand. Once they've got you, they'll never let you go.'

'It can't be that bad. There's nothing on the radio or in the paper.

'Censored. There's a completely different world out there.' He flicked his head backwards in the direction of the mountains and Sudan. 'Where you're free to choose who rules and change them if they're not doing the job you want. A world where people matter and governments care for their people. It's called democracy. That's what we fought for.'

'What about your family?' asked Osman.

'My father died fighting. My brother and cousins were transferred to Afwerki's military. In Nakfa we fought hard, sent the Ethiopians packing and celebrated our independence. Now women struggle to feed their families never mind themselves. We are slaves to the men who claimed our victory. Those who can, must run to survive.'

'Leave everything behind?'

'Take the important things with you – strength, determination, hope, honesty and goodwill. What more can people want?'

For the first time Osman felt ashamed of the protection he felt from his family, his father's job, their house, his mother's little patch of land.

'You'll stay?' asked his strange friend.

'I don't have the money or the will to get away. Nowhere can be as beautiful as Eritrea.'

'True, that makes it more painful to know you can't be your

own man here. I thought you were a student, someone who knows about the world outside Eritrea.'

'No, not me. I'm all right, but three of my school friends have talked about leaving. They want to get out of Eritrea.'

'Playing games or serious?'

'I thought they were playing games because I didn't think it was possible but they're frustrated by the way things are turning out for them.'

'Not everyone can find the funds and crossing Sudan and Libya without capture is no fool's game.'

'Their families aren't poor and they're not fools. Jamil's a conscript and he's seen too much of the way it works. Daniel's brother was conscripted and Hagerawi Agelglot, his national service, has no end. He's serving on construction sites and roads anywhere. Ariam, well, he's super clever and into IT. There's nothing here for him.'

'Be good to meet them if they're serious. You never know whose contact will be most useful when you're out in the field.'

He tore a strip from the top of his newspaper and scribbled on it. He pushed it across the table then tore off another and offered it to Osman with his pen. 'Yours?' he asked.

'Just an address, no phone,' muttered Osman bending over the paper. The man stood, watching and when he had finished, they stared at each other for a moment before Osman gave him the paper and he tucked it into his breast pocket.

'My name is Idris,' he said.

'Osman.'

They shook hands. Idris looked at the scrap of paper in Osman's hand, 'In case you change your mind,' he said. 'Our country is rich, our people strong but we are not free.'

Osman shrugged. 'My parents have each other, their work, their family, what more do we need?' He waved the thin ribbon of paper. 'For my friends, thank you. They are only around weekends; Saturdays okay for you?'

'Sure,' he replied thoughtfully. 'Couple of weeks?'

'Yeh, time to get them together.' Osman looked around. 'Here, same time?'

'Never the same place twice. There's a café at the end of the road on the other side of the roundabout from the stadium.'

'Stadium?'

'Joko Keren Football Stadium.'

Idris looked at his watch and shook his head. 'Too early, make it 14:00, week on Saturday.'

He stood and Osman scrambled up embarrassed and confused.

'I honour you,' he said quietly.

Idris shrugged. 'I have no choice. Be careful, the security forces are a deadly network intent on justifying their own existence.'

He laid a hand; big, warm, comforting, on Osman's shoulder and searched his dark, dark eyes with lighter, almost golden-brown ones.

'Take care.'

Osman watched his bulky figure thread its way through pedestrians and traffic then read the name on the scrap of paper, 'Idris Zaid.' The encounter left him unsettled.

He drained his glass of tea and chewed the fresh mint leaves until it was time for the bus. He was looking forward to showing his new clothes to Mariam.

He had left school early while she stayed the course. He'd tried different things before he settled with Sebhat: he had helped his mother on the land and at the markets, picked and boxed dates, bananas and oranges, even had a spell loading boats at the port, Massawa, staying with an uncle. He loved the Red Sea, swimming in its waters was so easy he felt as though he could swim to Yemen or Saudi Arabia with ease.

He was glad Sebhat had taken him in. He had found something inside himself he didn't know existed. Sebhat said he had patience and a creative eye, his fingers were nimble.

He took his glass to the counter and thanked the waitress who was squeezing lemon juice into a glass. She nodded without looking up. She was painfully thin under her loose kaftan. Osman hoped she had someone at home to look after her.

Back in the sun's glare, people passed along the pavement; busy, purposeful. Cars and buses glided up and down the wide road. Everything looked normal but it was not and he knew it. To ripple that still surface was dangerous.

He crossed the boulevard and waited at the bus stop. It was early afternoon so the bus was not crowded. He sat by the window and watched grand Italianate buildings and modern glass complexes with landscaped courtyards give way to older places with flaking exteriors pock marked by gun shots. The buildings got smaller and smaller, leading to terraced tenements. Spattered huts between stone cottages and daub covered dwellings interspersed with tiny squares. He saw an occasional camel and the odd dog. Finally, there was a line of small houses. He jumped off eager to see his sister and share his day with everyone. When the bus had departed, he felt a bit embarrassed by his big, black, paper carrier bag.

Lydia's place was third along a row of a dozen or more. Osman had only visited a couple of times before. It was always swept clean and tidy with decorated cushions on the floor and wall hangings. It consisted of an entrance room, two bedrooms, a kitchen and a shower with nylon curtains outside in the yard. Delina opened the door before he could knock. He dropped his bag, swept her off her feet and swung her round.

'Hi beautiful, here for the party?'

'Put me down.'

She was not laughing. His father was watching solemnly from a cushion on the floor with Wani close by his side looking close to tears. Osman gently lowered Delina to the ground looking at his father.

'What's wrong? Isn't Mariam here?'

His father gave a slight nod in the direction of the courtyard unable to speak.

'Where is she?'

'She's in the shower, she won't come out,' wailed Wani.

'Mama? Lydia?'

'They're with her.'

As he ran through the kitchen he could hear their voices. Lydia and Mama coaxing Mariam to join them, let them dry her, tidy her hair, dress her in fresh clothes. He burst into the yard. The water was trickling. Mariam was a shadow behind the curtain.

'Mariam!' He yelled, 'I'm so glad you're here. It's been so long. What's with all this shower? You're always clean and fresh as spring. Come on, come and tell us all about it.'

Nothing moved behind the curtain. He sensed she was cowering in the corner. Gently he said, 'Been looking forward to seeing you, star.' He looked at his mother and Lydia. They were staring hopelessly at the shower curtain.

His mother spoke, 'You must be tired Mariam, come and rest.'

'We've got chicken and hamli,[7] Mariam. You must be hungry, come and eat with us.'

The water trickled on.

The seriousness of the situation hit Osman. 'Mariam,' he begged, 'please let me see you. I've missed you for so long.' Saying it made him realise how much. This was worse than losing her – a tantalising absence – a sob rose. 'Big sister, I want to hold you.'

Silence.

'Please let me see your face, your beautiful eyes.'

A sob juddered behind the curtain unleashing a tide of tears.

'I'll turn my back. Mama has a towel to wrap you in. You'll dissolve if you stay in there, then where will we be?'

---

7 Greens cooked with garlic, tomato, parsley and coriander.

The plastic rings began to slide. Osman stepped back while his mother opened the curtain. She let Mariam sink her face into a towel then knelt to dry her feet and legs. When she got to her body Mariam cringed and bent double.

Her mother cooed tenderly, rubbing her back, reassuring her. 'Gently, gently, the towel is soft. Don't shiver, the sun is warm.'

Lydia held a big pink and lavender striped cloth to wrap her in and they led the tall, thin girl through to the bedroom. Osman followed like an automaton. Mariam sank onto the bed roll and curled up holding the cloth tight to her body leaving only her eyes, nose and mouth visible.

Her mother sat beside her.

'What happened?'

Silence.

'Do you need a doctor?'

The girl shook her head. Her mother looked at her friend in desperation.

'What can we do?'

'Nothing, Salma.'

Osman stared at the thin, defeated figure on the bed shivering in the afternoon heat. This was a nightmare. This was nothing like the brave, feisty girl who put him to shame when it came to dares, who charmed the world to do her bidding.

'Mariam,' he whispered, hardly able to speak. He crept round the bed to lie close to her back.

His mother continued, 'Mariam, please talk to us, tell us what happened. We can't help if we don't know.'

The cloth was pulled tighter round shoulders and face, her eyes staring into space.

'We are here for you, Mariam, let us help.'

Her mother looked desperately up to Lydia.

'You can stay here as long as you want, Mariam,' Lydia said quietly.

'We'll let you rest,' said Salma and looked at Osman to indicate he should leave with them. But he couldn't, he couldn't leave Mariam. He felt safer if he were close to her.

The two women left the room.

The bedroom was shady. Mariam did not move. Had she forgotten that he was here? He put a finger lightly on her back and traced the length of her spine. She wriggled away. He waited.

'I got my birthday present, I wanted to show you,' he whispered.

He felt her listen. 'Black T-shirt, jacket and great trainers, white. How cool is that?'

No response but he knew she was listening.

'Met a great guy, real badass, combat fatigues – big, good looking, not in the military, he's going to Italy.'

'Join him.'

She uncoiled and turned to Osman. He looked in her eyes caught between delight at having her back and fear at her words.

'No chance,' he said.

'Little brother, your life here will be hell the moment you're eighteen.'

'Don't be silly, a bit of military training an' I'll be set to extend our family.'

'That will not happen, Osman.'

'Why not?'

'The military isn't about protecting the country: it's about control. After the drill and the guns, you'll be set to work. You'll get little pay and less food and it won't end. I've seen it and the punishments they dole out.'

'No one would put up with it.'

'Complain and you're dead or tortured into submission. They are the law, there's no one to turn to.'

'Did they punish you?'

'They sent me to the officer's quarters where I was passed around.'

Shock paralysed Osman for a moment, then he groaned, 'Oh no.' He wrapped his arms around her and rocked them both together while Mariam silently wept.

'They called me dirty because I wasn't circumcised and used me like a dog.'

'Father was right, to cripple a girl for the sake of custom, is wrong Mariam.'

'Tell them that. I lost dignity instead of gaining it.'

'Come home Mariam. Come home, get better.'

Mariam sat up and dried her eyes with her fingers.

'I can't, little brother. I have to go back.'

Osman sat up. 'You can't, Mariam.'

'There is no way out.'

'Those men should pay. You should be free to do as you please, you've done your service.'

'I've another year but that means nothing, believe me you're conscripted for as long as you're useful.'

'They can't do that.'

'Who's to stop them?'

'It's wrong. It's against the law, what they've done to you.'

'They are the law. Whatever they want is legal and it has unfettered their cruelty. People are expendable.'

'You mustn't go back Mariam.'

'They will find me and punish me, probably kill me and who knows? My family. I have to go back no matter what but I don't want you to fall into the trap.'

'Let's talk to mother and father, Mariam. There has to be a way out.'

'I am ashamed, Osman. I can't talk about it.'

'The shame is theirs big sister. You haven't changed, you're just as special as you ever were.'

'Not to any future husband.'

'If he loves you, he will only be angry at them.'

'None of that will happen for me now. I am yoked to a

different world and must tread the path before me no matter what.'

Osman rolled to the floor and bent over her. 'Come, you're safe here, we love you, we are together, let's be together.' He reached out his hands to pull her up and she grasped them. He felt how weak she was as she struggled up.

'You need some good food. Mother's brought muhallabia, your favourite pudding.'

'I can't eat.'

'Perhaps when Mum and Dad have sorted things out.' He had genuine faith in their strength and wisdom. Still holding Osman's hands, Mariam looked at his young, innocent face and smiled at his optimism.

'They can't,' she said.

Osman led her to the sitting room. His father's face cleared into a smile. He stood and wrapped his arms round his precious girl and kissed her forehead.

'There's nothing left of you,' he said 'We'll have to feed you up, won't we Mama?'

Salma looked warily at Mariam. 'We'll see, Dawit. We'll do our best.'

They all settled down.

'I'll make some tea,' said Lydia and left them alone.

'You'd better tell us what has been going on,' said her father.

Mariam looked desperately at Osman.

'You want me to explain?' he asked.

She nodded. Osman looked warily at Delina and Wani then simply said that Mariam had been sent to serve the officers.

'That is the end of 'service' for you,' said Dawit.

'Can we stop them from taking her?' Osman asked.

'She's ill, she's done enough,' said Salma urging her husband on.

'They don't care, Dad. No one can walk out, or everyone would try,' said Mariam.

'But if you're ill?' he asked.

'You work until you drop and somebody fills your place.'

'All the people we know, is there no one who could pull strings?' Salma looked desperately at Dawit. They flicked through names and faces but no likely helper emerged. He shook his head.

'What about the hotel, your holiday job; the owner liked you?' asked her mother.

Mariam shook her head. 'No one is going to help, people are afraid.'

'Who can we turn to?' asked Salma.

'No one, the officers taunt us, 'who you going to complain to?' they laugh. It's Afwerki's law – judges rubber-stamp his grand plans and sweep the victims aside, backed up by the police.'

'How do you know?'

'The other students, they're angry, frustrated.'

The bleakness of the situation settled in Dawit's stomach. 'What has this country come to?'

'Can't we hide her and keep her safe somewhere?' asked Salma.

'Forget it mama, you'd be sent to jail. Allah knows where or for how long if I went missing. I have to go back but I don't want Osman to be trapped, he still has time, he can get away.'

Dawit and Salma looked at each other, resigned, they had heard rumours. All that they had heard and denied, chosen to ignore, was now in front of them. Dawit looked at Osman's troubled face, so innocent and his heart ached but he tried to put the necessary steel into his voice, the voice of desperation, 'Do you want to escape?'

'I don't know. I didn't…'

'Please Osman. There is a better world for you in the west. You can work and send money, help us all,' his father urged.

'A man I met says it costs eight thousand dollars to get across the Mediterranean. I'll stay and take my chances.'

'There are no chances for ordinary people Osman,' said his mother sadly shaking her head. 'Our life will change the moment you're eighteen, you have to go.'

His mother was strong, they were close. He did not expect to hear her pronounce his exile.

'Money is not a problem, Osman,' said his father. 'My wage is paid into the bank, and we hardly need any of it. Your mother's money is enough for us to live on. We have been foolish hoping it wouldn't happen to us, keeping you ignorant, trying to protect you, but I knew; people at work have 'lost' sons over the last few years. That's not going to happen to you. Better in Europe than a slave or dead. I'll see what I can find out,' said his father.

'And I'll speak to Birhane,' said his mother. 'He sees refugees passing through. He may know something.'

'It's too risky, Dad, if they find out you'll suffer too,' Osman said. 'I met someone who warned me about government spies.'

'We know who we can trust Osman, don't worry.' His father patted him on the shoulder.

Mariam lifted Osman's chin. 'Do it. If I can save you then it's worthwhile.'

'Nothing's worth what you've been through.'

Lydia appeared with tea and Delina took one for Mariam then settled by her side to watch her drink. Salma sat on her other side and Osman sank onto a cushion beside his father.

'Are we ready for dinner?' Lydia looked hopefully in Mariam's direction.

Salma nodded. 'I'll come and help,' she said.

Osman sucked on the hot tea in denial of the turn of events, all of it. Emotionally tangled in the web of family, with the restrictions of being guests in someone else's home, Osman couldn't think straight. It was claustrophobic, as if they were all under a microscope. Tensions seethed unresolved. They couldn't let Mariam go back to shame and abuse but she was on an invisible lead. They let her out and pulled her back.

The meal was a subdued affair. Mariam ate a little, more to encourage Osman than out of hunger. She watched his troubled face. He was too gentle for his own good. They were asking a lot of him, to travel so far alone. It saddened her to see him looking at her with pity and regret where he used to look up to her as his leader but she consoled herself that she was leading him away from captivity to freedom. She was determined he should escape her fate.

When it was time for Mariam to leave, Osman could hardly look her in the face for shame of letting her go back, let alone abandoning her by running away. He didn't know what to say. He couldn't cover up his misery with false cheer, he felt none. The rest of the family tried to cheer her and themselves up with the promise of Christmas together.

***

Home, with its familiar smell of woodsmoke and food, the precious objects of family life; his mother's sewing machine, Delina's school books, Wani's chalk board and his own basket of treasures, could not comfort Osman. Nothing could melt the tension in his chest. Their reassuring presence increased his fear of the unknown; he didn't want to leave. He didn't like change and this was a revolution. He put his bag on the mattress, took the magazines from under his pillow and tried to picture himself as part of that world before turning off his lamp but he couldn't sleep. His mattress felt hot, he threw off the sheet and crept away from the whine of mosquitoes.

Outside, land and sky merged in inky blackness. Osman felt the warmth, the moisture of plants, reaching out across the plain; lush, still, attentive. The mountains shouldered out the lower stars, but the highest peaks were drawn into infinity with them; so many brilliant, still but dynamic, their light twinkling, sparkling, taking over their space, their time; infinity, eternity.

He felt how small he was, how petty his concerns. He traced Leo's familiar markers, brighter than ever to him now and wondered what his sky would look like from distant lands. The mountains had been the end of his world, his protection, now they were a challenge to overcome. Sudan waited on the other side and on, on to the wider, broader sea that separated worlds so far apart as to be difficult to believe, but he had to, that was the only straw he had to cling to – a future full of promise. He breathed in the fresh night air marvelling at the luminescence of the dark. Whatever challenges he had to face, his home would not change, it would always be here for him. Mariam was part of that, she was suffering. He could not let that carry on, he couldn't leave her, but he had to go. The family he would miss was pushing him away, his friends were leaving. This little patch of precious earth, tended and loved, giving food to share, would carry on and he would return a free man. Who knows, to marry Hanna and keep it going forever. He smiled; he had come to a decision.

At breakfast the next morning he told his parents.

'I will go but Mariam must come with me.'

'She will never do it,' his mother said.

'We have enough funds for both of you, it would be good to get her out,' said his father, 'but, over the mountains – Sudan, Libya – it's too dangerous.'

'The man I told you about, who warned me about spies, he's preparing to leave. He's got his fare across the Mediterranean. He gave me his number.'

'Can you trust him?'

'He's from Nakfa. He's been living a guerrilla's life, moving from place to place making contacts. He sounded genuine.'

'Nakfa? If he's got their strength and determination, he'll not fail. Do you know how they won the war for us?

Osman shook his head. 'Not really.'

When the town was bombed, they dug trenches with

pickaxes and bare hands in the rock around the base of the mountain – a whole network. They shot down planes, trucks, troops and stayed on after Keren surrendered, even though they were starving, until Ethiopia and their allies gave up.'

Osman's eyes widened. 'I can see where he gets his determination and optimism from, if he can't do it, no one can.'

Salma smiled at her son. 'They're renowned for resilience, sacrifice and their sense of justice and independence.'

'But who is he? Who says he's true to that?' asked Dawit.

'His name is Idris Zaid. He will not tolerate Afwerki's tyranny. He's stayed out of the army and out of trouble for years.'

'How old is he?' asked his mother.

'He's about a year older than Jamil, twenty or twenty-one I suppose. He knows the mountains.'

'But can he be trusted?' his mother insisted.

Osman shrugged, half defeated. It was intuition, not proof that he relied on. 'He trusted me and he had more to lose.'

'So why did he trust a stranger?'

'Don't know. It was weird, he thought I was a student, a rebel and he was interested in my T-shirt, Italian oil in Libya. He needs contacts there.'

'Hmm.' His mother sniffed. 'It's a start, but not with Mariam.

'Jamil, Daniel and Ariam are going.'

'Your friends?' said Dawit, surprised.

'All three? Why didn't you tell us?' said his mother.

'I didn't want to talk about it.'

'And now?'

'Another reason to go. What would I do on Saturday afternoons?' He laughed and they relaxed a little.

'Jamil's older, he's already doing service,' said Dawit.

'In the end he saw how brutal the army is and he doesn't want to be part of it. The only way out is to run.'

His mother said, 'Jamil's a sensible lad. I'd trust him with the pair of you.'

'Ariam doesn't have to run,' said his father thoughtfully. 'His parents are rich and influential, they can keep him out of trouble.'

'He wants to learn about computers. He can't do it here.'

'He might come back then like Yusef.'

'So will I,' said Osman. 'I'll send you money and save enough to buy Sebhat's business.'

'You're like a son to them. He'll leave it to you.'

'I'd share the profits if he did but he has daughters.'

'And they have moved to Keren with their husbands. It's too backward here.'

'Daniel's going too? asked Salma. 'He has his father's garage.'

'So did Ibrahim and he's working on a building site. Daniel's father backs him and he supplies trucks and parts in Sudan, that might be useful. Idris said he's got contacts along the way. Don't worry about Mariam, I will look after her.'

'You may not be able to; Sudan, Libya, dangerous places, more so for girls.'

'The six of us together, we'll help each other out. Don't worry, we'll get by.'

'Your friends, I know, I trust them even with Mariam but this Idris, I'm not sure about him, Nakfa or not, I'd like to meet him,' said his father.

His mother was deep in thought, 'Birhane will be here for Christmas we'll ask him about getting across Libya. You must sort things out with the others. Now finish your breakfast, there's plenty of time for all that. '

'I don't want to lose you, Osman,' said Delina close to tears.

'Or Mariam,' said Wani.

Mariam and Wani were close. They both loved music and sang along with the radio. She gave him a kebero with beads inside so he could tap and shake it when they danced together.

Dawit pulled Wani to his side and looked at Delina.

'It's not safe for them here, we have to let them go,' he said.

'Life will get better, won't it? And we'll all be together,' said Salma.

***

Osman was first at the café on Saturday. He looked around the empty chairs and tables, the only person inside was talking to Zaid. Osman was about to slump into a chair when a large hand hit the middle of his back. He swung around tingling with shock and anger, to find Jamil.

'What you doin'?' he snapped.

'Woah?' Jamil cocked his head on one side looking at Osman. 'Surprise?' he said uncertainly.

'Surprise,' Osman answered lamely and sat down.

'What's wrong?'

Suddenly it was as if Osman's chest were too full, stoppered by a lump in his throat. He didn't know where to begin, what to say and he was afraid of crying.

Jamil bent to look up into Osman's face.

'Something happened?'

Osman nodded.

'Tell me pal, there's got to be something I can do.'

*Jamil, who idolised Mariam, what can I say?*

'I'm going.'

'Going? Where?'

'Out of Eritrea. I'm taking Mariam.'

'Taking Mariam?'

Osman finally lifted his head. 'Sawa, the army, Mariam's been attacked.'

Jamil sat up. 'Attacked?'

'Raped, abused.'

It was Jamil's turn to bow his head. 'Oh Allah defend us, no! Not Mariam.' He hit his forehead. 'Course Mariam…' He looked wildly at Osman. 'Where is she?'

'Back there.'

'We've got to get her out, they're animals.'

'I know.'

'Run and there's no end until you're out of the country.'

Osman looked at his friend. 'Are you serious about going west? Getting out?'

'Never more,' said Jamil grimly.

Daniel crossed the dusty square to join them. Jamil rubbed his sleeve across his eyes and turned to him. 'Hi Dan, how're you doin'?'

Daniel swung his arm out to swipe hands with Jamil and said to Osman, 'early buddy?'

Osman nodded squinting up at Daniel's profile against the sun and watched him sit entering their pool of sadness. After an awkward moment he broke the silence. 'Drinks?'

Jamil jumped up trying to brush off the gloom. 'I'll get them, usual?'

He returned with a couple of fruit juices and a coffee. Daniel looked at Osman.

'Any news?'

Jamil came to the rescue. 'He's coming with us.'

Daniel beamed. 'Great stuff!' He raised his hand and they hit a high five.

Jamil sat back and said, 'With Mariam.'

'Mariam?' Daniel looked confused. 'She hasn't finished Sawa.'

'Who hasn't finished Sawa?' Ariam appeared at the table.

Jamil swung back on his chair. 'You got weekend leave?'

Ariam nodded grimly. 'It wasn't easy.'

'Just for us?' laughed Daniel.

Osman saw Ariam was in no joking mood. 'What's happened?'

'They wanted me to tell Robel's parents he's a liar and a coward.'

'And you wouldn't.' Jamil stood and put his hand on Ariam's shoulder. He flinched. 'They beat you?'

Ariam nodded and slumped onto a chair. 'We're going, aren't we?'

Spontaneously they all clasped hands across the table. 'We're in,' they said together.

Ariam looked at Osman. 'You with us?'

'Sure am,' said Osman.

'And Mariam?' asked Daniel doubtfully.

'Mariam too,' snapped Jamil.

Daniel looked questioningly at Osman.

'She was sent to the officer's mess as punishment for being bright.'

'And beautiful,' said Jamil.

'Officer's mess?' asked Daniel.

'Raped.'

'No!' Daniel jumped up. 'I'll kill them!'

Ariam said quietly, 'I'm not surprised. It's another world in there, of course they'd choose her, Mariam! The bastards, we have to get her out.'

'It was months before they let her see us… they won't let her out.'

'We'll have to kidnap her,' said Jamil.

'Dangerous, if we get caught…' said Ariam.

'I can do it,' said Osman, 'but where? When?'

'You can't do it alone,' said Daniel.

'I'm with you,' said Jamil.

'Can you get messages to her?' asked Ariam.

Osman nodded eagerly; he was feeling better with his friends on board and planning something positive.

'We talked about contacting her without interference before she left; vegetable deliveries, mother knows the woman. Mariam has her name.'

'What's the best time of day?' Osman asked Ariam.

‘Their routine has to be the same as ours, lunch time’s the slackest; hot, free time after the meal,’ said Ariam.

‘Midday!’ said Osman. ‘There’s hardly any cover around the camp.’

‘We’ll just have to be extra clever,’ said Ariam.

‘We can disguise ourselves, pretend we’re delivering.’

‘I’ll grow a beard,’ said Jamil. ‘They’ll never recognise me with a beard.’

‘Not so simple or everyone would do it. They keep guard,’ said Ariam.

‘Mother can ask her contact, see if she can think of a way.’

‘Getting her out is only the beginning. They’ll be after her,’ said Jamil.

‘And anyone around her,’ added Daniel.

‘Nowhere will be far enough,’ said Ariam.

‘We’ve got to get her out of Eritrea,’ said Jamil.

‘With us,’ said Osman.

‘Too right. We need to get in gear, start moving,’ said Daniel. ‘Dad says he can get us in lorries to Khartoum.

‘And mother will ask Uncle Birhane to help us through Libya.’

‘Your uncle in the oil industry?’ asked Ariam excited.

‘That leaves the mountains and desert, the hardest bits,’ said Jamil.

‘I met a man from Nakfa in Keren. He’s leaving, going west. He feels betrayed, hates Aswerki. He’s organised the boat, got contacts in Sudan. Says it’ll cost eight thousand American dollars, do you have that much?’

Ariam smiled. ‘My parents saved to send me to University in Egypt, they’re okay for that and more.’

‘It’s a lot but my dad is more determined than I am. He says he doesn’t want to lose both his sons,’ said Daniel.

Osman looked at Jamil, the oldest and poorest. ‘What about you, Jamil?’

'The whole family is behind me. I was the first conscripted, now they know the truth, they have clubbed together to help me find a better life for my cousins.'

'Mother and father have enough for the two of us, all their savings but that is what they want,' said Osman.

'Will your man from Nakfa help us, Osman?'

'Idris? Sure, he says it's better to travel in a group, pool resources, look out for each other.'

'Makes sense, but why us?'

'He thought I was a student, rebel, wanted me to join him. I told him about you, he was interested, said he'd meet if you wanted, next Saturday in Keren. Can you make it?'

They checked each other's faces.

'Why not?' asked Jamil.

'Sure,' said Daniel.

'Shall we go together?' suggested Ariam.

'I'll see if I can borrow Dad's truck for the day,' said Daniel. 'I'll call you from the workshop,' he said to Ariam.

'What about me, how will you let me know?' Asked Osman.

'I'll call in after work on Thursday.'

***

Daniel stopped the truck outside Osman's house early on Saturday morning. Jamil and Ariam were up front beside him. They slapped hands over the window.

'Salem,' said Osman.

'Salem,' replied Jamil sleepily.

'Too early,' explained Ariam poking Jamil.

'Load of tyres and two batteries to collect,' moaned Daniel.

'But we've got the truck,' said Osman delighted. He pulled himself up and over to squat in the back. He was looking forward to seeing Idris now he was part of the venture. He felt braver, freer, more grown up.

'It's too early,' said Daniel.

'No problem, nothing better to do, have we?' said Ariam.

'S'pose not.'

When he got onto the highway, Daniel put his foot down and they were jolted into the air every now and again as they hit a pothole or the crumbled side of the road. In between, the truck whirred happily along and they looked out over bare ground, stones and cacti that stretched endlessly to distant, hazy hills, Eritrea seemed endless, neutral, theirs. Together for the day, away from home, the space around liberated their spirits and they felt exuberant. Four pals starting a great adventure.

After an hour Daniel spotted three old petrol pumps at the end of a long forecourt in front of a warehouse. 'Kahsai Haile' was written in faded red on a cream sign over a side entrance. No one seemed interested in the petrol pumps, but the warehouse hummed and throbbed with comings and goings. Cars, lorries, trucks, motorbikes and trailers were queuing on the roadside. Lines of defunct or repaired vehicles waited at the side of the building for their owners. Daniel ignored the queue and drove to a side entrance.

'What are you doing?' asked Osman.

Daniel looked at him sharply, 'We don't need any repairs and we haven't got time to be sitting around.'

Osman's eyebrows lifted and he shrugged. They jumped out to the sound of compressed air, creaking ramps going up and down, cars clanking over metal covers and engines coughing or roaring. There were mechanics in pits or over bonnets calling instructions to helpers. They followed Daniel to the shed. It smelt of oil, sweat and burnt rubber. Daniel circled while they hovered at the door dodging men rolling tyres, carrying batteries and oily cloths. Eventually, Daniel found the person who had spoken to his father and they were taken out to a tall stack of reconditioned tyres behind the garage. They formed a chain passing them up to the truck and loaded them, followed by the two precious batteries. When they had finished, Jamil looked at the tempting cargo and said, 'We'd better cover it.'

'It's all right,' said Daniel eager to get away.

'Abandoned in the back streets of Keren?'

'See what you mean, there's a tarp at the back,' said Daniel.

'Under this lot?' said Ariam.

'Afraid so.'

They climbed onboard and stacked the tyres to one side to free the tarpaulin then spread them back out with the batteries and tried to cover them; but the tarp was too small. They returned to their contact and asked for a polythene sheet. Anything big enough.

'To cover that?' He looked at the back of the truck. 'No chance, sorry.'

He turned back to his workbench. Daniel followed.

'We can't leave it like that. There must be something, somewhere.'

'Can't you see we're busy?' said the man rummaging through a box of cogs, springs and clips.

A horn started to blare; their truck was in its way.

'You'll have to move,' he said.

'Not without a cover,' said Daniel.

A mechanic came from the side of the workshop. 'Get that bloody thing out of here!'

A rusty white van joined the queue holding its horn on constant.

'We're not moving,' repeated Daniel.

'Right then, we'll see what we can do,' said the man through gritted teeth and walked purposefully to the back of the workshop. 'Follow me.'

He started to peel oily black polythene from the floor in front of a line of cluttered workbenches. It was trampled and oil spattered but big. He tried to roll it up while the others held the edges like bridesmaids. He thrust it into Daniel's arms and pushed it into his chest.

'Now get out,' he yelled.

They turned and ran, followed by a chorus of abuse. They flung it over the back of the truck and Jamil punched holes with his knife to thread nylon cord, from his pocket, through it to attach it to the sides of the truck. Daniel's arms and chest were covered in blotches of black oil and his shorts were filthy. Osman and Ariam looked at each other and decided not to say a word until they stopped to buy sambusas on the outskirts of Keren and sent Daniel to the toilets followed by Jamil.

'You and your clever ideas,' muttered Daniel as he used a paper towel and liquid soap to rub the worst of it off.

'Better than telling your dad that you lost the lot.'

'Fat chance!'

Water was not much use against the oil but they cleaned their skin and tidied themselves up.

Back on the road it was Jamil who directed them to the roundabout. He knew Keren Stadium.

'Saw my first football match there with my father and all the family.'

'Did you fill the stands?' laughed Osman.

'There's strength in numbers,' said Jamil. 'I'm proud of my big family.'

'Jamil's tribe,' said Daniel. 'My dad took us there too – Ibrahim and me, longtime ago.' He slowly shook his head to clear the sorrow and tried to concentrate on the route to distract himself.

The café was at the end of the road as Idris said and he was waiting for them looking cool in a navy-blue T-shirt, shorts, and sunglasses. Osman ran to him.

'Good to see you.' Idris grinned and shook his hand for a long time, looking over his shoulder at the other three.

'Oh yes, meet Jamil, Idris.'

Idris guessed they were about the same age, older than the others. Jamil was shorter than him but stocky, his wide chest and strong arms showed more than military training. Idris felt sure he had worked on the land with his family. Jamil was surprised, Idris was smarter than he expected, bigger, older, somehow stronger, he felt wary of him. Idris sensed his reluctance and smiled as he held out his hand, but Jamil kept his guard. When they had shaken hands, Osman introduced Ariam who looked Idris in the eyes; open, pleased, interested. Idris liked his confidence. Ariam's first impression was good. He was keen to find out more about this independent adventurer.

'And this is Daniel,' Osman continued.

Idris laughed, 'And what on earth happened to you?'

Daniel had to laugh. 'Long story, cover for my father's tyres and batteries.' Idris looked nonplussed.

'We came in his father's truck,' explained Ariam.

'And that was the price? You'd better cool down.'

Idris signalled to the waiter and ordered guava juice.

'Sit, everyone – good to meet you. So, what's new?' Idris looked at Osman.

'I'm in.'

'What changed your mind?'

Osman ducked his head and murmured, 'Long story.'

'He's bringing his sister,' said Ariam.

Idris stiffened, looking at Osman. 'The sister at Sawa?'

Osman nodded. Idris's face softened. He patted the top of Osman's arm.

'I understand but that doesn't make it any easier.' He looked at the others. 'What about you? What do you think about it? Is she up to it?'

'She's up to it,' said Daniel.

'She's more than up to it,' said Jamil. 'Good as any man.'

Ariam said, 'Mariam is clever and determined, strength of

character goes a long way on a trip like this.'

'And she's the only one who can make a meal out of a handful of rice and a couple of carrots,' said Daniel.

'A talent not to be sniffed at,' said Idris letting down his guard a little. It seemed to him that if they were all okay with it, then it would not be a problem. From here on in, solidarity was important; all they would have was each other.

'How serious are you?' He looked at Jamil.

'I went from being their ideal soldier to contempt for everything they stand for. It's nothing to do with independence or equality to them. It's power to do as they please with squadrons of young men and women. They're small minded, self-indulgent and some of them are sadistic.'

Jamil sounded more bitter and angry than Osman had ever heard him.

'And you?' Idris asked Daniel.

'My father's sending me away to save the family. He says he's lost one son, he's not going to lose another.'

'But what about you, do you want to go?'

Daniel nodded. 'My brother is the shell of what he was. There's no future here.'

Ariam spoke up, 'Don't worry about me, I know what I want to do. My future's mapped out and it can't happen here.'

Idris nodded. 'Okay, so that leaves you.' He turned to Osman. 'Big change of mind.'

'I saw what they've done to Mariam and I've heard things since. Yes, I love Eritrea and life at home but I know it's a dream that I can't have. As soon as you decide to leave you realise how much the government controls how little choice we have. Nothing will change because we are in their hands the moment we are useful.'

'You've seen the light,' said Idris dismally. 'Okay, hearts and minds solid, down to the practicalities. Did Osman tell you the cost?'

They nodded.

'Our parents can fund both of us,' said Osman.

'And the garage covers me,' said Daniel.

'My parents had enough saved for University abroad and my keep,' added Ariam.

Idris swung round to Jamil.

'My family have all clubbed together for me,' he said. 'I am to lead the way.'

'All set then. What we need most are contacts in Sudan and Libya.'

Daniel spoke up, 'my father sells trucks to a company with a branch in Sudan, he's already asked about transport. They're in Atbara if we can get there, they'll give us a lift to Khartoum.'

'Six of us?' asked Idris.

'We'll have to split up. They said it'll take two trucks, different days.'

'But we can get to Khartoum without much trouble, that's good.'

'My uncle comes back home for Christmas. He'll help us in Libya, I know he will,' said Osman.

'And I have a number to get us on a boat,' said Idris.

'Pity we can't get across the mountains in Dad's truck,' said Daniel.

'Don't worry about getting across the mountains into Sudan. I know the way and where the guards patrol on the other side,' said Idris.

'That's a start,' said Jamil.

'And the rest is up to us,' said Osman.

'And your sister,' said Idris.

'Mariam will be okay,' said Jamil.

Idris straightened up. 'We can only take what we can carry and water will be the heaviest item,' he said.

'And the most important,' said Ariam.

'True,' said Osman, the seriousness of the situation settling in his soul. 'And what we take is up to us?'

'Bare minimum, self-reliance is key. We can support each other but we can't carry anyone.'

'We have to get Mariam out of Sawa,' said Osman.

'It can't be long before we leave, they'll be looking for her as soon as she goes missing,' said Daniel. 'Ibrahim was a day late going back and they were at our door.'

'January, February is good. Everyone gets careless in the heat,' said Jamil.

'Into the lion's den. How the hell can we get her out?'

'Mother's contact says the men who deliver food to the camp are underpaid and detest Afwerki; they could be bribed to swap places,' said Osman.

'When were you thinking of going?' Jamil asked Idris.

'Sooner rather than later. Not long after Christmas, what do you think?'

Osman looked at the others and said, 'January, February is good with us.'

'Mariam will be allowed home for Christmas?' asked Daniel.

Osman nodded. 'I'm depending on it.'

'No reason why not,' said Jamil. 'They keep up a pretence of normality.'

Idris put his hand on Osman's shoulder and looked seriously into his face. 'If you can get away with it, the day you do, you will all be in danger. They will be round to your family, searching, threatening. As long as she is in Eritrea, she is in danger and so is everyone around her.'

'We can't risk driving straight from Sawa to Nakfa – if we're pursued it's all over.'

'Not sure about transport; we can't leave a vehicle on the mountain,' said Daniel, thinking of his father's precious truck.

'We have to be driven in,' said Ariam.

'Separately,' said Idris, 'less obvious than a crowded truck.'

'We have to get to Mariam the day before we leave.'

'She can stay at our house overnight, too dangerous at

yours, that's where they'll first look,' said Ariam.

'What about your parents?'

'They know what we're doing and why we're doing it. Difficult situations take desperate measures. They'll be okay.'

'We can get her out,' said Jamil.

'How are we going to get to Sawa, it's in the middle of nowhere?' asked Osman.

Daniel slapped his back. 'Haven't we got a garage? Leave it to me.'

'So when?' asked Jamil.

They all looked at Idris. 'I'll let you know the exact date after Christmas.'

'How?' asked Jamil.

Idris looked at Ariam. 'You have a phone?' Ariam nodded. 'I'll let you know end of January.'

The four looked at each other. 'I'll let you know, Daniel, as soon as I hear.'

'And I'll pass it on,' said Daniel.

'I wish you luck with that; one less in there has to be good. I just hope she can hold her own,' said Idris.

'She will, believe me she will, and some,' said Osman vehemently and the others watched Idris's scepticism dissolve.

'Anything I can do?' asked Idris.

'No, no, it's up to us now. You'll be doing your bit over the mountain,' said Jamil.

'Some food?' Idris summoned the waiter to bring dates and roasted peanuts. They talked about their families, what they liked, what they hated but not what they were looking forward to.

When they left the café, Ariam, Daniel and Jamil congratulated Osman on finding a treasure. They trusted Idris.

***

Christmas was an uneasy time for Osman. When Mariam came home, he pummelled her with reasons to accompany him until she surrendered. Then they shared the bittersweet welcoming of grandparents, aunties, uncles, friends – flurries of people bringing food and gifts – sitting under the trees in the courtyard. Routine, ritual, timetables no longer dictating. Every day a friend day, a love day, a giving, sharing, chattering, drinking, dancing day. Pots stayed full, warmed one after another and a table under an awning was kept supplied with every colour of fruit and vegetable. The whole family ran to and fro, filling gaps on serving plates, topping up drinks and providing music.

There were two waves; 25*th* December and 7*th* January. Birhane came in the bigger second wave. It was not until Thursday 9*th* that Salma and Dawit could take him out for an early morning walk. Birhane stopped dead when he heard what they were contemplating.

'No, no, no. You can't let them do that.'

'He must.'

'Mariam too? It's too dangerous for girls.'

'We know,' said Salma, 'but nothing's worse than what she's suffering here.'

'Impossible. There are slavers looking for young girls, she won't stand a chance.'

'They are prepared. There are people ready to meet them on the way,' replied Salma.

'And they'll have enough to keep themselves,' said Dawit.

'Can you help them?'

He looked at their grim, determined faces and said, 'Of course I'll do all I can but it's not easy in Libya. I don't want to lose my job. I can get lifts in the company's oil tankers and maybe beds for a night or two.'

'Thank you Birhane. I knew you wouldn't let us down,' said Salma.

Under the bright, jingling surface of Christmas festivities, the plotting and planning continued. Each giving a surreal quality to the other. Osman, Daniel, Mariam and Ariam met at the café and arranged meetings in the open where they could not be spied on. Idris arranged to meet them outside Keren. He was pleased with progress. The other three were impressed by Idris's matter of fact attitude. He told them he knew a safe route over the mountain into Sudan, hidden from border guards. The more they tapped into their escape route the more they learnt; new contacts, new stopping places emerged day by day.

Mariam went back to Sawa with the promise of an early release. Jamil and Osman planned to 'kidnap' her at the end of the month. Ariam too, had to return to his military training centre. Daniel and Osman went back to work. Osman felt guilty when Sebhat praised his baskets and taught him more complicated techniques.

In the evenings at home, Wani helped Osman water the vegetables and Osman followed his mother around like a lost lamb; passing her things before she knew she needed them, picking oranges and lemons, pruning the hibiscus bushes, and digging dung into the ground for the next crop. He ran home after work in time for his father's return. In the evenings by the fire, Dawit would slip his arm over Salma's shoulder so she could snuggle closer. Delina was restless until her mother gave her some cloth to sew.

The four boys felt like conspirators and started to take precautions in ordinary everyday activities. To be caught trying to leave the country was imprisonment, torture, death. They clung to their dream of escape.

When Daniel appeared at their entrance on Thursday 29*th* January, Osman's heart jumped. Salma and Dawit felt a gulf in their stomachs. Only Delina, combing her long hair and Wani, doing his homework, remained oblivious of the tension. Salma looked nervously in their direction and Osman signalled that he would take Daniel out into the garden.

They stood between Dawit's motorbike and Salma's donkey at the front of the house, watching the lane.

'We meet Idris in the trenches facing Nakfa on Sunday. He'll be looking out for us. We must go in separately, different times, not to draw attention.'

'Sunday trip to the trenches,' laughed Osman nervously. 'Mariam?'

'Tomorrow – Friday will be work routine, normal deliveries. Saturday is too risky.'

Osman gulped. 'How can we let her know?'

'Will your mother be at the market tomorrow?'

Osman nodded dumbfounded. 'That's too late.'

'The market starts early. If can she get word to Mariam before midday we're okay.'

'Tomorrow is our best chance?' Osman asked desperate to know if his mother could do it.

'Our only chance,' said Daniel grimly.

'She can't stay at Ariam's for two nights!'

'Stop worrying, Ariam's parents want him to get away, they're ready to help, and they're so rich and upright, no one will suspect them.'

'What about tomorrow? Do Ariam and Jamil know? Are they up for it?'

'Course they are, she's like a sister and a weekday fits best for Sawa deliveries that's for sure.'

'How're we going to get to Nakfa, it's a long way?'

'You can come with us, Dad's taking me.

'And Jamil?'

'Yeh, he'll make his way there after us. I've got to go, few things to sort out,' said Daniel with a wry smile.

'Thanks Daniel, see you tomorrow.'

'Dawn!'

Osman shivered and went inside. Time had seemed endless while they waited and terrifyingly short now it had begun.

'We have to get Mariam tomorrow.' He looked desperately at his mother. She was up on her feet in an instant. 'I have to tell Fatima, she has the drivers, she needs to get word to them.'

'And to Mariam,' said Dawit. 'I'd better take you to the village.'

'Look after Delina and Wani, Osman.'

The engine revved and Salma climbed behind Dawit. 'Let's go…'

Osman heard her voice and they roared into the night. He looked around. There was nothing he could do. It all seemed so tenuous, out of his control. He couldn't rest, couldn't leave the hut.

Delina was combing her hair looking in their tiny mirror. 'Do you think I should braid my hair?' she asked holding her hair up behind her head and checking the mirror.

'Does it matter?' replied Osman.

'Asmarina has a thick braid down her back. She's beautiful.'

'So what?'

He turned away and Delina watched him lay a yellow T-shirt, underpants and jeans beside his bed then add sunglasses and a wallet.

Wani came over. 'What are you doing?' he asked.

'What does it look like I'm doing?'

'Putting out clothes.'

'So?' Osman snapped.

Wani looked questioningly at his brother then took the sunglasses and put them on.

'Don't touch,' shouted Osman and swiped them off Wani's forehead.

'You're not my brother.' Wani stamped out of the hut.

Osman sank onto the bed and hugged his knees. Delina came over, sat beside him and turned her back.

'Will you braid my hair?'

Osman pushed her away. 'Leave me alone,' he snarled and she too ran outside. Again, he clenched his body, gripping his knees until he heard the motorbike and ran to know the worst.

'It's all right. They will let Mariam know first thing tomorrow morning.'

'And the drivers?'

'They expect you at half past eight.' She went to a tin box by her sewing machine and took out a wad of notes, counted five hundred nakfa and handed it to Osman. 'This is what they're expecting. Here's another two if things get difficult.'

'Thanks Mum.'

Osman put the five hundred into his wallet and the extra two hundred in his jean pocket.

'Good luck, son,' said his father. 'Now get some sleep.'

'Where's Wani? He should be in bed.'

'I'll find him,' said Osman.

Wani was sitting on the wall behind the house tickling Lemlem and Genet's noses with the fronds of a reed. Genet sneezed and snorted. Osman took a big nobbly carrot from the reject bin.

'You shouldn't be tormenting them. Here give them this to make up for it.'

'Why can't I have your sunglasses?'

'Because you don't need them.'

Osman looked up into the sky, laced with stars and put his arm round Wani's shoulder, 'Daniel and me, we're going a long way tomorrow. There's more to sunglasses than stopping the sun. You don't need them.'

'But they're sure cool, man.'

Osman looked at Wani. 'Don't you grow up too quickly. Come on, time for bed.'

***

Daniel's father beat his head with his fists, eyes popping out of his head. 'Madness!'

'It's only for a day.'

'It's not the truck. What if you're caught? I lose you, my business – who knows? We could all be shot.'

'We're not going to get caught.'

His father looked at his son in despair. 'Sawa's a military training centre with only an airport and high security prison for company – the area is deserted. How are you not going to be seen?'

Daniel smiled. 'Osman's mother has a contact with the suppliers there; food deliveries.'

'So, what can you do with a crate of canned tomatoes?'

'It's more than that, there are thousands there.'

'So?'

'Deliveries twice a week.'

'And?'

'That's our cover.'

'You think they don't check?'

'Course they will. We'll change places, dress like them so it'll all seem the same.'

His father put his hands on his hips and stood back shaking his head.

'Just like that!'

'Mariam's father and mother are paying them.'

'And what chance has Mariam of joining you?'

'She's already had messages from us.'

Daniel put his hand on his father's arm. 'It's Mariam, Dad and she's gone through worse than Ibrahim.'

His father looked at him sadly. 'She'll be sent back in days, to Allah knows what punishment.'

'No, she's coming with us.'

'Over the mountain?'

Adem Musa stared open mouthed at his son and then shook his head.

'There's nothing for her here either,' said Daniel urgently.

Adem laid his hands on Daniel's shoulders and looked into

his eyes. 'Be careful; plan like it's a military campaign until you're free of Eritrea.'

Daniel lowered his head. 'I know, Dad, I know. Don't worry, Jamil's onto it and Idris is a survivor, he knows all the ropes.'

'Please Allah, let it be true.'

'Not for long…'

'The truck's yours but bring it back.'

***

Osman heard the soft crackle of stones under tyres as the truck slowly nosed along the side of Salma's plot in the dark. Daniel pushed open the door and Osman swung up to sit by his side with just a nod. They stopped outside Ariam's garden and waited, staring at its black and white chequerboard front. All was still and silent behind its black windows, no reassuring flicker of light. Suddenly a hunched figure appeared behind them carrying a soft bundle. Osman moved along and Ariam joined them.

'What you got there?' whispered Osman.

'Clothes.'

An explanation that explained nothing but Osman did not pursue it. On the outskirts of the village, they stopped by a cluster of huts and Jamil climbed into the back.

They tunnelled through darkness zigzagging around rows of houses and sheds big and small. They didn't speak until they turned from the bumpy track to a smoother straight road heading away from Asmara, past the hills to the plain. Black lightened to grey, then trees, fields and rooftops came alive in colour. They shifted their bottoms and let go of the dashboard and handles. Osman passed his water gourd round and they drank, loosening their jaws. Their eyes scanned every building, parked car or bin. The further they sped inland the less there was to see. A convoy of army trucks, packed with sleepy looking soldiers passed in the opposite direction. They were overtaken by an old white Toyota and tried not to duck or hide their faces. There were no buses, bikes or animals. There was nothing to see but the road for a while, then, up ahead there were shops and houses on either side; a small settlement.

'It must be there,' said Osman.

Daniel hunched over the wheel searching for a name.

'What was it called again?' asked Ariam scanning both sides.

'Brinesh Stores,' replied Osman.

It was not on the highway. They turned round and headed back to try the back streets. Parallel to the road, there were small shops, a garage, a mosque and a café but no big grocery and vegetable depot. They tried the other side of the main road where there were more larger buildings and not so many houses. They found a grey building with a glass front showing tills and shelves of fruit and vegetables surrounded by a sea of tarmac. A refrigerated lorry sat along the side and three large vans were parked behind the store in front of wide roll up doors. There was no sign of life. They parked in a far corner of the car park feeling exposed.

Eventually a motor bike puttered to a halt by the door. A young man slid from the back and the middle-aged driver rummaged in his pocket for a key. They looked furtively in their direction then rolled up the shutter and disappeared into the darkness. Osman slipped out of the van and followed them. After a moment he waved Jamil over. The older man gave Jamil keys to the end van nearest the doors and told him to back it into the store. He clicked the light switch and they were overwhelmed by the enormity of the enterprise. Bulging sacks of grain, flour, lentils stacked high up into the roof, dwarfing them; onions and potatoes in plastic netting were piled high in a corner. White plastic drums of water filled a wall along with towers of square tins of coffee and tea. The older man took a list from a shelf and indicated a pile of sacks – '25,' he said and all four of them set to work, heaving them into the back of the van without exchanging a word. The young man jumped in to push the sacks as far back as they would go. The older man pointed to another. '15.' They shouldered the sacks and pushed them tight together into the back of the van. '10.' They heard each other's heavy breathing as they hurried to load the van in silence. Cardboard boxes of tins came next, then drinks and finally a few fresh fruit and vegetables.

Jamil carefully closed the big doors of the van. The two men stood stiffly side by side, waiting. Osman stepped in front of the older man and pulled the five hundred from his back trouser pocket. The younger one's eyes widened at the sight.

The older man quickly counted while his eyes darted furtively around.

'I was told six hundred,' he said and stared at Osman, stubborn, determined.

Osman slid one of the hundred Nakfa bills free and handed it over.

The man pocketed it with grim satisfaction and nodded to the other. They jumped onto their bike, revved loudly, and roared away. Daniel joined Osman watching their departure.

'Father and son?' asked Osman still looking in their direction.'That's what I thought; you're the son.'

'And I'm your father,' said Jamil rolling up his shirt sleeves. He went to the hedge, scooped earth and dust and rubbed it into his hair, hat and shirt then loosened his belt and pulled his shirt to hang over it.

'Any fatter?' he asked.

Osman looked doubtful and laughed. 'Not as fit, that's for sure.'

Jamil tucked his hair under the hat and they were ready.

'Good luck,' said Ariam and he joined Daniel in the truck.

While they waited to see the van emerge from the gloom of the warehouse, they heard cars arriving at the front, voices greeting each other, then dispersing inside. Eventually the big van crept out, chassis close to the ground. They couldn't look at Jamil or Osman's faces. They watched it turn left towards the military base.

Osman looked at his watch. 'How long will it take?'

Jamil shrugged. 'Dunno,' He banged the steering wheel. 'This old lady ain't goin' anywhere fast.'

The road seemed endless and the area barren. An occasional army vehicle passed on the other side but nothing followed in their direction.

'What's the drill again?' asked Jamil.

'Drinks first – door at the end of the canteen. Cans second – door in the middle. The rest down the end.'

'Like feeding dates to a camel,' said Jamil. 'No problem.' He settled himself more comfortably behind the wheel.

A fighter jet split the sky overhead followed by another's loud swish. In the distance they could see a grim concrete building with high barbed wire fencing and sentry posts.

'The prison,' said Jamil.

Another half hour of dust, grit and stone and Jamil saw the barracks.

'Sawa,' he said.

The distant lines of huts came closer. Between them in some places there were squares of ground, some with assault courses set out and equipment stacked. They were awe stricken by the enormity of the operation. Line after long line of identical huts extended to the horizon in every direction.

'I didn't realise,' muttered Osman.

'Room for eighteen thousand to lay their heads.'

'It's as big as a city,' whispered Osman staring through the window incredulous and afraid.

'Where's the bloody entrance?' shouted Jamil, slowing down and peering through the windscreen at the uniform rows of huts. Eventually they saw a few smaller buildings close to the road and turned into a wide entrance with a kiosk at one side.

They wound down their windows ready to answer questions and heard a regimental voice yelling staccato instructions followed by the pounding of feet behind a building on their right. They caught glimpses of a group of youngsters; girls and boys, turning and wheeling around a bare patch of earth. The guard came to Jamil's side of the van.

'What we got today?' he asked with a toothy grin. 'Anythin' special?'

'Couple o' watermelons,' said Jamil.

'Won't be for the likes o' me, no sirree,' he whistled through a gap in his front teeth.

Jamil shoved his papers into the man's chest. He took them, waved them in the air then elaborately stroked the creases out leaning against the truck but he didn't read them. He knew the truck and what it contained. He slapped its side and handed back the papers.

'See you later,' he shouted.

And they were off into the unknown. They stared at the lines of identical huts and Jamil slowed down.

'Which one, for the sake of Allah?' hissed Jamil afraid to stop in view of the guard, equally afraid of missing the place and having to turn back. The van crept forward.

Osman went through his conversation with the man at the depot. 'Storage at the end of this line, fifth and sixth huts and a barn at the end.'

'Two, three, four, five, this it?' Jamil was looking at a closed, dusty building.

'Has to be,' said Osman. 'The first few huts were offices. I saw through the windows.' He examined the fifth, no door, no boarding around and high slit windows. 'Turn down the side,' he said.

Jamil turned into the alley way and sighed with relief to be out of view of the guard. There was a wider door but no sign of life.

'This must be it,' said Osman.

He jumped down and opened the door. In front of him there were large plastic drums of water and a couple of large square tins of coffee. To his left there were bags of powdered milk and big wooden boxes of tea. No one appeared. He listened to the stillness, nothing. It was almost noon, siesta time, if only they were all asleep, impossible but it was mercifully still and quiet. His sea of adrenalin stopped crashing on the rocks. He went back to Jamil and they carried in enough drums, pails and tins to double what was left around the walls.

A slit of light appeared in the corner. They raised their heads to see a figure in uniform standing in an inner doorway.

'What do you think you're doing?'

'Delivery,' said Osman carrying a tin of coffee on his shoulder.

'Not so fast, they have to be counted off.'

Jamil stopped in his tracks with two big drums of water in his hands.

'Aw, come on boss, give us a break. We got two more deliveries after this.'

The man closed the door behind him and advanced on the two of them.

'That's none of my business.' He tapped a clipboard with his pen. 'This is.'

'Okay, okay,' said Jamil and set his load down with the rest by the door. 'This lot is this morning's.' He indicated their newly delivered, carefully stacked piles.

The man bridled then bent to count.

'We've got more,' said Osman.

The man stood up, stuck his pencil behind his ear and went to lean against the wall.

'You'd better bring them in, hadn't you?'

Jamil and Osman took it in turns to breach the door with load after load until their shirts were sticking to their backs. Jamil dumped the last crate of cordials down.

'That's it.'

They turned to go.

'Aren't you forgetting something?'

They looked at each other, then in his direction. He was waving a sheet of paper at them. Osman went to collect it.

'Oh no, not until I've counted.'

They stood by the door feeling cornered while he laboriously counted and ticked and finally signed their release.

Outside Jamil muttered, 'I'd like to ram his bloody paper down his throat.'

Osman wiped his forehead with the hem of his T-shirt.

'Not finished yet,' he said grimly.

Jamil rammed the gear stick into reverse and they lurched back onto the centre path and the next shed.

'We'd better find someone this time,' said Osman.

They knocked on the door, opened it and called. There was no one in the store but they could hear voices in an adjoining room.

They shouted, 'delivery.'

'I'll go.'

A man, with sleeves rolled up, came through and looked them up and down.

'Delivery, huh!' He shrugged and turned to go.

'Where shall we put it?' asked Osman.

He scanned the room impatiently and pointed to a space at the far side. 'Over there.'

They carried boxes of large catering cans of everything from tomato puree to beans, stacking them higher and higher until their shoulders ached.

'All done,' shouted Jamil through the door, resigned to a repeat of the same rigmarole.

'Okay, see ya,' someone called back.

Osman and Jamil looked at each other. Osman raised his eyebrows and shrugged, Jamil turned to get out.

Back in the van, their excitement mounted as they headed to the cold store.

'Will she be there?' asked Jamil.

Osman looked at his watch. 'Give it half an hour unloading. She'll be with us at lunch time – 1:30pm.'

'Allah willing.'

A high wooden building straddled the end of the rows of huts. They turned right looking for the entrance and pulled up in front of wide wooden doors at the end. The sun beat down on Osman as he opened a door and waited while Jamil checked the narrow, dusty roads and buildings for movement, wondering where Mariam was.

Inside was a different world, lofty and dark, cool after the burning sun and still. Straw spread out from a corner, muffling their steps. They shuffled slowly around, admiring the space, the sense of order and calm, feeling small.

'New, are you?' A man in tight blue jeans and a white long-sleeved shirt open almost to the waist was leaning his elbow against a fridge, legs crossed watching them.

They jumped.

'No,' said Jamil.

'Yes,' mumbled Osman.

Their interlocutor eased himself off the fridge and stalked towards Osman.

'Thought so,' he said. 'So, what have you got for us today?' He asked circling Osman.

'Usual,' said Osman.

'Nothing exciting?'

Jamil stepped in front of him. 'Watermelons?'

The man eyed Jamil suspiciously. 'Okay, that's a start, let's see them.' He turned towards the van and they followed. Jamil opened the doors and exchanged a look with Osman over the man's back.

On top of the sacks there were a couple of trays of peppers and lettuce.

‘Jirjir,’ the man said delightedly, fondling the green leaves.

‘They won’t go far,’ said Osman.

‘Not for the troops,’ replied the man. ‘Officer’s only.’

‘Yours too?’

‘A bit here, a bit there. They’re not going to miss that are they?’ He patted his hair. ‘Let’s get it in before it fries!’

Osman’s yellow T-shirt was clinging to his chest.

‘Why don’t you back the van inside. It’s cooler in the shade,’ he suggested.

Jamil and Osman looked at each other, incredulous.

‘Good idea,’ said Jamil. He ran to the cab and reversed the van into the barn. Osman opened the back and grabbed a sack of lentils. The man loaded a sack of potatoes onto his shoulder and Jamil followed with a large paper sack of flour. The three of them arranged the melons on the straw. Osman took off his cap and ran his hands through his hair. The store man stopped on the way back to load up, staring at Osman’s young face, framed by glossy, dark hair. His sudden attention sent an electric shock of alarm through Osman. Had he realised they were fakes?

‘All right?’ he asked.

The man relaxed, laughed apologetically.

‘Yeh, good,’ he said. ‘Better.’ Obviously delighted. Osman wiped his forehead with the bottom of his T-shirt in relief and the store man noticed his taut, lean diaphragm.

‘Would you like a drink?’ The man asked.

Osman looked at him, surprised.

‘Yes or no?’

There was no way to get rid of him, he nodded. ‘Thank you.’

The fridge held water and flavoured milks.

‘What do you fancy?’ he asked.

‘Water’s good,’ said Osman.

‘That looks tempting,’ said Jamil behind them pointing to banana milk.

He passed back their drinks.

‘Thanks’ grinned Jamil and slapped the man on the back making the silver chain on his chest jump. Their mouths were dry with thirst and fear. They drank quickly.

‘We’ll soon have this done, won’t we?’ The man looked at Osman and grabbed a sack of lentils. Osman and Jamil stared helplessly at each other; how could they get rid of him? Mariam would be with them any minute. They toted their sacks so quickly they outstripped the man and he said, ‘You’re used to this, strong, aren’t you?’

‘Okay, only potatoes and onions left,’ said Jamil. ‘We’ll look after that.’ He hoisted a bag of potatoes on his back and Osman stacked nets of onions against his chest.

‘Please yourselves,’ the man replied and disappeared into a space at the back of the barn.

‘He fancies you,’ said Jamil bent under his load.

‘Creepy,’ said Osman, onions rustling as he shuddered.

When they had finished it was past 1:30pm and they had not heard or seen a sign of anyone. There was no door guarding the space where the store man had gone. They felt self-conscious, unsure, as if they were being watched. Their ears strained, sifting sounds of movement, voices, all muffled by distance, midday sun and siesta.

They heard the van door click and swung round to see a slim figure slide across the front seat. They looked at each other. Jamil ushered Osman to the van while he checked around.

Osman opened the van door and hissed, ‘In the back and get those clothes off.’ Mariam looked confused.

Osman peeled off his T-shirt. ‘Put this on.’ Mariam grabbed it and ran to the back. Osman wriggled out of his jeans looking around. He threw them into the back and grabbed Ariam’s bag of clothes. He pulled a grey hoodie over his head. Jamil joined them ready for take-off.

‘Changing? What’s that for?’ said the store man staring at Osman’s bare legs and Ariam’s white jeans. ‘Party?’

Jamil and Osman froze, the back of the van was still.

'Yeh, that's right,' said Jamil.

Osman put his arms through the hoodie and picked up the jeans. The man advanced. Osman looked desperately at Jamil who walked over to the man as Osman zipped himself up.

'Wanna come?'

The man looked at Osman. 'Why not? Not far, is it?'

'No.' Jamil took aim and landed his punch in the middle of his chin. His teeth clattered and his eyes rolled up into his head as he dropped. 'Not far.'

They dragged him inside and covered him with straw.

Jamil uncovered the wheel well and Osman curled up inside while Mariam took his place in front. She tucked her hair under Osman's cap and put on his sunglasses. Jamil passed the one piece of paper they had to Mariam and she passed it to the guard at the gate.

'Afternoon off now, is it?' He asked enviously.

'We hope,' said Jamil tapping the steering wheel.

'Some people have all the luck,' said the guard as the wheels kicked up dust in a rapid take off.

***

Sebhat was pleased with his protégé. Osman was interested in their customers, chatted pleasantly and was popular. On his last morning, he sold two big, intricate baskets with lids to a well-known trader from Asmara. In his delight, Sebhat insisted on giving him a bonus which made Osman regret his betrayal. He longed to explain but he couldn't implicate Sebhat or risk a careless word and jeopardising everything, his loyalty was to the others now. He tried to refuse but Sebhat muttered how he was like the son he'd never had. Faven and Sebhat had been good to him. The moment of departure was a wrench. He couldn't leave without saying, 'Dehan kunu,'[8] to Faven so while Sebhat was clearing the front and closing the door, Osman pretended he'd forgotten something so that he could poke his head round the back door and call, 'Dehan kunu, Faven.' It was even harder to say a final, 'Dehan kunu,' to Sebhat who was expecting to see him the next morning.

***

His journey home was strange, as if he'd never seen the path before. Bare, trampled earth studded with low grass and an occasional bush or cactus; ordinary, familiar, safe; nothing, no one, had ever posed a threat here but he felt alienated, as if he were letting everyone down. The ultimate betrayal; Sebhat, his family, friends, neighbours. He watched his feet treading the dust, one before the other making their way home for the last time. They would have to take him three thousand kilometres before he could smell the salt air of freedom. One step at a time, he would do it, they would all do it; Idris, Ariam, Jamil, Daniel and Mariam; all different but united in hope.

His final day at home with his mother and father, Delina and Wani, was too precious to know how to spend it or what to say. It was impossible to tell them what they meant to him, how grateful he was for their love, their unselfish love. Some feelings were too big for words. The only farewell they had known was Mariam's departure for Sawa. That was sad and didn't get any better. To lose the two of them together was cruel and he still didn't know if he was strong enough to leave their love and safety for the unknown.

His mother was already back from market when he arrived. He was so pleased to find her there that he hugged her for a long time and Wani joined in. Osman had no sooner rinsed

8 Tigrinya for goodbye.

his hands and face, when they heard his father's motorbike. He went outside rubbing his hair with a towel and his father gave him a brief silent hug. Delina followed them inside; heavy, slow, thoughtful. Her eyes followed Osman's every move.

'How about a picnic in the foothills tomorrow?' Salma suggested.

Delina's face lit up. 'Great idea, mama.' She clapped her hands. 'Can we take Mariam's tripod and kettle?'

'So long as you carry it. And the coffee. Now do you think you can make some shiro?[9] We'll be hungry by the time we've climbed the mountain.'

'I can, I can.' Delina started to bustle around the stove finding what she needed.

'Plenty of berbere for me,' said Osman.

'Oh no, not too much,' wailed Wani.

'I'll make some orange juice to cool you down,' said Osman and went to the outdoor shed where the oranges were stored.

'I'll put some yoghurt in too,' said Salma.

'Did you bring prickly pears home from market?' asked Wani.

'I did, lots.' She ruffled Wani's hair and held his forehead in the palm of her hand for a moment.

'I'll bring my knife,' said Dawit, 'and find a rug.'

When he had squeezed enough oranges to fill a couple of bottles, Osman found the enamel mugs that he and Mariam used to warm their hands on out on their expeditions early in the mornings and gave them to Delina. 'Here, we'll need these.'

'Thank you.' Delina held one in the palm of each hand, missing Mariam and thinking how much Osman loved his expeditions with her and those mugs. All over, she thought, everything is changing. She looked at Osman quietly folding his clothes and a wave of loss overcame her. She was transfixed by

9 Onion and chickpea powder in water seasoned with berbere spice.

grief and acceptance, the inevitability of their family break-up.

They were ready within minutes and set off to the foothills with Wani holding Osman's hand, skipping along then running impatiently between them, kicking stones, urging them on.

'Stop that!' Yelled Delina as a shower of grit and dust covered her legs.

'He's excited,' said Salma.

'Come on monkey,' said Osman and lifted him onto his shoulders, but not for long as they headed uphill separating into single file like a camel train. Small animals skittered away as they passed and birds of every size and colour flew up in front of them.

They spread a bright cloth on a flat spot shaded by overhanging rocks and Salma set out the shiro, yoghurt and injera. They helped themselves in silence. No one knew what to say but the silence drew attention to all that could not be said.

'Not too spicy Wani?' asked Salma. 'More yoghurt?'

The freedom of being outdoors, the climb and hunger took over and Wani replied, 'Another please, not too much shiro.' He drank Osman's orange juice. Talk was limited to the here and now. They couldn't think of the future, not even tonight and especially not tomorrow, when there would no longer be anything shared to talk about. Now they were celebrating being together here, in a land they loved, sharing a meal, pretending it was not their last.

Salma tipped prickly pears onto the cloth. Dawit took out his knife and peeled them, passing them round. Delina filled Mariam's kettle and set it on the primus. Osman was restless after the excitement of the kidnap; he was missing Mariam even more. He knew she would be happy with Ariam's sisters, especially his mother, a woman who was loved by everyone; round as a ball, happy and bouncing with her family. He circled the site looking up at the mountain and the endless blue of the sky then started to climb. Salma nodded to Dawit in the direction of his retreating back and Dawit followed. Wani set off behind and Salma called him back.

'I wanna go be with Osman.'

'I know but Osman needs a bit of quiet time. He won't be long, don't worry. I brought your ball, how about football?' Salma swept up the cloth and picnic things to clear the site.

'Can't play footie with girls.'

'Don't you believe it,' said Delina getting up.

She took the ball from her mother and threw it to Wani. Instinct made him catch it.

'Come on then.' Delina crouched like a goalkeeper. 'Between these two cacti.' A tall cactus stood on either side of the track up the mountain. Wani couldn't resist. He dropped the ball to his feet and kicked with all his power but it was heading up hill and landed short. Delina ran for it and started to dribble towards him. He tackled, she swerved and passed it to Salma but Wani was quick. He stepped in front of his mother and kicked the ball away. He dribbled and dodged their tackles to kick the ball up the track.

'Five points.' Applauded Salma and Wani was won over to the game. They played fiercely and intently, circling around under the rocks. Salma lost herself in the game. All the anxieties of the past year evaporated as she focused on the ball. Dodging her younger son and daughter gave her back her energy until the heat of the sun sent her looking for shade.

'Half time, come over here and cool down for a bit.'

'Ah Mum,' moaned Wani.

'Good idea.' Delina joined her mother.

Wani rubbed the sweat from his forehead and dropped in the shade of a stone. 'Not long…,' he muttered.

Osman found a shelf with a wide vista and looked out across the plain where the river Barka ran. Clusters of bright pink and black flamingos stalked the shallows, heads in the water, egrets flew up and settled on the banks and smaller birds poked the earth. Not far below, there were more round, thatched houses like theirs. A young man was herding goats with a stick. On either side of the river, down the valley, thick green umbrellas of banana trees ran in swathes between the higher, airier doum palms with their bunches of young rust-coloured dates. Two camels made a stately progress along a path between fields of sorghum and maize. Their humps piled high with palm leaves, following a man in a beige robe and terracotta coloured turban. This seemingly idyllic picture of peace and plenty, filled Osman with anguish at the thought of leaving. His love for Eritrea, his family, friends and neighbours pulled him back from the precipice of flight.

'What are you thinking?' asked Dawit.

Osman rubbed the water from his eyes. 'It looks so peaceful and prosperous, safe and familiar.'

Dawit put his hand on his son's shoulder and looked into his face. 'But it's a lie, Osman. Even this will be out of reach if you're a conscript with no choice of what to do, where to go. There's not a lot of land for farming anymore. It is barren from over production, mis-management under so many occupying powers.'

Osman straightened his back. 'It's hard to believe when you look down there, but Mariam proved it.' Osman turned an agonised face to his father. 'There can't be anywhere as beautiful as this.' He spread his arms towards the coast. 'And the sea, our sea; so many fish, beaches, beautiful shells…'

'Out of reach,' said Dawit sadly.

'But not to you,' said Osman.

'My youth was war with Ethiopia, not Eritrea. Yours is different.'

'Osman turned back to look up the mountain. 'What's over there? Anything better?'

'Nothing can be worse. You know what democracy means, justice, freedom, opportunity. You have to find it.'

'I'd like to bring it home for you.'

'I'm protected by the mining company; our life is settled.'

'Only as long as you work and give up your children.'

'That's why you have to go. That's not a sacrifice we are prepared to make, you have to go, Osman, keep our hope alive.' He scooped up a handful of earth. 'Take this with you, then it'll always be part of you. You're not leaving your country; you're taking it with you.'

Osman held out his cap and watched the precious powder pour into it.

'Thank you, Dad, our mountain together. It won't be so bad with that in my pocket. It's a promise to come back.'

They could hear Salma laughing and Wani taunting her. The sound of their feet running and as Osman emerged from behind a rock, the ball landed at his feet. He set down his hat, picked it up and threw it in between them.

'Come and join us, show him how to do it,' called his mother out of breath.

'I can do it better than you,' shouted Wani and hooked the ball into the air with his toe. Delina ran to catch it but Osman was too quick and the game took off with all of them running and kicking when they could, to whoever they wanted, haphazard and exhilarating.

At home the precious earth was tipped into a cellophane packet and his mother sewed it into his jacket pocket. She had made a canvas satchel for Osman and filled it with biscuits, dried fruit, meat and cheese. Osman folded his Christmas outfit into a paper bag and tucked it in. Salma rolled up a habesha[10] and netela[11] for Mariam and put them in her bag with a T-shirt and underwear then she collected soap, a comb, toothbrush and cloth into a little zip bag that Delina had made and put it on top with some perfumed oil to rub into her skin and hair.

---

10 Cotton tunic.

11 Shawl.

'The heaviest thing you have to carry is water. You'll need so much,' said Dawit.

'We can carry it and we'll find supplies, don't worry,' said Osman pushing a couple of water gourds into his bag.

***

The next morning at the far end of the mountains, Idris chose a vantage point under an acacia tree to scan the roads. Deep, narrow trenches cut out of the stone, circled the foothills in jagged lines. He followed a land rover winding its way through the town and out towards the hills. It bumped alongside the first row of trenches, disappeared behind a dip and when it came back into view he stepped out and waved his arms. It pulled to a halt beneath him on the other side of the trench. Idris pointed to a plank further along. Ariam's father jumped out followed by Ariam and a third person descended on the other side so Idris could not see Mariam until she came round the bonnet of the vehicle. A tall, slim figure in a yellow kaftan with green embroidery at the neck and hem was looking at him with large, steady brown eyes. Her hair covered by a dark green shawl. Her cheeks were hollow under high cheek bones. He drew a long slow breath, shaking his head, feeling suddenly self-conscious.

Ariam rushed across the plank to shake Idris's hand. 'Good to see you,' he said. Idris held his hand in both of his looking over Ariam's shoulder at Mariam standing behind, waiting. When Ariam moved aside, Idris faced Mariam. He spread his arms and said, 'selam aleykum,' in a solemn voice.

'Selam aleykum,' she replied returning his stare. His eyes were respectful, honest. Mariam lowered her eyes feeling suddenly at peace.

Ariam's father shook Idris's hand and held his arm. 'Look after them, won't you?' he asked earnestly.

'We will all look after each other.'

'Thank you.' The older man's throat thickened.

'I am sorry but there aren't many land rovers in these parts and parked on the hill here?'

'I mustn't make things difficult for you, I'll go.' He turned to Ariam. 'I'll be in town for a couple of hours if you need me.'

'We'll be all right now, Dad, honestly.'

'Be careful, won't you? We'll wait for news, keep us posted.'

'You'll keep Osman and Daniel's parents up to date, won't you?'

His father nodded solemnly. 'Of course I will, good luck, son.'

Ariam put his arms round him. 'Goodbye, Dad.'

His father turned back to the car followed by Ariam. When the engine started, Ariam joined Idris and Mariam waving his father 'farewell'.

'I'll wait here for the others,' said Idris looking at Mariam. 'You two can sit in the shade. There's room back that way.' He indicated a curve in the hill. 'We'll eat and sleep there tonight.'

Ariam and Mariam made their way along the trench until it widened to make enough space for a group of soldiers to sleep, plenty of room for the six of them. They sat leaning their backs against the stone wall listening for voices.

Idris had his eyes on a battered white truck that rattled through the town and out towards the hills. When it was close enough, he stood and waved. Daniel's father called, 'He's there!' Delighted to see him at last. He checked his rear-view mirror again and again before drawing to a halt close to Idris.

'Here we are,' he said.

Osman slid out to meet Idris. Daniel's father jumped down and waited at the door watching them but Daniel lingered. He felt a sudden pang at leaving the security of his father's cab, its warm manly smell. He looked around for the last time; at the old navy sweatshirt that he hardly ever wore draped over the back of his seat and the carved wooden amulet hanging from the mirror. Perhaps he needed protection now? He touched it and watched it swing. Why hadn't he thought of something like that?

His father saw the look on his face. 'Would you like that?' He unhooked it. 'Here, you take it, you have more need…'

'No, Dad, I can't do that.'

'I need it looking after you, more than I need it here. Keep it safe.' He pressed it into Daniel's hand.

'Thank you, Dad, I will.'

They jumped out of the truck.

'You must be Daniel's father,' said Idris offering his hand and looking him in the eye.

The father looked at the confident, strong young man, along the stone trenches and up at the bleak mountain they had to scale. Suddenly their little group seemed small, facing something huge, hostile, unpredictable. Would their youth and confidence see them across this continent to another?

'Everything all right, sir?' asked Idris concerned.

Daniel's father looked at his pleasant, earnest face and relented. 'Yes, sorry.' He took Idris's hand and shook it long and hard. 'Yes, it's a big thing…'

'Don't worry sir, we have it planned and we have contacts along the way. We'll look after Daniel.'

'All by yourselves under cover…'

'We'll keep our heads down. Don't worry, we've got each other.'

'Yes, yes, of course. You're young, my heart goes with you.'

'We're not the first,' said Idris confidently.

'True, true and you'll not be the last.' He looked along the deep stone trough. 'Your father fought here?'

Idris nodded. 'And my uncles and cousins sir.'

Finally, he turned to Daniel and said, 'Well, you couldn't find a better man to lead you over the mountain.'

He clasped the young man in his arms. 'Thank you. May Allah grant you a safe and blessed journey.'

Daniel lightened the mood. 'These trenches are fantastic, how did they do it?'

'Pickaxes and shovels, oiled by determination,' said Idris relieved. He looked across at Osman and they smiled like old friends.

Both said, 'Hi,' together.

'Where is Mariam?' asked Osman.

'Your sister? Further down. Don't worry, they're all right.'

'Daniel has numbers for travel in Sudan then you're on your own,' said his father.

'My uncle will see us through Libya,' said Osman.

'You're lucky,' said Daniel's father. 'Make the most of it son and take care. Allah be with you.' He placed his hand on top of Daniel's head, embraced him and turned away. He waved to Osman and departed. Daniel watched his father rattle, jolt and bang his way down the hillside into town and out back towards home. Idris put his arm round Daniel's shoulder.

'Only one left. I'll wait for Jamil, you go join the others. Follow the trench, it widens, they're waiting for you.'

The sun was dropping when Idris saw a solitary figure with a heavy backpack climbing towards him. He waved and Jamil ran down a slope and up the other side to the tree where Idris waited. They gripped each other's forearms yelling, 'Selam aleykum.'

'The others here?' asked Jamil.

Idris nodded. 'Follow me.'

Mariam had spread injera, biscuits, dates, bananas and water on her shawl. Idris passed his gourd so they could rinse their hands and he spoke the Dua, 'Allah bless us with what you have provided and keep us from the punishment of fire.' It settled their excitement and sharing the food sealed their delight at being together. Both Idris and Jamil were attentive to Mariam. This stage of the journey was up to Idris, Sudan to Daniel, then Osman but they would depend on Ariam and Idris for their phones all the way. Easy going Osman, with no ambitions to be a leader, realised that he was the one who had brought them together and the one who had changed the dynamic by adding his sister.

It was Osman's first night away from his family. He realised that all the others apart from Daniel, had made that break, even Mariam was used to communal living. They settled, head to toe along the trench. Mariam laid her shawl at the end of the line and Osman dropped his satchel beside her. It was a huge relief to have her back, to be close in the darkness. The walls of the trench made him feel safe and the network gave them privacy when they had to relieve themselves. They lay in silence looking at the stars, adapting to their new life as nomads. Looking up into the luminous dark thinking of their goal, Osman felt more like a pilgrim. The trench was quiet, they had talked themselves out after supper. The tension of preparation had dissolved into satisfaction at the accomplishment of stage one.

After a breakfast of bread and dates with Idris's coffee, he led them up and around the foothills. Jamil walked beside Mariam and Osman, Daniel and Ariam stayed close to Idris.

They climbed over pale bare earth dotted with sparse grass and spindly trees. There were few birds or animals of any kind. The path narrowed, got steeper. The boulders grew bigger and all that remained was lifeless grit and stone, broken by the drone of flies. They sheltered behind rocks for a hasty break in full view of Eritrea, hoping not to be seen before pushing on higher and higher. Sliding on gravel, climbing over boulders until the sun was slipping down the sky, Idris told them to look out for a resting place. Osman spotted patches of level ground among boulders just ahead.

When they assembled, Idris said, 'We'd better light a fire.'

'Won't it be seen?' asked Ariam.

'Not behind these rocks.' He patted a line of three high boulders leaning against each other.

‘There’s not much wood around,’ said Jamil.

‘Dry grass, twigs, whatever you think. Keep snakes and scorpions away.’ He looked around and they all listened to the sound of birds settling, their different calls, some muffled by distance. Most of all, they listened for the rustling of grass, the snapping of a twig or the sound of feet on stone. The sun was slipping rapidly down the sky.

Mariam shivered. ‘It’s cold.’

‘We need more than grass,’ said Jamil and set off stumbling into the dark.

‘It’s dangerous. I’ve got a torch,’ said Idris retracing their path to bushes below. They spread out and collected what they could. Their eyes adjusted to the dark and the familiarity of the mountain helped them to find pockets of spindly bushes surrounded by twigs. Osman and Mariam pulled up some dry grass, loaded their arms with sticks and dropped them in the centre of their campsite. More was added and they soon had fire enough to boil water for tea. They emptied what little food remained onto Mariam’s shawl, rubbed their hands on their sides and waited for Dua. Biscuits and dried bananas relieved the gnawing in their stomachs. They loaded the fire and curled up. Bare stone and grit could not prevent exhaustion and satisfaction from sucking them down into dreamless sleep.

Cold ash greeted them in the morning but they were safe and together. Mariam, like the others, found a private place to relieve herself. They were all aware of her and tactfully avoided embarrassing her.

Once assembled over water with biscuits and dates, they craned their necks to see the summit.

‘We should make it today,’ said Idris.

They packed and started quickly determined to get as high as possible before the heat slowed them down. They walked in silence, concentrating on every step, climbing over rocks, squeezing between boulders, higher and higher. Suddenly the path became a ledge around a ravine.

'There's no other way,' said Idris. 'I'll go first.'

He faced into the mountain so his backpack didn't get in the way and shuffled sideways, his big feet leaving his heels over the edge in places. Dust and stones trickled down the gulf. From the other side he called, 'Come on.'

Daniel turned his backpack to his chest and leant back against the mountain edging across, watching his toes at the brink. Idris caught his arm at the end. Ariam looked at Osman, lost and confused. 'Which way?' he asked.

'Depends on where you want to look,' said Osman.

'I can't do it.'

'You can, of course you can. You know you can – look, Daniel's okay.

Daniel and Idris were watching eager to get on.

'I can't,' wailed Ariam.

Osman put his arm round Ariam's shoulder. 'Should I go with you?'

Ariam was shaking his head to and fro. 'Can't, can't,' his voice rising a pitch.

'It's not so bad Ariam. Look, if I can do it, so can you.' Mariam lifted the straps of her bag round her neck to the front and inched out over the ravine.

Jamil stepped forward. 'No!'

'It's got to be done,' she replied.

Jamil and Osman stood paralysed. Ariam stared, then followed. Everyone held their breath watching them creep around the ravine. Osman pushed his body against the mountain's breast and shuffled across, his long feet overlapping the edge. Once over, they looked for Jamil but he had disappeared. After a few charged minutes they started to call, 'Jamil!' one after another.

Eventually he returned, wide eyed and shouted, 'I'm too big, it's not wide enough.'

Idris turned back, pushed past the others and called, 'You can do it. Focus on your centre of gravity. Put your bag in front, lean into the mountain, now slide, slide, slide your feet…'

Jamil took a deep breath and edged out leaning back into the mountain, turning his head from side to side, afraid to look down, desperate to see the foothold for each step.

'Look at me, look at me!' called Idris.

Jamil lifted his head and staggered. His knees bent then his back hit the stone behind and he spread his hands, fingers gripping it. He steadied himself and stared at Idris's hand out towards him. He focused on Idris's golden eyes holding his and shuffled rapidly to reach him, sending grit cascading down, down, down.

Climbing boulders and rocks was nothing after that, nor the steep ascent. Eagles circled abreast of them and vultures swooped below. They had to find individual pockets of space to sleep that night and assembled in the morning for biscuits and water. They rationed the water. There was little conversation, they were conserving their energy. They shared a purpose and they needed each other, together they would get there.

'Top this morning,' said Idris.

'The other side of the mountain,' said Daniel.

'Sudan,' said Jamil.

The prospect of the summit lightened the final climb. They set off eager to pass their first frontier and reached the summit within the hour to stand looking in awe at the vast reaches of Sudan – dirt and stone, bushes, and trees, a seemingly endless plain, hinterland to the Sahara with little sign of humanity.

Osman contemplated the scene. Somewhere out there was the Nile, gathering riches to pour into Egypt. Nature knew no boundaries; he was glad of that. There was an occasional cluster of dwellings, a road, even a railway line. Each looking isolated and at odds with its surroundings.

'Peaceful,' said Jamil.

'Don't be fooled, Darfur is being bombed into submission. This is a country in ferment, too many factions, too many would be leaders,' said Idris. 'Locals follow the nearest who they think will keep them safe.'

'And the outside world?'

Idris shrugged. 'Not interested; too poor, too big, too split.'

'Not the place to stay,' said Jamil.

'No longer than we need but there's a lot of Sudan before we get to Libya.'

'We can get a lift for some of it.'

'Your father's contacts?' asked Idris.

Daniel nodded. 'In Kassala.'

'Are you sure they'll help?' asked Jamil.

'Dad has bought and sold their trucks for years. They owe him.'

'Can they get us to Khartoum?' asked Idris.

'That's where their main outlets are.'

'Good.' Idris unfolded his map, found Kassala and traced back to their end of the mountain. 'We'll head to Gadamai and jump a train to Kassala,' said Idris.

At their feet lay the steep body of the mountain; impassive, eternal, harsh. Idris shaded his eyes to search the terrain for a route and a secure place to spend the night.

'We must keep our heads down,' said Idris. 'Border guards patrol the mountains.'

'There, down there. There's a small ravine halfway down. If we can make it in time, we can sleep there.'

They followed his finger and traced the ground back to where they stood.

'It won't be easy,' said Osman.

'You can't expect a direct road,' said Idris.

'We can try,' replied Osman.

Jamil searched the mountainside below. 'It's steep. We have to go sideways.'

'We'd better try to get to the ravine before sunset,' said Osman.

The descent was quicker but not easier. They slid into boulders banging their shoulders and elbows. They were silent and stopped every now and again to listen and look for guards. A shared sense of danger drew them closer. Jamil was always ready to help Mariam off a boulder or stop her sliding too far. Ariam joined Idris, planning their route, his phone was long out of charge. Osman's long legs and Daniel's stout muscles kept them abreast of each other, concentrating on every foothold, weaving round stones, an occasional stunted tree or sliding down steep dusty gullies. They made their way across and down in silence.

Mariam, looked warily along the lower slopes. A few huts lay below and a compound with a goat looking desolate on bare ground. So dry and hard the land, brutal, she thought, nothing like home. Suddenly her mother's plot, Lemlem and Genet, their suppers round the fire, summer picnics by the river seemed so blessed. Her heart ached to hear her father's quiet voice. To have her mother's practical common sense to rely on. She had never felt so alone. Osman took her hand and squeezed it. 'We'll be all right,' he whispered.

The sun towered over the mountain and burnt the rocks. They sipped more and more water.

'Be careful with the water,' said Idris.

They had been guarding it but need overcame reason while baking in an oven.

Mariam's feet were sore. Her sandals were no help over stones and dry grit. She clenched her toes to keep a hold on the ground. The water could not satisfy the thirst that scorched her throat. The struggle to keep going in the heat was almost unbearable. The pace slowed and aches and pains from the punishing climb made every step a challenge. There was no shade just rock all around. They had to get further down to rest. Osman's legs began to feel weak, they trembled like jelly and he was afraid that they might pack up. His lower back ached. Jamil adjusted his rucksack and Daniel stripped off his T-shirt.

'Don't do that, you'll get burnt!' snapped Idris.

Daniel draped it over his shoulders.

'Not far now, we're almost there!' called Ariam.

Idris stopped and spread his arms as a barrier. One by one the others lined up behind and looked over. They were on the edge of the ravine. Far below a spring trickled into a little pool surrounded by millet, star grass and a tall, tufted grass.

'Do you believe that?' whispered Daniel.

'I saw the crevasse,' said Idris, 'but I never dreamt we'd get this lucky.'

'Down!' hissed Jamil nodding his head to the pool. A guard stepped from behind the tree zipping up his trousers and went to another guard hidden behind the reeds with his feet in the water.

They all hit the ground and lay on their stomachs looking over the rim.

'Back,' whispered Daniel.

They wriggled back and back. Behind the cover of rocks, they stood and dusted themselves off, shaken and lost.

'We've got to get away from here,' said Idris.

They retraced their steps around the mountain, tired, hungry and thirsty. Mariam's face was closed, intent on the next step, her mouth tight. Osman knew that look. His legs were almost giving way. They needed to eat, drink, rest.

'Stop!' he called. 'We're far enough away, we need a break.'

They dropped where they stood, grateful for an end of footfall. They mopped their faces and carefully sucked in one mouthful of water each, swirling it round and round before swallowing. Packs were opened, meagre supplies pulled out and spread on a rock to share as was their custom.

'Bastards!' said Daniel. 'We could have filled our bottles there.'

'They knew what they were doing,' said Ariam. 'Perfect spot.'

The sun was sliding west with the heat less intense as they set off.

'Soon be time to pitch camp,' said Jamil.

'Better below if we can make it,' said Ariam.

The mountain spread its apron below. The slope eased and rocks gave way to trees and low grey plants.

'Somewhere to stretch out,' said Mariam.

Darkness fell without warning. There was no slow sliding of the sun down the sky. They stopped in a clearing, leant against rocks to pull off their shoes and T-shirts to cool down. Mariam fanned herself and wiggled her toes in the cooling air. Their eyes grew wide adjusting to the gloom.

'Watch out!' Idris shouted.

'What is it? What's the matter?'

Ariam shone a torch towards his voice in time to see a large rock python slithering around a rock. They turned their torches to the ground and stamped and shuffled sending scorpions and lizards scurrying. Another snake with turquoise scales edged in gold and head erect, slowly wound its long, thin body around a bush and up between the rocks.

'Beautiful,' murmured Osman. *Terrific design for a basket.*

'But we don't know how deadly,' said Ariam.

They shone their torches all around and set down their bags nervously.

'Pity we can't light a fire,' said Idris.

'Damned guards,' agreed Jamil.

They settled as close to each other as the rocks would allow and exhaustion released them into sleep.

Breakfast was meagre. Idris led the way down the mountain. The descent introduced more and more diverse wildlife; from insects, shrubs, dusty plants and birds to shrews and lizards.

At the base, Idris took out an old compass left to him by his father; he muttered to himself as he took a bearing for Gadamai, 'North-north-west, it has to be.' They skirted the mountain for an hour before seeing mud huts with flat rooves, red patches of fenced ground, low trees and rows of plants.

'Can you see what I can see?' asked Ariam.

'Goats,' said Osman grinning. A nanny with a kid, a whiskered billy and a couple more nannies were watching them from a tiny bare paddock.

'Not where I'm looking,' said Ariam.

They followed his outstretched arm – low fruit trees; orange, lemon, guava and sycamore fig.

'They're not ripe,' said Daniel staring up at small yellow and green oranges.

'Look, look at the top…'

Plump deep orange fruit dangled closer to the sun.

'How're we going to get them?' asked Mariam, thirsty at the thought.

Jamil looked around. 'I can't see a ladder.'

Idris checked the farmhouse. 'We've got to be quick.' He crouched and cupped his hands. 'On my back, Ariam.'

Ariam put a foot in his hands and levered himself up to stand on Idris's shoulders. Idris gripped his ankles and slowly rose. Ariam leant across the branches and pelted the others with fruit. They scrambled to collect them in Mariam's shawl. The sycamore fig had a divided trunk. Osman scaled it and filled his hat and the hem of his shirt before lowering himself within reach to pass them down. Idris plucked a couple of guavas from the one precious tree.

They checked the house. Not a murmur in the still morning air, not even a child's cry.

'Fancy some goat's milk?' asked Osman.

'How are we going to get it?' asked Ariam.

'No basin,' said Osman crestfallen.

'What about my canteen?' said Jamil. He took out a small rectangular metal container with a handle.

'Too small,' said Daniel.

'It'll go all over the place,' said Mariam.

'Daniel, you hold the canteen and I'll go gently and take aim.'

'We can all have a drink if she'll stand for it,' said Osman.

'We don't have time,' said Mariam looking anxiously over her shoulder.

'We don't want to be caught,' agreed Ariam.

Idris looked towards the house. 'There's nobody moving.'

They followed his gaze. 'No, it's too quiet, for my liking,' said Ariam.

'We need this, let's take it while we can,' urged Osman and squatted by a curious nanny who had joined them, followed by a kid. She stood watching them. Osman stroked all along her side, gently reassuring her, then held her teat. Daniel quickly pushed the canteen underneath. Osman squeezed and milk splashed noisily into the canteen. Daniel gave the first to Mariam then, one by one, they drank relishing the warm, light milk, watched by the kid with its head to one side.

'Eish, that's good,' said Daniel wiping his lips.

Jamil saved a little for Mariam.

'Finish it,' he said. 'You need it.'

'Thank you,' she murmured.

It took her back to home, with Lemlem and Genet and restored her a little. The privations of the mountain had made her limbs weak and now she felt heavy and depressed. Neither her mind nor her body wanted any more of this alien struggle. It all seemed pointless. Jamil's kindness lifted her but she still felt shaky and bloated, a sea of hormones in her body was rising to high tide, an internal clock that could not be stopped.

The sound of a truck brought them back to reality. An uninterrupted vista of red earth and barbed wire fences offered no shelter apart from a hut two fields away.

'Run!' yelled Idris and they followed him across the fields, heavy bags and full shawl bumping their backs.

'Just in time,' they laughed once inside.

There was an open slat along its side looking away from where they had come. They peeped through and saw a long shed with piles of dry grass and reeds.

Ariam looked at Idris. 'Same farm or another?'

'Another I think,' said Idris.

'Shall we try it?' suggested Jamil.

They emerged tentatively and looked around. There was another thatched house far to the right. They walked towards the shed. Between it and the house, there was a cultivated plot with baby ochre, tomato, aubergine and onion plants.

'Where do they get their water?' asked Mariam, full of wonder at the health of the plants.

Osman joined her. 'Not so lush as mother's,' he said, 'but not bad.'

They crept between the buildings towards the house.

'A well!' cried Daniel.

'Shh,' hissed Jamil.

They had come to an open square with a raised mud brick circle in the middle surrounded by a couple of sheds with tin rooves, a lean to full of grasses and a thatched barn. A cultivator, plough and several drums of gasoline sat outside one shed and on the other side of the clearing, empty bags of fertiliser and pellets were stacked in front of the other. A couple of old chairs set in front of the thatched barn reminded them of the owners. Plastic bowls, dented buckets, lengths of rope and coils of wire stood around the sides of the square.

They stared into the open space afraid to expose themselves. There wasn't a sound.

'Can't stop us, water's for everyone,' said Daniel. He crossed the courtyard and peered down. It smelt of rust and dry clay. He pulled on the rope; the winch creaked as the bucket rose. A young girl came out of the house and stared at them followed by a naked toddler. She didn't call anyone or move. They were all transfixed watching each other. No sound came from the house.

Mariam took a step towards the door and gently asked in Arabic, 'Where are Mummy and Daddy?'

The girl studied them considering her answer.

'Gone to market?' asked Mariam softly.

The girl nodded.

'Are you all right?'

She took her little brother's hand and nodded.

'May we have some water?' asked Mariam.

The girl nodded graciously and took her brother indoors.

Once satiated they filled every container they had with water.

'Desert soon,' Idris reminded them.

As they passed the shed and lean to with grasses, they heard a squawk followed by clucking.

'Hens!' said Idris. They leapt over the stacks of grass by the entrance gathering eggs like jewels. They wrapped them in T-shirts, underpants and anything soft they could find.

'How're we going to cook them?' asked Mariam.

'The sun will do that for us,' said Jamil.

They headed out to the road and looked longingly at its long straight line out.

'Wrong direction,' said Idris. 'Gadamai's northwest, that's south. There's no easy way. It's the desert when we've freshened up.'

They found an outdoor pump and took turns at washing. Mariam had first chance. She sent them away and slipped out of her kaftan and pants. She debated using her precious piece of soap but didn't want to keep the others waiting too long or leave tell-tale suds, so she crouched to soak her hair and wash the bottom half of her body. The water was cold and a bit brown, but it was luxury. She patted herself with her shawl, found new pants, dressed quickly then washed her shawl and pants and hung them over the top of her bag. She found the others leaning over a fence looking at the desert. When they had finished, they ate slices of guava as they set off.

It felt alien to leave the road and turn their feet to a limitless expanse of sand without sign of human existence, plant, or animal life. No landmarks or way signs, no transport other than their feet. It didn't seem daring or exciting, it was scary. The desert's enormity belittled them. The second stage of their journey had begun. Idris checked the map and let the sun guide them.

The sun had passed its peak by the time they were surrounded by sand. They barely registered the first ten kilometres, adjusting to the silence and the enormity of sand to the horizon whichever way they looked. The blankness of the sky; impossible to relate to, no storybook clouds, no banks of grey, threatening storms to give it recognisable life. It stared across the desert, alien, impassive, beyond human time, beyond human comprehension.

Milk, water and fruit had refreshed them. Civilisation had restored their spirit. They ploughed purposefully through the hot sand for a couple of hours while the sun descended.

'We'd better eat while we can,' said Jamil.

There was no special spot to look for, no shelter, no people, no threat. They dropped onto scorching sand. Jamil took out his thin metal canteen and set it in the sun. Mariam tore the last two pieces of injera into six.

Jamil cracked two eggs into the canteen and said, 'Get ready.'

He transferred the cooked eggs onto the tiny pieces of injera in each person's hand and let the metal heat again.

'Mariam,' he called and she held out a plastic lid. He scraped out the eggs with his knife, scrubbed the pan with dry leaves and began again. They were soon all fed and almost happy. They had managed the mountain and were a third of the way across the desert. When the sun plunged into the horizon they curled up or spread their tired limbs in the soft sand and slept as the temperature dropped.

Full sun woke them. They had slept too long.

‘We’d better eat our oranges on the way,’ said Idris. ‘We can’t walk at midday.’

Too sleepy to speak, they followed with their oranges, dropping the peel for scavengers.

By noon their heads pounded, their tongues stuck to their palates and sweat stung their eyes.

‘Time to stop,’ said Ariam and dumped his pack on the sand.

‘Yeh,’ said Daniel sinking onto his knees. ‘Ouch, ow!’ He leapt up. ‘It’s scorching.’

Idris and Jamil surveyed the emptiness. ‘No shade. We’ll have to sit on our bags whatever we can. We’ve got to rest,’ said Jamil.

‘We mustn’t walk at midday or we’ll overheat. We have to stay still,’ said Idris.

Still was what they needed. Their calves ached from pulling their feet out of sinking sand and their backs from their bags. Their heads were boiling. The high white flame in the sky streamed unimaginable heat down on them. There was no escape. The heat intensified minute by minute. They were beyond thirst and mere weariness into blind, suspended animation, burning within, trapped in a vast expanse of scalding air and scorching sand under a torch of exploding gas. There was no escape; survive or die. They spread their bags. Mariam folded her shawl, too thin to stop the heat but with her kaftan, she could lie down.

‘Don’t take your T-shirt off,’ said Daniel to Ariam.

They all tried to hide their heads from the sun’s onslaught – paper bags, underpants whatever they could find before settling on their rucksacks.

‘We can be seen for kilometres,’ said Osman feeling exposed. There was no corner to hide in.

‘And we can see for kilometres,’ said Ariam. ‘No ambush is possible or likely.’

They sipped water and settled in silence.

Osman saw the red veins of his eyelids and drifted back home. Lemlem bleating a welcome, the whirr of his mother's sewing machine, the clunk of a ball hitting a bat and Wani shouting, 'Not again!' in disgust at his miss.

His father's voice, patient, 'Next time.'

Why did it sound so wise and calm now? Osman opened his eyes and saw the inside of his cotton hat which was covering his face. He touched his pocket. The cellophane crackled, Eritrea, betrayed, he would plant it somewhere new, make it grow. *Playtime is over. This is reality but you're with friends. What more do you need?* The spectre of the free world seemed unreal but he knew that what remained at home was a nightmare for his generation. For him there would be no family, no basket making, fresh fruit or vegetables like his parents had.

Mariam stirred beside him. 'All right Osman?' she asked.

'We're right, aren't we sis?'

She groped for his hand. 'We wouldn't be here…'

'We had so much.'

'To be taken from us. That's what makes it worse.'

'Hard to believe when you're away.'

'We're not alone.'

'No.'

'Rest.'

Mariam was holding back a tide of emotion, feeling vulnerable, fragile, depressed. Her body was following its rhythm. Her womb was not nursing new life, its lining had to be shed. Hormones bloated her body, her ankles were swollen. She missed her friends, her mother. She felt isolated in her femaleness.

The others started to move. The rest had helped and the sun's glare had softened when they rose, sipped water and silently carried on. They trudged, two by two over sand dunes, along valleys of rippled sand, hour after hour. The sand pulled them down, sapped their strength.

'Are you sure we're going in the right direction?' asked Jamil.

Idris showed him the map. 'Northwest,' he said.

'Are you sure Gadamai is northwest?'

'We're only halfway, maybe a bit more. We won't see it for another couple of days.'

They plodded obediently on until a curtain of shadow was drawn across the desert. Too dry to talk, too tired to move, each dropped on the spot. Mariam was glad for an end to today's march. Pushing her leaden limbs and bloated body through the hot sand had become so painful that her only way on was in a trance, mechanically chanting, 'On, on, on...' Numbing herself, pushing her barriers further and further. She dropped her sack and shawl and collapsed. She couldn't speak. She didn't want anyone to know.

One by one they offered up their eggs without the sun to cook them.

Jamil joked, 'Raw egg anyone?'

He emptied them into his canteen and stirred them with his knife until they were thoroughly mixed and passed it round for anyone who was hungry enough to swallow a little.

'We've got a few figs,' said Osman.

Mariam delved into her bag and shared the figs. There was nothing to say. They were halfway there. The desert would not defeat them. They dug away the sand to get under its burning surface to cooler layers below and squirmed their bodies to sculpt it around them.

Ariam stirred first, relieved himself a little way from the others and returned. They forced themselves up and looked at sand and dust without break; yellow, red and grey.

'Camels!' shouted Daniel.

The sun blinded them as they followed his finger.

'Down!' hissed Osman.

'They're not interested in us,' said Jamil.

'Not bandits or spies?'

'Not the Bedouins,' said Idris. 'They have their own government. Our politics don't interest them.'

'Maybe they can help,' said Ariam staring enviously at their stalely progress.

'They're not going to give us a lift. What more can they do?' asked Jamil.

'Check we're on the right route.'

'Waste of time, theirs and ours. They're too far away.'

Without points of reference, the camel train seemed achievable but they looked small, too far to reach.

They shrugged and peeled their oranges as they walked on grateful for the cool of morning. Mariam felt the first contraction – lower stomach through to her back. The pain gripped her and she longed to curl over it, to bend and rub her back but she had to hide it. Her mouth dried with pain as well as the sun. The change of hormones made her feel wobbly, vulnerable but above it all she was ashamed, embarrassed. They had treated her with respect. Now the reality of womanhood was upon her and she felt embarrassed, menstruation was messy and disgusting to men. She longed for a place to hide and stared outraged at the blank expanse of sand and sky, feeling as exposed as if her skin were flayed. She felt sticky blood ooze into her pants. The dampness and despair overwhelmed her and she had nothing to soak up the flow save her spare pants and a tiny wash flannel. She daren't let it stain her kaftan, to announce her condition to the world was humiliation beyond reckoning.

'Stop,' she pleaded.

They stopped and looked at her. Mariam had never interrupted their progress before.

'You all right?' asked Jamil.

'What's the matter?' said Idris.

'Sorry I need to go…' She indicated a sand drift high enough to hide behind.

'Okay.'

'I'll mind your bag,' said Osman, taking a handle. She pulled it tight to her chest.

'Oh no, it's all right. I might need it.'

Osman felt concerned, she didn't look well. Had he believed too much in her big sister's strength? He watched her climb the dune, feet sinking into the sand, dragging her down. Mariam knew they were watching her. She hated holding them up. Once hidden from view she examined her blood-stained pants and the tops of her legs, what was it going to be like at the end of the day? She panicked, rolled up her spare pants and put them inside the others. She had bought a little time, temporary comfort, that was all she could hope for.

The others waited in silence too dispirited by the heat to talk. The sand was already too hot to drop onto and rest. Minutes passed. Everything piercingly illuminated by a sun alive with energy, flaring light and heat. They squinted at the interminable ahead. Mariam slid back down to them afraid of jolting her aching, bleeding body. She couldn't speak, she avoided their eyes.

They moved on, one foot after another across the sand. Monotony numbed their brains, thought became as slow as progress. Higher and higher the fireball, hotter and hotter their skin, flesh, and bones. Their eyes saw only light and glare – sky and sand merged into light. Perspiration dripped from their chins. Mariam's contractions subsided into a constant dull pain. She was miserably aware of the claggy roll of material between her legs.

'Midday, we'd better stop,' said Idris.

They stopped like automatons – rest meant burning sand under the body, light boring into your face, respite for legs and feet, no more. They sipped water.

'Supplies gone?' asked Daniel.

'I've been keeping this for an emergency.' Idris went to the bottom of his bag and took out some vacuum packed biltung.' He slit the packet with his knife and divided the meat equally between them.

'You're full of surprises,' laughed Jamil chewing. 'Better and better.'

'Thank you, Idris,' said Mariam hardly able to believe the miracle.

'Thanks,' said Daniel taking a piece.

Ariam said, 'Better than tsebhi derho.'[12]

'Better than sojee,[13] said Osman chewing the rich, salty dark red meat.

After they had savoured the meat, Mariam took an orange from her bag, peeled, and segmented it.

'Here we are,' she said. 'The last piece of fruit.'

'Perfect,' said Daniel.

'Ten segments, one and a half each,' said Mariam.

Jamil cut three into two and gave Mariam the extra whole.

They searched the horizon in the direction they were travelling, no sign of habitation.

'No sign of Gadamai,' said Ariam.

'Tonight, we'll see the lights,' said Idris. 'Rest now.'

Again, they found their own places, further apart than before. They took out things to place between their bodies and the hot sand and settled down to garner their energy. Osman sat by Mariam hugging his knees.

'You all right, sis?'

She nodded.

'You're quiet.'

She nodded again. 'Tired,' she said.

'Here, have this.' He offered her his peeked hat to shield her face.

'Thank you.'

---

12 Chicken cooked in tomato, onion and peppers.

13 Semolina cake with honey.

She tried to escape her predicament and the pain while she slept, terrified of getting stains on her kaftan.

There was no escape from the burning heat: the sand scorched their skin; the air was oven hot, intense, unrelenting. The sun seemed to fill the sky, radiating white heat, exposing their frailty, their smallness in the face of the vast desert and enormity of the sky. They each suffered it in different ways. Ariam lay on his side, to lessen the surface area touching the burning sand. By his side Idris lay on his back, knees up tight with a T-shirt making a tent over his body and face. At their feet, Jamil lay stoically on his back, head on his bag with a shirt over his face. Daniel carefully covered the ground with his spare clothes and lay on his front, cheek on his bag. Osman curled up by his sister's side. Her cramps and fear of sitting on her kaftan made her pull her knees to her chest and stay on her side. When they woke, she felt the fullness in her padding.

'Osman, I need help.'

'What is it?'

'I've started my period; I need cloth to soak up the blood.'

'Underpants okay?'

She nodded. 'Please.'

She went last over the sand hill to relieve herself. Everyone was having a final sip of water before the afternoon's trek.

'Not much water left,' said Osman shaking his flask.

'Save as much as you can,' said Idris.

They set off in single file, one hour, two, three; nothing to see but someone's back and the sprays of sand kicked up by their feet. They trudged on with the task; walk to Gadamai. Dusk fell and night dropped them in their tracks; no ritual, no meal, no talk. Each one watching their own inner space; their aches, pains, thirst, hunger, dwindling energy and hope.

Merciful dark descended, sweet, cool, secure black night with its distant diamonds twinkling and benevolent moon. Mariam's eyes were wide staring at misty veils of tiny stars, tracing brighter ones into patterns. Then the moon; so big, its gentle light beamed down, familiar, benign, yet she wondered at its power.

'You pull great oceans up to your light and send them crashing back, is it your power that drains my womb month by month? Am I part of a lunar cycle?' Bathed in its light, feeling at one with nature overcame her anxiety at being at odds with her companions. The stillness and beauty released her into sleep.

Safely wrapped in night's cradle they all slept and woke to stiff limbs but less acute pain. Mouths dry, lips peeling, silent, grudging, they set off again. On and on, feet through sand.

After a while with no change of view, Ariam said, 'Are you sure we're going in the right direction?'

Idris took the map from his pocket. 'According to this, look.' He gave it to Ariam who spread it out and traced their supposed route from the mountains to the desert and found Gadamai.

'Northwest,' he said. 'The sun rose over there so we have to turn our backs on it but it is North, that's left, so that's the angle we have to take.' He extended his arm. 'This has to be the right direction.'

They all followed his arm but every degree of the 365 looked identical.

'The desert plays tricks,' said Jamil.

'But the sun doesn't,' said Idris. 'Keep it on our right shoulders and we're okay.'

The sun as their friend and ally seemed strange when they cursed it every day.

'Let's get it over,' said Ariam.

Reassured and resigned they walked on and on. Sipped their last drops of water, and tried to quell the rising despair.

'Camels!' Idris's voice was hoarse.

They stopped and stared as if at a mirage as four turbaned riders on red and green rugs sailed above a dune and their camels emerged at the end of the rise. Still as rocks they watched and waited.

'Where are they heading?' whispered Daniel.

'They're coming this way,' said Ariam in disbelief.

'Let's go to meet them,' said Idris.

'Nothing to lose,' said Osman.

They pressed forward focusing on the colourful rugs and waterskins dangling from the sides of the camels and the calm faces of their riders. Their mouths were so dry they couldn't shout. Jamil pulled off his shirt and waved it. Osman and Mariam flapped her shawl. The camel drivers plodded sedately towards them taking in their shrivelled faces, glassy eyes, and empty bags. The first man silently unhooked a water skin from the back of his saddle and threw it down. Jamil passed it to Mariam who sipped and passed it back.

They each took a sip and thanked the man.

'How far is it to Gadamai?' asked Mariam in Arabic.

The man pointed back the way he had come and shook his head. They had been travelling in the wrong direction. The first two had a conversation above their heads.

'South westerly direction,' said the first. 'On foot it's better to travel at night.'

'We can't navigate at night,' said Jamil in halting Arabic.

'To travel Southwest, keep the pole star behind your right ear, choose a star south of that line and head towards it, checking all the time to keep the line – west and south, pole star, guiding star.'

'How long will it take?'

'Two nights.'

'We have no food,' said Idris in perfect Arabic.

The camels lurched down, the riders dismounted and opened bags. They filled Mariam and Idris's water bottles and gave them flat bread, camel's cheese, and dates. Mariam rummaged in her bag, and gave them a hair slide, comb and ribbons. The others saluted the men and wished they had something to add.

When Mariam shared out the food. Osman checked her portions afraid she might deny herself. It was a relief to walk at night and concentrate on the stars. It was not easy to keep their trajectory but their lives depended on it. They walked and corrected, walked and corrected until they were rewarded by the sight of spiky plants and scrubby bushes, followed by a few square mud dwellings and finally a child, a couple of men and a donkey.

'Gadamai!' yelled Idris. 'Sorry about the map.'

Jamil slapped his back grinning. 'We're here.'

'There has to be water,' said Mariam.

'Further in,' said Ariam.

They felt alien as they walked along a road lined with mud houses. The odd person they passed showed little interest.

'How many people have they seen emerge from the desert the worse for wear?' asked Mariam.

'Too many from the looks of it,' said Jamil.

'We need water,' said Idris.

'Follow the houses,' said Mariam.

At the end of the road there was a cleared space with a well. They clustered round, pulled up a bucket and cupped their hands to drink and drink.

'Be careful, you'll get stomach-ache,' warned Idris.

Daniel started to fill his bottle.

'Don't drink too much and don't fill up yet, you'll only have to carry it. We'll come back for more when we have eaten,' said Osman.

It seemed odd to see people doing ordinary things. They found a café, ordered juice and sat in the shade. Their eyes hurt and they ached; backs, shoulders, legs. They sat in exhausted silence for a long time until Jamil said, 'We'd better check the station.'

'Yep,' said Idris, standing up. They all followed.

The station had two platforms, two tracks and a siding with a rusty old engine and flatbed wagon. Metal containers and pallets were stacked under a high tin roof on thin metal legs beside their platform. The far platform had a makeshift shelter with a form, a simple wooden fence and a stack of plastic crates. Either way the tracks stretched to the horizon.

Three donkey carts and a few old vans were parked in front of a small wooden shed with a low window.

'Ticket office,' said Ariam.

A bleached, curling timetable was tacked to the wall of the office. They clustered around it.

'Not many passenger trains,' said Mariam.

'That's good,' said Idris. 'Mainly freight from the port.'

'How can we jump one?' asked Daniel.

'Night time's best,' said Jamil.

'Will they stop?' asked Ariam.

'We'll have to see,' replied Idris looking down the track. He followed it out of the station back towards Port Sudan. There were no sharp bends or steep climbs. Trains could keep up speed. 'We've got to wait for one to stop to unload.'

'They won't stop at night,' said Ariam looking at a couple of insect spattered lights, one on either end of platform.

Idris checked the line out towards Kassala. It was bare apart from a water tower surrounded by metal drums, coils of wire, a couple of hand carts and a few bald rubber tyres.

'We'll have to hide there.'

It was a little way from the station.

'It'll have to be a long train,' said Daniel.

'We'll have to check,' replied Jamil.

'We need times,' said Osman.

'First we'll eat,' said Idris.

They went back to the same café and ordered ful medames[14] and mutton stew with gourrassa.[15] They shared their meal in thoughtful silence drinking and moving as one. Osman was

14 Fava beans with onion and tomato.

15 Flat bread.

happy to see Mariam relaxed, even smiling as they helped themselves and each other.

'We'll get stomach-ache,' she laughed.

Daniel grinned happily stuffing a wadge of meat filled gourrassa into his mouth.

They sat back in their chairs. The world felt less alien and the journey less difficult.

'What shall we do now?' asked Osman.

'I'd like a shower,' said Mariam.

'I'm with you on that,' said Ariam.

'We'll find a room for the night,' said Idris. 'We need to stay out of sight.'

'And out of the sun,' said Daniel fanning his face with his hat.

'Near the station,' suggested Jamil.

'Cheaper,' agreed Daniel.

They followed a beaten track behind the station car park, past workshops and houses, yards and motorbikes, to a long terrace of mud brick buildings. A woman was making coffee in front of a narrow two-storey house. When she saw all six of them staring at her she gestured them to join her. They squatted round a small table and watched her ceremoniously pour and hand out tiny cups of treacly delight. They were in front of her late husband's workshop, she explained. Since his death, she had rented out rooms as much for company as money. Her name was Suma and she was happy to let them share a room and water no problem. Gadamai sat on a water source.

The room was small, but they were used to stretching out together. Mariam took her precious piece of soap from her bag and was first to try the shower in the yard. She dried herself on her shawl then washed it and spread it on the fence to dry. The bleeding had stopped. Her hair felt light and frothy, her body free and supple again. She was almost happy; they were safely on their way to Khartoum. She passed her soap to Osman.

They all felt the same, Jamil and Daniel went to celebrate.

Ariam wanted to check the trains and Idris went with him. Osman and Mariam were left to wander into town. They passed leather workshops, bread makers and little stalls of olives and oranges, okra, and gourds. They filled Osman's bag with dried meat, flat bread, onions, dates, and figs.

Dusk was gathering as they sat drinking tea in a café watched by children and beggars. Strings of tiny lights sparkled and gradually, bigger ones flooded the darkness with garish light as they walked back to their home for the night. Idris and Ariam were waiting for them and the other two were not far behind.

Suma welcomed them like family, fussed over them and served a meal of so many dishes it took hours sharing it round. They persuaded Suma to join them. They made her taste how delicious her food was, feeding her tasty morsels. Suma laughed, shy and happy, loving them.

'One big happy family,' she said holding her juice aloft. Life was good, they had come a long way and they were all together.

Osman wished he could feel it but there was a hole, an ache in his middle for the family he had left. The strength of his mother, the patience of his father. Mariam made sure everyone had what they wanted but it was mechanical. This was not her family. Osman caught her eye and they recognised each other's pain.

'There's a goods train from Port Sudan going through at 5.30am,' said Ariam.

'It'll still be dark,' said Daniel.

'We can't miss it!' snapped Ariam.

'No, but how do we find places to hide on it?' said Daniel.

'There'll be people unloading, they'll need light,' said Idris.

'They'll see us,' said Jamil.

'It's up to us to make sure they don't,' said Ariam.

Idris surveyed the group. 'Are you up for it?'

They nodded.

'Not much choice,' muttered Daniel.

'You can't climb onto a train dressed like that,' Idris said to Mariam. Her thin cotton tunic felt light and comfortable, but he was right.

'I haven't anything else,' she said.

'Jeans are better,' said Ariam. 'I have a spare pair.'

'It's sharia here. We're in trouble if she's seen,' said Daniel.

'She can't climb onto a train like that,' said Ariam.

'She's a woman, hijab or suffer the consequences,' said Jamil.

'I won't be a woman; I'll tie up my hair and hide it under a cap.'

Jamil looked at her. 'You look like a woman.'

'Not in men's jeans and top,' said Daniel.

'Thank you.'

'I've got a T-shirt to go with it,' said Osman.

It was too hot for Osman to sleep in the room packed like sardines with the creaking paddles of an old fan stirring the air. He crept downstairs and stretched out in the yard. When Idris joined him, he explained, 'I'm more used to the stars.'

'Me too.' Idris settled down, put his hands behind his head and looked up.

Mariam came down at 4:30am with a hat pulled over her forehead, in Ariam's jeans and Osman's T-shirt. They woke the others, drank water from the pump and left money for Suma.

'We must separate,' said Idris.

Mariam and Osman looked at each other. 'We'll go together,' Osman said.

'That's up to you. We can't help,' said Idris.

'We understand,' said Mariam.

When they got into the deserted street Idris said, 'you're on your own.'

'Good luck,' Jamil whispered to Mariam and Osman.

'And you,' whispered Mariam watching him go.

'Make for the water tower?' asked Osman.

Mariam shook her head. 'The others will be there, better go for the back of the train at the other end of the station.'

'There's no cover.'

'It's dark. If we cross the track the train will hide us.'

There were lights on the platform. A couple of workers were sitting on crates in sleepy silence. The end of a cigarette rose and glowed, faded and dropped with dull regularity. Osman and Mariam gave the ticket office a wide berth passing the trucks and carts behind it. They ran, backs bent, beyond the end of the platform and scurried across the track.

The lights of a train appeared in the distance. They crouched beside the track under cover of darkness until it groaned and creaked to a halt with a flatbed stacked with building timber in front of them. The driver jumped down and shouted to the two men. One climbed onto a truck and passed boxes down to the other. They prayed the unloading wouldn't continue beyond the platform to the building timber. Osman nodded towards it. They crawled to the end of the truck. It was too high.

'Climb on my shoulders,' whispered Osman.

Mariam stepped on his knee then shoulder. He rose and she crawled on top of the wooden beams. Osman went to the end of the car, climbed on the link and hauled himself up against the ends of the beams. Mariam reached down for him. They had made it. They lay side by side thinking of the others, dreading alarmed shouts.

'We'll be seen,' hissed Mariam.

The beams were strapped together in packs of four.

Osman lifted a pack. 'Can you take the other end?' he asked.

She nodded.

'Stack the middle two onto the sides and we can lie between them.'

The train began to move as they were about to lift the far side pile. They ducked down as it left the station then moved the last into place before it gathered speed.

When the excitement had worn off, Osman felt his bones rattle against the hard wood and Mariam began to feel the cold despite her jeans. They lay in silence shuttling through the night and surrendered to the rhythm of the wheels on the tracks. Before long the sky glowed grey, then pink, orange and blue. They plucked up courage and peeped over their barricade to watch the dusty plain studded with an occasional umbrella acacia. Eventually, up ahead they could see huts, bushes, barbed wire fences, bits of machinery and rectangular mud houses. They shifted stiff limbs to face the next problem; how were they going to get down unseen?

'Kassala,' hissed Mariam.

Osman nodded. 'We'll have to jump,' he said.

'Yes…'

The train started to slow down. Cars were parked behind yards stacked with wire and timber, sacks of cement and wheat guarded by railway employees. On their right, two warehouses were set back, doors closed, with barred windows looking ominous. The train slowed, brakes screeching.

'Jump!' yelled Osman.

They hit the dirt hard, stunned, got to their knees and looked at each other then all around. No one had seen them. The station was half a kilometre further on. They stood up; stiff and shaky.

'We'd better find the others,' said Osman.

'Yes.' Mariam slipped her bag over her back.

'Hide that,' said Osman. 'Too girlie.'

'I forgot,' said Mariam and tucked her hair tighter under her cap.

'Give it to me,' said Osman.

'You can't carry it.'

'It'll go in here.' He said tucking it into his bag.

'Not much left for either of us,' said Mariam. 'Where do you think they'll be?'

'They won't hang around the platforms.'

'The other side of the car park?'

Idris was sitting on a petrol drum in the corner of the car

park, smoking a cigarette. Osman smiled. 'You look cool,' he said.

'Good to see you,' said Idris looking up at Mariam.

'Have you seen the others?' she asked.

'Not yet.'

A ghostly figure appeared from behind the ticket office; Ariam, covered in pale dust. 'Been looking for you,' he said.

'Good to see you,' Osman grinned.

'Where did you hide?' asked Mariam banging the dust from his clothes.

'Under the cover of a hopper full of wheat. I kept sinking, couldn't breathe and couldn't get a foothold 'til I waded to the end.'

'Have you seen Daniel or Jamil?' asked Idris.

'No, but I didn't go near the platforms or office.'

'Should we go and look for them?' asked Mariam.

'Why not? I'll wait here,' said Idris.

'I'll check the car park,' said Ariam.

'We'll try the station.'

It was good to stretch their legs and be among people again. It amused Mariam to adopt the swagger of a boy. There was no sign of Jamil or Daniel. Defeated they returned to Idris. Ariam and Daniel were there. Osman hugged Daniel.

'Glad you made it,' he said.

'Where was he?' Osman asked Ariam.

'Can't you guess? Touring all the cars checking their dashboards.'

'Never seen so many SUVs,' said Daniel.

'No sign of Jamil?' Ariam asked.

'No, I'll do a tour,' said Osman.

Jamil was nowhere to be seen. The train had been emptied and shunted into a siding. It was close to midday and there were fewer passenger trains. The platform was empty.

Exhilaration at their success was clouded by the loss of

Jamil. Osman returned to the others to break the news.

'Jamil didn't make it.'

Mariam put a hand on his arm. 'Another day. He'll get here, you know Jamil.'

Idris stood up. 'Breakfast boys?' It made him smile to see Mariam as a boy. She looked cheeky like that, more approachable.

They found a busy café in a back street. Ariam looked for a table near a socket so that he could charge his phone. They ordered a plate of tamayya[16] and a bowl of tomato, onion and parsley covered in lime and peanut butter sauce with gorassa.[17] Their minds were on parting and the vastness of their quests so they tore their bread and scooped up the tomatoes funnelling them into their mouths in silence, then made their way into the centre looking for accommodation.

Kassala was big and busy; cars, carts, people and animals all on top of each other. People's faces were tense, harassed, everyone was in a hurry, few stopped to chat. A city of strangers? Who could you trust here? To breach a door and ask for accommodation was daunting. Who? Where? Which entrance would not lead into a trap and return to a cruel death. After two hours of tramping the streets they stopped for coffee and Daniel used Ariam's phone to dial the transport company. Khartoum was possible but they would have to split up; three in a couple of days time, the others four days later. All the lorries left at dawn.

They found a dusty room with a double mattress on the floor surrounded by dead flies. They dumped their bags and used a deep latrine in the far corner of the yard. Mariam heard cockroaches under the ledge at the top of the wall. There wasn't much of a yard. Not enough space to sleep outside in peace and the cacophony of traffic was unnerving but there was a gas hob in a corner where they could heat water or cook.

'We need to find out what's going on here,' said Idris.

16 Chickpea fritter.

17 Soft, doughy flatbread.

'Do you want your jeans, Ariam?' asked Mariam, they were hot and heavy to wear compared to her cotton tunics.

He shrugged. 'I'm all right, what do you think guys, should Mariam be a girl or a boy?'

'It's too risky, forty lashes if she's discovered and return for all of us.'

Mariam was glad to give them back and the cap. She shook her hair free, before covering it with her shawl.

'Do we need to tell people where we're going?' asked Mariam.

'No, we need to get the buzz and say nothing,' said Daniel.

'Cafés,' said Osman.

Kassala was a lot bigger than Agordat. The roads bustled.

They passed tourist cafés and worker's pit stops – exposed at the side of the road, under trees or faded umbrellas selling fruit juices, tea and shakes, fritters or biscuits. One long side street was lined with stalls selling fruit or sesame seeds, dried okra, powdered chickpeas, chilli and spices. Open doorways displayed lengths of brightly patterned cotton, some jalabiya[18] and chadurs.[19] Daniel stopped by a display of hammers, rough string and tiny metal tripods. Mariam saw another with goblets and bowls made from painted gourds. The aroma of roasting peanuts stopped Idris in his tracks.

'That smells good,' he said.

'We need to find a place to sit,' said Osman.

'Get to know what's going on round here,' said Ariam looking warily around.

'There are seats up there,' said Mariam pointing to a couple of small tables with stools outside a dark doorway.

They headed towards it and watched a man emerge, hitch up his trousers and straighten his shirt before passing them on his way to the centre.

Idris looked at Ariam. 'Should we try it?'

---

18 Men's long tunic.

19 Women's draped covering.

'I'm thirsty,' said Daniel.

They filed into the gloom and followed the sound of voices to a courtyard at the back with four or five tables seating a strange mix of people. Some in western clothes looking like businessmen, a couple of tables with younger men in jeans and T-shirts. Conversation was sporadic, low, melancholic. Osman thought that the groups had known each other for a long time, it was routine, nothing much to say. One by one they began to register their arrival and take an interest. At a table by the wall, four older men in jalabiya and turbans stopped playing cards, laid down their hands and sat back to watch them. Osman felt unnerved by their sullen, heavy eyes but made himself smile confidently in their direction.

He put his hand on Daniel's arm and whispered, 'Let's get out.' Without taking his eyes off the men.

Outside they breathed easier and were glad to sit on stools beside the road. Idris ordered two kerkede,[20] two chai and a mint tea from a young man in a baseball cap turned back to front. They watched the passers-by. A couple of men with Ethiopian features came to sit at the next table. They ordered a Fruto and a Lemonada and carried on their conversation.

'It's Tigrinya, listen!' said Mariam. 'They're Eritrean!'

They listened in silence and Ariam nodded to Idris. 'They must be Eritrean.'

'What are they saying?' Idris asked Mariam, who was closest to them.

'One's got to go to work, the other's telling him not to be seen.'

'They're like us,' said Osman.

'They came in on a bus,' said Mariam still listening.

'From where?' asked Idris.

Mariam shrugged and concentrated. 'Talking about different

20 Hibiscus tea.

people, a community. Some help them but there's one they don't trust. He took money from Yonas, the one in the green T-shirt.'

'How long do you think they've been here?' asked Daniel.

Mariam shook her head. 'Don't know but a while I think. They know too many people.'

'And one has a job,' said Ariam.

Suddenly the conversation at the next table stopped. The two men were staring at Ariam and the others.

'Sorry,' said Osman, 'you speak Tigrinya. We come from Eritrea.'

Yonas hissed, 'Shush.' He looked nervously over his shoulder up and down the street. The five stiffened. The other young man, in a short sleeved shirt, said quietly, 'You don't know where the spies are.'

Yonas nodded his head indoors to the café's courtyard. 'In there, everywhere, everyone wants to keep the police on their side.'

'What should we do?' asked Osman.

'Just arrived?' asked the man in the shirt.

Osman nodded and murmured, 'This morning.'

'No papers?'

Osman shook his head.

'The only way to stay safe and get papers is at the camp.'

'Camp?' said Daniel.

'Shagarab,' said Yonas.

'Shagarab?' repeated Daniel.

'You haven't heard of it?'

'No,' said Ariam impatient.

'I have,' announced Idris.

They stared at him. 'What do you know?' asked Ariam.

'It's overcrowded and you never get out.'

'Not true. It takes time but you can get a work permit and apply for refugee status there.'

'What does that mean?' asked Daniel.

‘That you can’t be sent back to Eritrea,’ said Yonas, ‘and they help you find work, money to save.’

‘Is the camp far from the centre?’ asked Ariam.

‘There’s a bus that brings us in every day. It’s not that far,’ replied the other man.

‘It’s a shuttle between the two,’ said Yonas.

‘Be careful, if you’re discovered on the streets without the camp behind you, you’re finished,’ said his friend standing up.

‘We must go,’ said Yonas. ‘Be careful.’

They watched them pay at the counter and step into the street to merge with the crowds.

‘It’s not safe here,’ said Mariam speaking their common fear.

‘What’s Shagarab like?’ Daniel asked Idris.

‘Too many people; women, children, old people. Thousands like us; young and looking for work. Too many to process with too few to do it.’

‘But they must be looked after…’ said Ariam.

‘Oh yes,’ said Idris. ‘Western governments pay to keep refugees in place; Sudan, Libya, anywhere but Europe and the West. You’ll be fed but not much and housed but under canvas with others you don’t know and can’t choose.’

‘He said you can get papers there.’

‘How long are you prepared to wait, six months, a year?’ asked Idris.

‘I want to go to University. I can’t go underground and hide. I need proof of who I am. I’ll wait,’ said Ariam.’

‘I’m not worried about University but I don’t want to be sent back. I want to get out of Africa and find somewhere decent to work,’ said Daniel. ‘I don’t have a passport, not even a birth certificate; papers are the key to freedom, I’m with you, Ariam.’

‘I’m not hanging around waiting, it could take months. There’s a boat waiting for me,’ said Idris.

Osman and Mariam looked at each other, they felt the same.

‘Camp? Life without privacy, surrounded by strangers, fed

by charity, waiting, waiting. Girls will be last on their lists if there are any,' said Mariam.

'You'll never cross two countries without papers, proof of identity,' said Ariam.

'You don't need a passport to hitch a lift,' said Idris.

Osman listened, taped to his body he had enough for a ticket across the sea. That was precious, he wasn't going to fritter it away in cities. He had to get across the desert into Libya and through. The people in the camps were happy to have escaped, prepared to sit and wait, not planning a future. He and Mariam were passing through, moving on. Across the Mediterranean human life was precious, people mattered, work was paid, you were free to do things you never dreamt of.

'I don't care about Sudan or Libya,' he said. 'I'm happy to keep my head down.'

'We'll get our papers when we arrive, meanwhile we'll keep a low profile,' said Idris.

'Fly under the radar,' echoed Mariam.

'Are you sure you want to stay in Sudan?' Osman asked Daniel.

'I'll be safe in the camp and I can find work here, lots of old bangers around. I'll follow when I have papers to get through.'

'Will the lorry still take us to Khartoum?'

Daniel nodded. 'They don't know what I look like, Dad set it up and you're turning up. We're the only ones who know about the arrangement.'

Khartoum was a milestone and a lift there made them feel blessed.

It was a huge relief to Mariam to get back to their empty room and hide. She was happy preparing a meal of lentils and rice which they ate in silence, deep in their own thoughts. It seemed as if Daniel and Ariam had drifted into a separate orbit, they would forever pass but never touch. The loss of his friends hurt Osman. He felt bewildered, as if they had let him down but a new life was their only bond now and each had to find it their own way. Kassala did not impress Osman. He didn't like the city, it seemed alien and treacherous. He was passing through, in travel mode, not looking for a home, not here. He was impatient to get on with the main task – getting to the Mediterranean.

Tired though they were, the hot dusty room with Osman and Mariam on the bed and the others on the floor was too crowded, too hot. The rattle of trucks and rumble of distant traffic did not drown the rustle of cockroaches or the whine of mosquitos. Osman longed to stretch under the stars but the proprietor was an old, thin man who only had eyes for the notes in their hands. Osman didn't trust him.

Daniel and Ariam set off early hoping to catch a work bus returning to Shagarab. Mariam and Osman wandered the streets collecting things for the journey and ingredients for their last meal in Kassala. Idris set off for the café again after tidying his backpack.

They had to be at the transport depot by dawn so the next night was shorter yet seemed interminable to Osman and Mariam who put their arms round each other for comfort until the heat separated them. It was a relief to rise at 4.00am, rinse their faces in the yard and creep away. Mariam had packed them a stuffed injera each and left two for Daniel and Ariam.

The owner of Omer Hassan trucks was a sullen man who hardly looked them in the face before leading them to the lorry where a round, middle-aged man with a shiny face and moustache was stowing a sack under the driving seat.

'This is Abdu,' he said.

Abdu showed his broken front tooth in a wide grin. He looked from face to face.

'Idris,' said Idris offering his hand.

'Osman.' Osman held the man's plump hand.

'Mariam.' Abdu eagerly reached for her hand.

'You'll have to go in the back,' Mr. Hassan told Osman.

'I'll do that,' said Idris.

'So, you'll sit up with me,' said Abdu delighted that he would only have to share his space with the thin boy in simple clothes and the equally thin young woman.

They left a grey, sleepy Kassala unseen. Mariam asked how far it was to Khartoum.

'Over six hundred kilometres. Sit back and relax,' laughed Abdu.

'How long will it take?' she asked.

'All day, welcome aboard,' he shouted over pounding pop music.

Abdu took half the seat but their early start meant that the first couple of hours were cool enough. As the sun rose and tedium set in, the monotonous jolly music jangled Mariam's nerves and Abdu's hot body made Osman uncomfortable. Outside was nothing but a flat, arid waste with an occasional tree or glimpse of a distant camel train or goatherders. Eventually an occasional hut appeared, then fences, sheds and lines of low buildings set in the red sand.

'Al Qadarif,' announced Abdu.

It was no more than a roadside shed with a latrine behind and a water pump. Inside there were breads and pastries and every kind of dried food for sale. They had ful medames and orange juice. They paid for Abdu's meal then, while he smoked a cigarette, they stretched their legs around the compound.

'You all right in the back?' Osman asked Idris.

Mariam watched Idris. He smiled. 'I'm better in my own space, even if I am sharing it with a load of motorbikes.'

Mariam laughed, 'Should have been Daniel.'

'Do you think they'll stay in Shagarab?' Idris asked Osman.

'Ariam's straight. He'll stay for the papers and Daniel, he's not ready to cross Libya or the Med. They'll stay.'

'So, they won't catch us up in Khartoum then,' said Mariam sadly.

On the next leg of the journey, Abdu was content to sit back with a hand on the bottom of the wheel and let the lorry jump and jiggle its way along the pitted road. Mariam gave up bracing herself and Osman stopped trying to support her, it was too hot. The sun smouldered through the dust on the windscreen. The cab was stifling. Mariam opened her window; the air scorched their throats. They sucked their water wondering how long it would last. The rattle and roll of the lorry threw their sweating bodies together.

'I hope Idris is all right,' said Mariam looking up at the enormous ball of fire overhead.

'He's got a hat,' said Osman.

Mariam passed her thin shawl through the rear window and Idris spread it between two bikes to shelter under.

The unbearable was born for three hours until, in the distance, they could see not only huts and sheds but trees, palm trees. Mariam wondered if they were real. Abdu grinned.

'Wad Madani,' he shouted.

'An oasis,' Osman whispered, 'not a hallucination.'

Abdu coasted to a halt in the shade of a wooden emporium. They headed straight to a pump and ducked their heads under its warm murky water grateful to sluice away sweat and dust from arms, legs and feet. It cooled their boiling blood. Inside they ate fresh tomatoes, cucumber, rice and eggs followed by fresh pineapple. They treated Abdu who bartered down the price, happy to show his influence. The place was quiet, the waiters attentive and pleasant.

The joy and relief of this stop carried them on, that and a cooler truck, the sinking sun and finally the glowing lights of Khartoum – three cities sprawling between the arms of the White and Blue Niles. It spread as far as the eye could see, punctuated by tall, modern buildings; pointed towers, circular arenas of offices and flats, museums, shopping malls petering out to flats and high-density housing. The three areas were connected by long, spidery bridges.

They passed no dust tracks, no side streets bordered by crumbling houses, no vacant lots with donkeys or camels as they expected but glass and concrete, paving slabs, tarmac, structured roads, tall buildings, and wide highways. Abdu drove to an industrial site not far from the airport and let them down on the roadside.

'Thank you,' said Osman and shook Abdu's hand vigorously. Mariam gave him biscuits and dates then they wandered the streets on stiff, wobbly legs in awe of the enormity of the capital. Threading their way to a four-lane highway lined by palm trees with elegant shops and smart cafés, they didn't know which way to turn. They drifted right hoping it was away from the centre and looked down every side street hoping for dust, sand, ragged awnings and friendly smiles only to find cut stone and brass plates. They walked until weary, trying to get away from the glamour, looking for humble and friendly faces and finally came to a more crowded district with people overflowing onto the street. However, they were still afraid to expose themselves in a café.

They knew no one here, they were rudderless. Every small decision seemed crucial. Libya had never seemed so far or so impossible. Osman felt insecure, without anchor, no familiar point of reference. He was afraid of dangerous currents dragging him off course. He touched his money pouch and looked nervously at Mariam. Idris straightened his shoulders.

Hunger gnawed at their stomachs. Finally Mariam stopped in front of a shop with wilting veg and dry looking fruit.

'Let's get something to eat and find somewhere to sit,' she said.

The man inside the shop ignored them as they toured the shelves. They gathered a couple of tins of fish, a cucumber and a packet of flatbreads. Idris added chocolate bars and Osman a bottle of orange fizz at the till.

'Nakfas all right?' asked Idris showing his money.

The man shrugged his shoulders and dropped the coins into separate drawers without looking up.

Outside Mariam said, 'he wasn't very happy, was he?'

'Do you think he knew we are refugees?' asked Osman.

'It's late. He was probably ready to close,' replied Idris.

As they walked away the blind came down over the door and the weak yellow light behind was extinguished.

'Where to now?' asked Osman.

'Somewhere quiet,' said Mariam.

'The river,' said Idris.

But they didn't know which way it was. They passed in front of the wide steps and pillars of a glamorous hotel with uniformed staff at its doors.

'This is a rich city,' said Osman.

'Abdu dropped us by the airport, a tourist area. The poorer suburbs with the Southerners, must be on the other side,' said Idris.

'We stand out,' said Mariam frightened.

'Not for poverty,' said Idris looking at Mariam's white tunic with azure and turquoise embroidered braid around its neck and down the front and her soft blue shawl draped over her head and shoulders. He didn't know how she managed to look so tidy.

'We don't look Sudanese,' said Osman.

'No,' said Idris watching three Arabs pass a group of Westerners at the doors of the hotel, 'neither do they.'

Not far from the hotel, there was a park where they sat on the grass between bushes to share their meal. They longed to stretch out and sleep but the noise of traffic encircled them.

'Do you think it's far to the river?' asked Mariam longing for peace and quiet and the reassurance that one side was protected by water.

'Can't be far,' said Idris.

It wasn't long before pavements and concrete gave way to bushes and trees and they saw lights rippling on water. The riverside was busy with families walking, men securing their boats, women selling fruit and pastries, cyclists and children playing. They were too tired and purposeful to feel envious. All they needed was a safe place to sleep. They carried on upriver away from the centre until the sound of monkeys chattering and birds settling overtook the clank of heavy vessels on the water, human voices and the hum of traffic. Then they slept by the waters of the White Nile disturbed only by the whine of insects and ripple of wakes as boats moved silently past.

The roar and whoosh of a plane woke Mariam. She opened her eyes to bright sun and white sky.

Their breakfast of leftovers became a war cabinet. They had to find a room and Idris wanted to find out more about life in Khartoum and to plan the next leg of the journey before phoning his contact.

'We' d better get to know the city,' said Osman.

'Three cities,' said Mariam sitting on a stump looking over the Nile, its bridges and the island where the two Niles met.

'We're in the centre,' said Idris.

'Not where we'll meet our sort,' said Mariam.

'No, but it may be safe for a while. No one's going to look for refugees where they're expecting tourists,' said Osman.

'We'd better head away from the river,' said Idris.

The Nile was wide, its bridges already full of traffic. Small boats were tethered on either side and people were stowing provisions or loading cargo. Traffic hummed all around.

They walked away from the glamour further and further into a labyrinth of streets and little squares with stalls and crowded housing until they found a café where young men were talking or earnestly reading newspapers.

They drank their coffee watching the comings and goings of women and children, waiting for the strangeness to wear off. Then they moved on closer to the University and stopped for lunch at a café with a tiny, tiled courtyard shaded by a palm tree.

The place was alive with animated conversations. There were students from China, Egypt, Saudi Arabia and Sudan; some quiet and studious, some relaxed and chatty, some political and volatile. They sat in a corner listening to the different languages, interpreting by gesture rather than words. Mariam's bit of English helped, it seemed to be everyone's default language. They heard nothing of any use to them.

By evening their feet had mapped a wide area from the river to the University and around but they hadn't found a likely place to stay or gained enough confidence to ask, so they headed back to the river and walked along the bank until they came to Al Sunut Forest. They walked in silence, picking their way between trees and bushes, each processing their myriad impressions of Khartoum and its people as they trudged in single file through the forest with the river at their side. Leaves trembled as birds flew in to roost and monkeys climbed to watch their approach, lizards scurried up tree trunks and ants filed across their path undeterred. It was a struggle to get through the undergrowth.

Mariam stopped and called to Idris in front, 'We can't sleep here, there's hardly room to put a foot.'

The three of them stared around in the diminishing light.

'There's nowhere else safe to spend the night,' said Idris. 'We'll be well hidden.' He kicked a bush, it sprang back and a monkey screeched away.

'We can clear it,' he said.

'How?' asked Osman in despair.

Idris grabbed a small bush, kicked his heel into the earth around it, pulled and twisted with such force that he almost fell over when it came free.

'Like that, if need be,' he said out of breath.

They set to – pulled, cut and stamped a clearing for the night. Mariam gathered dry leaves and grass to cover the soil.

They washed in the Nile and settled in their nest with

branches overhead and a screen of bushes all around sinking into silence, peace, calm. The only sounds they heard in the night was the occasional gibbering of a monkey and muted calls of owls.

In the morning the others were woken by Mariam calling frantically, 'Where's my bag? I can't find my bag!'

'Mariam's sack of many colours?' asked Idris smiling.

'It's all I have; everything is in it.'

He looked where she had slept. 'Not there,' he said suddenly serious.

They looked around their tiny camp; no colourful sack. 'Our things are here, it can't be thieves,' said Osman.

They searched between the bushes around and retraced their steps back.'

'I didn't drop it,' she cried. 'I had it by my side when I went to sleep.'

They checked by the river where they had washed but there was no bag. Mariam sank onto the floor shaking her head in disbelief. 'All my money, toiletries, all our food, gone.'

A monkey snorted above their heads and another replied in a rising scale of screams.

'The monkeys!' she jumped up and started to run between the trees looking up into the branches too desperate to cry, too shocked to shout. The others spread out, determined to search around the trees where the monkeys had travelled in the night.

'You go on,' Idris called after her. 'I'll cover the river.'

'I'll try inland,' said Osman.

They covered a wide area without success and came back to the same spot an hour and a half later, each one hoping for good news from the others.

'Sorry, Mariam,' said Idris.

Her own unsuccessful search had prepared her for the worst. Hope was snuffed out.

She said, 'Monkeys can travel fast when they want and go anywhere and they're clever, they'll have emptied it, eaten the food and left it – up in the trees, down among the bushes – they may even have played with it until it was buried under leaves, who knows? You've done all you can, thank you.'

'Don't worry Mariam, I've got money,' said Osman.

'I'll find work, get it back,' she vowed.

Idris held her shoulders and looked into her eyes.

'We won't leave you; we share, our only strength is sticking together. It'll be all right.'

'We can't sleep here, we have to find a safe place,' said Osman.

They returned to the centre, even more wary than before and searched an area adjacent to where they had been, away from the University, beyond the tourists and had breakfast in a café. The proprietor was a large, commanding woman in a black hijab and heavy make-up. Khartoum was host to many nations, its people were used to strangers, they didn't need to be afraid. They asked where they could find a room. She looked at the two men then Mariam disapprovingly.

'My brothers,' Mariam reassured her.

She gave them the address of a guest house.

The man who showed them their room was polite and formal. He asked no questions. They paid him for a week. He said, 'selam aleykum' and departed. There were a couple of men at breakfast, one in western clothes and the other in a white jalabiya, fingering prayer beads as he waited to be served.

'We can't keep this up for long,' said Idris.

'I must find work,' said Mariam.

'Not easy without papers,' said Idris.

'I can speak English, the place is full of foreigners. There must be a hotel that can use me.'

Idris looked at her beautiful face and said, 'You'll get a job, no problem.'

Osman and Mariam went to hotel after hotel, Khartoum was

full of them but all asked to see her papers until they tried a tall, glass and steel structure close to the airport, 'Hotel Senopper.' The manager tested Mariam's English and was visibly impressed. A girl at reception had failed to turn up and several flights were expected with one and two-night bookings, turn over time was pressed. Mariam explained that her bag had been stolen and she had applied for replacement papers, it would take a while. She was hired and when they got back, Idris had toured building sites the other side of the airport, chatting to labourers. They told him about a new build that was taking on labour a couple of kilometres out of town. His big, healthy body said it all, he was hired on an hourly basis. Dinner that night was a celebration.

With the other two at work, Osman felt wretched and useless. He was too thin for building work; he spoke mainly Tigrigna and nobody wanted baskets even if he could find the materials. The city was noisy, alien, claustrophobic. The river was a magnet. He wandered along its bank watching its traffic. No two boats were the same; feluccas vied with ferries and big motor cruisers, fishing boats and skiffs.

Dividing the great expanse of the White and Blue Nile was an island. It looked green and peaceful, unspoilt, without high rise buildings or heavy machinery on its wharf, just small boats. He crossed the bridge to Tuti Island. The roads were beaten earth, there were no luxury limousines. He was passed by a couple of dusty vans and a rusty truck. *That's seen some work.* He watched the battered vehicle rattle and jump along the road ahead. The houses were simple, single storey dwellings with earthen walls. He breathed easier, relaxed into his usual loping walk and stopped to watch half a dozen men working around a mud bath mixing straw into clay. Hundreds of brown clay bricks were stacked in rows behind them. One mixed, two filled moulds, one tipped them out, two stacked and turned bricks baking in the heat. They worked seamlessly together without speaking. *I would like to be a part of a team like that.*

He was dwarfed by sorghum plants in a small field by the road, their pale green foliage looked lush, just like home. He passed goats and stood on a grassy shelf where a rusty pump dipped its tail into the Blue Nile. Osman looked down the wide stretch of peaceful water forever moving, travelling thousands of kilometres to the sea, the Mediterranean Sea, just like him and the way leading back to Ethiopia, Eritrea, home far, far back along those waters, seemed a dream. He thought of its long journey, how this living water knew no boundaries; desert, mountains, rivers, seas; they belonged to everyone and wondered why mankind splits the planet up, breaking it into false chunks with frontiers, making boundaries to imprison people. He sat on the bank feeling detached from society like a satellite in orbit.

It was Friday, a day of rest. A couple of colourful, canopied boats passed by full of curious visitors secure in their freedom, following the Nile. Someone waved, he waved back. They looked just like him but for him, it was like looking at fish in an aquarium, creatures in a different world. He missed Mariam, Idris, Daniel, Ariam and Jamil but most of all his family and Sebhat who had such patience and belief in him. He got up and walked on past a small field of grass with a few grazing cows. The quiet and familiarity of the island reassured him.

He heard voices, young, eager voices, and the sound of a foot against a ball. A group of boys were playing football in front of a long, low house with a verandah. The ball rolled towards him, and he kicked it hard to their makeshift goal, straight between the posts. They applauded and grinned at him.

Play started again, and a short, spiky-haired boy dribbled quickly past his friends to kick the ball to Osman, who lobbed it back.

'What are you doing, Bashir?' yelled a tall boy. 'He doesn't want to play.'

'Spoil sport, Mohammed, who says?' Bashir looked defiantly at Osman.

He replied, 'It's okay, I'll give you a game if you want.'

Mohammed shrugged.

'My team.' Bashir grinned at his brother.

'Then I'm having Faheem and Asim,' said Mohammed, picking up the ball.

'I'll kick off,' said Bashir.

'Why not give the newcomer a chance?' replied Mohammed.

Osman took aim and kicked the ball to a tall, lanky boy who swiftly passed it back.

Osman dribbled and dodged past the others on his way back to the goal, but Mohammed tackled him and side swiped the ball to Faheem, a big, strong young man who evened up the score. Osman didn't want to dominate the game as the eldest, but it was not a problem – he was out of practice and they were quick and clever. They all lost themselves in the fight for the ball and targeting their goals. Bashir kept close to Osman, always ready to take a pass. He enjoyed showing off his ball control. Together they scored another goal and became instant pals. At the end, the boys shared their water with Osman and asked his name.

'What do you do?' asked Bashir.

'I make baskets,' said Osman.

'That's girls work!' laughed one.

'What with?' asked another.

Osman looked at the rushes by the river. 'Things like that.'

'How?'

'I'll show you.'

He started to select reeds moist enough to be pliable, then long grasses. They quickly got the idea and helped. They took them back to sit under the shade of the thatched eaves of the house. One of the older boys from Osman's team sat by his side. A few who had helped gather reeds wanted to weave. Osman showed them how to tie them together with grass to start. They tried to copy his twisting and plaiting, some gave up, a couple started again. Osman's young friend carried on plaiting reeds together.

'How old are you?' Osman asked him.

'Eight.'

'Same age as my brother.'

'Where is he?'

'In Eritrea.'

'That's a long way.'

'It's on the Red Sea, isn't it?' asked Mohammed.

Osman nodded.

'We've only got desert,' said Faheem, sitting at Osman's side carefully plaiting his reeds as Osman had shown.

'We've got Tuti Island,' shouted Bashir.

'You've got the Nile,' said Osman, looking from Mohammed on one side, to Faheem on the other. 'Lots of it. It's good here.'

'There's not much going on,' complained Mohammed.

'You've all of Khartoum over there,' Osman nodded to the bridge.

'Only the rich can enjoy that.'

'Mohammed, Bashir, dinner!' A woman in an ochre-coloured sarong with brown patterns down the side, came round the side of the house and stopped in surprise at the sight of Osman halfway through building a basket, surrounded by boys.

'I wondered what was going on,' she laughed.

Osman looked up and smiled.

'A bit of basket making.' He indicated a couple of boys tying reeds.

'Isn't he clever?' asked Bashir.

Mohammed got up and Osman's new-found friend groaned, 'Ma.'

'Can he join us?' asked Mohammed.

If he wants to.' She looked at Osman.

He put aside his work and stood. 'I don't want to be a trouble.'

'No trouble, there's plenty for all of us.'

She reminded Osman of his mother.

Three of his pupils stood and said, 'Thanks.' Before departing, leaving two who were competing with their baskets. Osman inspected their efforts.

'You've got the hang of it, well done,' he said feeling guilty at abandoning them. 'Hadn't you better go home too?'

'Soon,' mumbled one engrossed.

'In a bit,' said the other picking up another reed.

'Come on,' called his young friend from the entrance.

'I'll leave you to it, then,' said Osman.

Inside the house was dark and cool.

'Abdul, this is…' His wife looked to Osman.

'Osman,' he said and put his hands together in greeting, 'Selam aleykum.'

'Wa-alaykum salam,' replied Abdul and signalled Osman to sit next to him.

A girl in a green sarong set their meal platter on a low table. Osman was beginning to feel at home. Bashir's sister was a little younger than Delina.

'Alia, this is Osman,' said their mother. Alia smiled and lowered her gaze.

'Look what I made,' shouted Bashir holding up his reed rope.

Alia's big eyes followed Osman's every move.

'Osman showed us how to weave baskets,' explained Mohammed.

'Did you see that, Zina?' Abdul asked his wife.

'Usin' reeds and grass,' she said.

'We've got plenty here.' Abdul dipped a piece of fried chicken into spicy sauce.

Osman took a roll and dipped it into mint yoghurt.

'Osman played football with us,' said Bashir.

'Bashir's good,' said Osman.

'He's got a brother like me,' said Bashir pointing to Osman.

'Where is he?' asked Abdul.

Osman bowed his head. 'Eritrea,' he said quietly holding his breath, waiting for their reaction, afraid of anger and exposure.

'Do you aim to stay here?' asked Abdul.

Osman shook his head, embarrassed. 'No.'

Alia looked disappointed.

'Where're you heading?'

'Europe.'

'That's a long way and a dangerous journey. Do you think you'll make it?'

'My family made sacrifices to send us. We've got to make it.'

'Who's we?' asked Bashir's mother.

'My sister and a friend.'

'Three of you,' said Abdul thoughtfully.

'Be careful,' said his wife, 'we hear things. There are people making money from your family's sacrifices – kidnappers demanding ransoms, smugglers who abandon their 'customers' in the desert and worst of all young girls, captured to sell to traders as slaves for sex.'

'You can't cross the desert alone, you'll need help. Choose wisely and Allah be with you,' said Abdul.

'How long will you be here?' Asked Zina.

'A couple of weeks to set things up and earn money. The others have got jobs.'

'Your sister?' asked Zina.

'She speaks English.'

'A clever family,' she said offering Osman the plate of chicken.

'Good luck, young man. I admire your courage,' said Abdul.

'And determination,' said Zina. 'We're lucky, Abdul likes his work and I have my vegetables and goats.'

'Just like my mother.'

'Really?'

Osman turned to Abdul, 'What is your work?'

'I'm a manager at the brick factory. We send our bricks all over. There's a bit of Tuti Island all over Sudan.'

'There'll be no Tuti island left for us!' wailed Bashir.

'No, son, it'll always be here. The earth's a great giver – clay, minerals, fuel; the Nile – she gives life to every nation along her course.'

Zina picked up the empty platter and Alia collected the glasses.

'Can I go to Amina's?' Alia asked.

'If you've finished your chores,' said Zina.

Osman stood ready to leave and said 'hatur nuhun.' But Bashir said, 'Can I show Osman the goats?'

Zina looked at Osman, he didn't seem in any hurry. She nodded. Bashir took his hand and led him out into the sun. The goats were pleased to see them. They nuzzled Osman's hands and shoved each other for attention. Their udders were full. Osman did not want to interfere, but he felt their discomfort in the heat.

'Who milks the goats?' he asked.

'Alia.'

'When will she be back?'

Bashir shrugged his shoulders.

'Should we do it for her?'

'I've never milked the goats,' said Bashir excited.

'Go and fetch buckets.'

Bashir handed one to Osman then ran inside and came out with a washing bowl.

'That'll do,' said Osman. 'Do you know how to do it?'

Bashir shook his head.

Osman stroked his goat talking to her as he tucked the bucket beneath her. He took the teat firmly in his hand and started to squeeze and pull.

'Grip, squeeze, pull,' he said and Bashir followed suit delighted to see the milk flow.

'Don't let go. Squeeze, pull but not too hard.'

As they were storing the milk in the shade, Osman noticed people making their way along the lane to the bridge.

'Time to go,' he said to Bashir.

'You'll come to see us again, won't you?'

Osman grabbed him under his arms and swung him round.

'Maybe,' he said and headed off to the bridge.

Mariam worked shifts, early morning, mid-day or late. Today was late so Osman stopped at the supermarket for peanut butter, oil, tomatoes, onions and gorassa. There were newspapers on a stand in languages he couldn't read. He had never paid much attention to news at home but suddenly it mattered and he couldn't fathom it. Feeling cut off from a world he depended on made him uneasy.

Idris worked long hours for little pay. It was the only way to get a job without papers. Mariam returned a little before him. The meal was set out when Idris returned with the news they had all been waiting for.

'He replied,' he said. 'My contact, we met at lunchtime. The only way to cross the Sahara is in a four by four. There are set routes, none official. We have to pay people to get us into Libya.

'Does he know anyone reliable?'

'Yes, he'll put us in touch. We'll be part of a group.'

'How much?'

'You can get the complete deal here, Libya and the Med.'

'How much?'

'8,000 American dollars like I said.'

'Where can we change the money?' asked Mariam.

'Western Union. They're everywhere, give and get back, simple business exchange,' said Idris.

'How do we know he'll see us through?'

'Half now, half at the port.'

'We've got my uncle in Libya.'

'There's no transport in Libya, it's just the desert and the Med.'

'You trust him?'

'I looked at others. He seemed our best bet.'

'When can we go?'

'End of this week or next.'

'We won't have enough by the end of the week?'

'Damned monkey. We'll have to wait until the end of next week.'

'I must get work,' said Osman.

'There's nothing on the building site and there are probably half a dozen in line for every waiter's job in Khartoum.'

'I've got to try.'

Instead of feeling relieved at the prospect of moving on, Mariam felt uneasy. Daily interaction with the hotel's guests and an employer who appreciated her smile and willingness, gave Mariam all the identity she needed but she knew that she couldn't live life as a smiling shadow.

The next morning while she slept, Osman returned to his haven, Tuti island. Bashir was delighted and Alia, shamefaced, thanked him for milking the goats.

'Can we play football?' asked Bashir.

Osman looked around. 'There's no one to play with.'

Zina was pulling up spent plants in her veggie patch. Osman stopped to watch.

'Can I help?' he said. 'I worked behind my mother, digging the rows she cleared and planting replacements.'

Zina knelt back on her heels and looked up at him. She realised he was home sick.

'You know what to do then, okay. You can put those corn plants in.'

Bashir grabbed his hand. 'You don't want to do that, come on,' he said dragging him aside.

'I do,' said Osman, 'sorry Bashir, later.'

Zina went to tend her tomato plants. Osman had never enjoyed wielding a spade so much and the row of little green plants in their neat bed gave him real pleasure.

When Zina returned, she said, 'Well done, you've earned your lunch.'

Abdul was pleased to see him. They were the nearest thing to family Osman had.

Over lunch Osman told him about the prospect of transport and the story of the monkeys in the forest.

'Al'ama, abil monkeys, they make mischief everywhere[21].'

'I need to get a job but who's going to give me work without papers?'

'Leave it to me, I'll think about it,' said Abdul.

'That's good, Abdul. Osman planted our corn,' said Zina patting Osman's hand.

'We won't forget him then; we'll say a special prayer for you when we eat them.'

Abdul helped himself to one of Zina's sweet pancakes.

Mohammed passed the platter to Osman and said, 'all the way from Eritrea, you're brave and clever too, I wouldn't know where to start.'

"You would if you had to, like running into the sea to escape a fire.'

Osman stood, 'Thank you for the lunch, Zina, your pancakes are delicious. Should we play footie?' He asked Bashir. The two brothers were up on their feet quickly licking sugar off their fingers and heading for sunlight. They dribbled and passed the ball then sat and drank water plaiting reeds until Abdul came home, washed his hands and face and said abruptly to Osman.

'Let's go,' he said.

Osman was surprised and grateful, then nervous as they crossed the island to a beach with boats lined up and two or three fishermen mending nets and painting hulls. A thin old man was massaging his back outside a ramshackle shed. A small

---

21 Al'ama is the equivalent of damn. It actually means blindness in Arabic. Abil means stupid.

bleached boat lay on its side by the river with a tangle of nets beside it.

'Selam aleykum, Zair. How are you?'

'Wa aleykum salam.'

'Not the man I used to be,' said Zair. 'Dry rot, wet rot, always something in the way.'

'Brought you some help, Zair,' said Abdul.

The man looked suspiciously at Osman's fine features.

'Not from these parts?' he asked.

Osman shook his head.

'You'll not find work here.'

'He's not looking for anything steady, he's young and strong and willing. He can clear all your jobs in a week.'

'How do you know what jobs I've got?'

'How many years have I known you Zaid? Did my father grow up with yours? How many times have I heard you complain about setting up for the season?'

Zaid looked at Osman. 'A week, just a week?'

Osman nodded.

'Can't pay much.'

'Whatever you think,' said Osman

'Is fair,' added Abdul.

'3,000 pounds.'[22]

'That's a niggardly sum,' said Abdul.

'4,000,' said Zair grudgingly.

Abdul looked at Osman.

'Thank you,' Osman said.

'Start tomorrow. This keel needs scrubbing and varnishing.

From Sunday to Friday Osman worked from dawn 'til dusk. He repaired baskets, mended nets, made oars and sorted Zair's smelly shed. It started with Zaid complaining of his aches and pains and loading his work onto Osman but as Osman listened

22 2,000 Sudanese pounds is equal to 4.04 euros.

and did the jobs without complaint, Zaid joined him more and more, enjoying his quiet, positive company. By the end of the week, he and Zaid worked well together. The old man was enjoying Osman's company. Nothing seemed too much for the boy. Osman was driven by his purpose. Nothing here was part of him, nothing permanent, all was part of a greater end. Zaid confided his disappointment that none of his children wanted to follow him in the business. His boat would be sold. He complained that people did not eat enough fish.

'They don't like fish here; decent food for a family. No, they prefer camel and goat; fools!' He spat.

He complained that life was getting harder instead of easier. 'Progress?' he snarled. 'No such thing. People are poorer, sicker, worse off. I'm sick of promises, one after another, they stir up rebellion on the promise of better and we get killed or imprisoned – win or lose, it's all the same to us.'

'What did you want to leave your family for? Why did they let you do that?'

'The Government in Eritrea has its hands round everyone's neck. You are their slave, until they throw you on the scrap heap without funds or family.'

'Depends on what you want from life,' said Zaid.

'Same as most people I suppose. To work for your family, make a home where you want and pass a peaceful future to your children. Most of us want the same things.'

Saying it made Osman realise that he was sacrificing one of his major wishes. He could not put down roots in Eritrea, his beautiful homeland that was part of his DNA. He was losing touch with his childhood, his family. His friends were all dispersed. The football team had gone. Meetings at the café were over but Eritrea was part of him, he would go back. Close to his heart he still had a sprinkle of their hills, their precious earth, his father's gift. He touched the packet, the heavy sand moved under his finger, full of riches, promise, and heartbreak.

Zaid was sorry to have no more to offer Osman than the 4,000 but he sent him away with a knife he used for scaling fish and a couple of guavas.

'From my tree,' he smiled proudly.

Osman said, 'Shukran.' Feeling almost happy.

He put his gifts into his bag and headed for Abdu's house brimming with love for the people of Tuti Island. Mohammed, Bashir and Alia were all out watching for him. 'He's here,' shouted Bashir.

'Come on,' called Alia to their mother and she ran out drying her hands on her kaftan.

Abdu followed. 'What are we doing?' he asked feeling silly.

'Saying 'goodbye' to Osman,' said Bashir crossly to stop himself from crying.

'Okay, okay,' said Abdu, pleased to see Osman's slim figure emerge from behind the reeds and bushes by the track.

'Welcome, welcome,' Abdu shook his hand grinning. They were all grinning. They herded him into the house for tea and cakes.

'What was it like on the river?' asked Bashir.

Osman laughed, 'I wasn't on the river.' Bashir looked disappointed. 'Well not often anyway.'

'Did the old grouch give you a hard time?' asked Abdu.

'He was fine,' said Osman. 'We got a lot done and he helped.'

'Where are you going Osman?' asked Mohammed.

Osman looked at Mohammed's serious face. 'A long way, Mohammed. A new world.'

'Why don't you like this one?' Mohammed lamented.

'This is not my home, Mohammed. Eritrea is my home but I can't stay there.'

'That's where your family is isn't it?'

Osman nodded solemnly. 'They are.'

'Don't you miss them?'

'Of course, I miss them,' Osman spoke more vehemently

than he intended, 'but they want me to be free and have a better life.'

'Than you can in Eritrea?'

Osman nodded, 'While The General rules…'

'Try this Osman.' Zina offered a dish of halawa simsim.[23]

He put one in his mouth and crunched. 'Oh that's good,' he said. Alia clapped her hands with glee. 'I made them, I made them, didn't I mama?'

Zina smiled. 'You helped treasure, you helped.'

'Would you like my catapult?' asked Bashir.

Osman turned in surprise and lifted Bashir's chin. 'That's generous, Bashir. I know how much you like it. Thank you for the thought but we travel light. The most precious thing I'll take is my memory of you and our game of football.' He looked at the family. 'Thank you, all of you.'

Zina stood. 'We have some food for your journey.'

In a cool corner was a packet of biscuits, gorassa and a little pile of onions beside tomatoes, ochre, courgettes and peppers.

'Shukran, shukran,' Osman said hugging one after another and finally Abdul.

They walked to the end of the allotment and the square where they had played football and Osman said, 'Wait.' He disappeared round the hedge and returned with a basket he had woven while chatting to Zaid at lunch times.

***

They were to be collected in the middle of the night outside a deserted children's playground. When they arrived, a woman was already waiting with a little boy. She edged back to the fence and pressed her back against it when she saw them coming. The boy's eyes widened as he gripped her hand, staring at them

23 A crunchy, sweet dessert made from roasted sesame seeds in caramalised sugar.

through the dark. Her hunched shoulders relaxed when she saw Mariam.

'Are you waiting for the bus?' asked Idris.

She nodded and pulled her little boy close. A couple of young men emerged from a side street opposite and quickly crossed the road.

'Desert trip?' asked the first newcomer.

The five looked at each other and then at the two youths.

Osman said, 'Maybe.'

'So're we,' said his companion.

'Where you from?' the second asked the woman with the child.

'Somalia,' she replied holding her son to her and lifting her chin.

'Thought so,' he replied.

A door opened at the end of the street and light shone on a man with a child in his arms while his wife carried bags, followed by two children. They joined the group. Osman felt uneasy, a group this large with baggage looked suspicious. Further down the street, he saw more dark outlines walking towards them. They looked sinister, perhaps soldiers in disguise, or police. The four strolled confidently past the houses and took their place by the fence nodding silently to the assembly. One leant against it and lit a cigarette. They were all quiet. The new, confident arrivals made everyone withdraw inside themselves wondering how many more and how long they would have to wait exposed. Before long, a full family arrived; grandparents, two couples and four children all under nine, Mariam guessed. The three generations passed along the line, whispering, 'Salem Aleykum.'

Some responded and they began to feel more like a group. It crossed Osman's mind that from now on they had to look after each other. Files of people began to pour in from different side streets. The more arrived, the quieter they all became, shuffling closer to make room. There were no more greetings, no conversations just silence and increasing tension. They had all paid their money, would the truck arrive?

The distant sound of a heavy engine throbbed through the dark growing louder. Headlights peered at them from the end of the road and Osman made out DAF on a chrome radiator. A red lorry with a canvas cover stopped at the corner. Osman expected a rush, a great surge of people but everyone waited for the driver to jump down followed by a second who unbolted the back of the truck and pulled down a crate to act as a step.

He lifted the canvas and said, 'Get in quick.'

'You first,' said Osman to the elderly couple. Their family followed.

'I'll pass your boy up to you,' said Mariam to the young mother. She climbed aboard and took her son from Mariam. The three of them followed. The canvas muted the streetlights reducing those seated along either side of the lorry to silhouettes. Osman and Mariam followed Idris to the end behind the cab where they joined the others sitting on a bank of water containers. The last few to climb aboard dropped their bags in the centre and sat on the floor. Osman pitied those crouched on the floor and hoped there were no more pick up points.

They crossed the Nile and entered the desert unable to see the stars or each other under the cover. The intermittent glow of electric lights ceased and the darkness became funereal. No one moved or spoke a word as they churned on and on, further away from Khartoum. The canvas became grey and gradually started to glow into daylight and they were thrown against each other as the lorry surfed drifts of sand.

'The Sahara,' someone whispered.

People shifted in their seats, tried to stretch cramped limbs and drank from their water bottles. Osman thought about the network of escape routes they were crossing. Their little ark was no more than a fraction of fleeing humanity. So many others had trodden these paths before and so many more would follow. It seemed as if half the world were on the run from dictatorships – religious, political, commercial, it didn't matter. They all ground down the masses, sapped their strength and hope, gave fear instead of pride, slavery instead of independence. No matter how different they looked, how different their stories, they were his brothers and sisters; brave enough to say 'no,' escaping together, dreaming, hoping, believing in better; called by the flimsy flag of democracy.

After five hours, the lorry pulled into the side and the back was dropped. They clambered out to plough through sand, find drifts to crouch behind, dig holes with their hands and return relieved. Mariam broke Zina's bread into pieces and they ate, happy to be on their way.

Less than half an hour later the truck pulled over again. The back was unbolted, and the canvas lifted. A group of Syrian families, some with babies in arms, were standing beside a pile of bags, rugs, pots and pans, accompanied by a man in jeans and sleeveless jacket. The drivers of the lorry complained loudly about the number of the group and their pile of belongings. The shouting continued until the man made a phone call and passed the phone to one of the drivers. He listened, looked at the other, shrugged his shoulders and gave it back in disgust.

'Get in, get in,' he barked.

They bent over their luggage. 'Leave that,' snapped the other driver.

'No room,' said the first.

A couple of women wailed and a man tried to argue. He was pushed aside. They started to unpack and stuff things into their clothes.

'Stop that, no time, we have to go.' The first driver looked nervously along the highway.

Inside people shuffled back to make space on the floor and one of the women unrolled her carpet over it. Women and children were helped up, some wore burkas, some jeans and

T-shirts and were joined by their men. The back was secured and they were on their way again into the gathering twilight.

Once the truck had gathered momentum and the newcomers had adapted to the space, all sat still and silent, relieved to be propelled to the coast and freedom. The children slept and babies were comforted at their mother's breasts as they sped through the dark. Anxious faces mellowed in the gloom, breath steadying, the canvas cavern was their sanctuary. Osman felt part of something big, touching countries and continents, carried on a wave of humanity. These people were his people. Their breath was his breath, their hearts beat like his – a little quicker with excitement, fear and hope. They had done what they could, now they were dependent on the men they had paid. No one could cross the Sahara alone or the sea. No government sanctioned flight from their own country or into any other. They were alone. The only people to turn to were those who learnt to circumscribe institutional cruelty and outwit unscrupulous rivals.

Hours later the black roof started to lighten, changing from grey to orange and yellow. Faces emerged from the gloom and Osman recognised Somalians, Sudanese, some like himself, Ethiopian or Eritrean but no Jamil, Ariam or Daniel. There were a few young Syrians too. As daylight and heat gathered strength, families amused their children playing what games they could with a child on a lap and the others watched, grateful for the diversion.

People started to fidget, get restless and a child begged to pee. It had been spoken; a wave of relief was followed by another of urgency. Infants were passed to the side of the truck and held up by the young men there. The men followed while the women suffered until the truck stopped. The back came down and they all poured out into the desert sun to struggle through the sand in small groups. Mariam with the young mother and son, Idris and Osman with the men of the family. They ate Zina's vegetables cut small with Zaid's knife and stretched their limbs before climbing back on board to their original places. No one had the courage to overturn the established order.

They headed off towards midday. The canvas stopped the sun's glare but under it, thirty-five bodies sweltered. Children became tetchy, old people struggled to breathe. A woman in a burka fainted. A Syrian came forward and told her husband to remove what he could of the cloth enveloping her. The man looked up afraid to expose his wife and terrified of losing her.

'I'm a doctor, cool her body.'

The man removed the hood, her hair clung to her head, then lifted her robe. Her body streamed with sweat. They fanned her. The old woman in the corner close by feverishly unwrapped her shawl and tried to stand. She fell back and her husband leant over her holding his water bottle to her lips. Her daughter fanned her but the old woman's head sank onto her chest. Her husband shouted her name and rubbed her hand to bring her back. The doctor among the Syrians tried to get to her but couldn't pass. The families in the middle struggled to keep their children quiet. A man cried out seized with cramp. Idris banged on the back of the cab. It stopped. The driver came round and lifted the canvas.

'What's wrong?'

Idris showed the old woman struggling to breathe. 'She's ill.'

'Give her water.'

'The people in the middle can't move, the heat's too much.'

'Nothing I can do about that. There's water in the tanks, pass it round.'

Tin cups were stacked beside the tanks. Idris and Osman filled them and Mariam passed them along a line of hands. Young men from the sides offered to swap places with the women and children. After a general re-shuffle, they set off again. The old woman revived a little as they flapped the canvas sides to circulate air. Her husband watched her full of anxiety.

It was not long before dusk deadened the intensity of the heat and darkness settled the children. It blurred the claustrophobia and calmed everyone. They were speeding to freedom. At ten o'clock they stopped to stretch out on the cooling sand and sleep, only to be woken before dawn by torchlight flashing in their eyes. Everyone guarded their own water and rationed their food. Osman, Idris and Mariam ate dried banana and Alia's biscuits. Mariam and the mother with the child left the group to relieve themselves then they were all herded in and set off again. Sleepy from the early waking everyone was quiet, glad to be covering the ground towards their goal.

They drove relentlessly on, until just before midday the lorry started to judder and hiss and stopped. Osman felt the vibration of the cab doors slamming as the two drivers got out.

'What's happening?' asked a Syrian woman.

Idris looked through the cab window.

'The bonnet's up,' he said.

The back was let down and they all jumped down onto the side of the road.

'Problem?' asked the Syrian doctor.

'Overheating,' muttered the short driver.

The two drivers were joined by half a dozen passengers; mechanics, engineers, farmers; each one wanted their say but the lorry had the last word. It needed to rest and cool down. They were stranded without shade. The elderly and mothers with babies sat in the meagre shade of the truck. Osman and Idris tried to block the sun from Mariam, other husbands and fathers did the same. Some even went back on the lorry.

The old man sat with his wife in the lorry's shade, loosened her clothes and flapped air down her body. Sweat rolled down his face and the vein in his temple stood out. Their son and daughter squatted in front of them with their families watching the children play. The bigger boy kicked sand and it went in the little boy's eye who went crying to his mother.

'Mama, it hurts.'

She lifted his chin and licked the surface of his eye.

'Oww,' he howled. 'Ahmed hurt me.'

'No, the sand hurt you but it's gone now.' She looked at the shamefaced older boy. 'Say 'sorry,' Ahmed.'

The younger boy stopped crying and waited eagerly for his reckoning.

'Sorry,' mumbled Ahmed and quickly turned away.

His grandfather dried the younger boy's cheeks with the end of his head dress and sat him beside him in the shade.

'There now, he didn't mean it. Would you like a story?'

The boy nodded and took his grandfather's hand.

'Long, long ago,' he said,' there was a little boy called Samir. The day he was fourteen, a grown up, he was told to take the cattle to graze and watch over them. If lions or tigers came, he had to blow the cow's horn slung over his shoulder and they would run from the village.'

The story drew other children who sat around Solomon. He smiled a welcome and carried on.

'His first day was fun. He watched zebra and monkeys and there were plenty of parrots to aim his catapult at. The second day was boring, the same old picture, the same old cows. He thought he would try out the horn to see if it worked. He took a deep breath and was very proud of the great bellow he produced. In his excitement he followed the drill and ran to the village shouting, 'Tiger, tiger!' People dropped their tools and ran to the field but there was no tiger, no lion, not even a hyena. Only contented cows. They were cross and Samir was very sorry.

A week went by before the monotony and his sense of mischief, as well as the temptation of the magnificent horn, got the better of him. He blew and ran and called, 'Tiger, tiger!'

More children joined Ahmed and his brother, adults too. Solomon was a good storyteller and the tale was so familiar it was like home. Solomon's wife heard the magic of his voice and came to sit with the children accompanied by their daughter.

'The people ran, Samir's parents ran, afraid for their son. They found nothing but cattle peacefully munching the scrub and a family of monkeys laughing at them.

'You bad boy, stopping our work,' yelled the men.

'Ruining our meals,' shouted the women.

'Concentrate on the cattle not running off, never mind playing games,' they said.

Samir hung his head in shame and tried to be a good herder. He shooed the cows circling further and further away from the village in search of richer pasture. He watched them eat and chew, look for shade and sit, day after day. One morning, slinking down the hillside Samir saw a big orange and black striped body. He held his breath praying for the tiger to pass around the little hill to the other side, but no, it headed down towards the cattle.

He grabbed the horn, heart pounding and blew and blew and ran shouting, 'Tiger! Tiger!'

The people in the village heard the distant call and said, 'That Samir, he's at it again.'

So, no one came to rescue the cows or their tender tasty keeper.'

The children were rapt, the adults applauded. Solomon's face contorted with pain, he hunched his shoulders, held his chest, his arm dropped and he fell forward. His son leapt to his side.

'Papa! Papa!' He laid him flat, removed his head dress and sprinkled water on his father's lifeless face. The children backed away and ran to their parents crying. The doctor raced over and knelt at his side trying to find a pulse. He looked up at the shocked family and shook his head.

'I'm sorry, heart attack.'

Everyone froze. His wife howled and threw herself down beside him and clung to his body.

'Allah's will be done,' said one man before leading his family away. Osman couldn't leave, he felt part of the family. They had been together throughout the journey. He wanted to help, Mariam and Idris hovered too.

The driver appeared and asked the doctor, 'Dead?'

The doctor nodded. The driver went back to his cab and took a spade from behind the seats. He thrust it into Solomon's son's hands.

'Bury him.'

The daughter tried to pull her mother away but she wailed and clung to her husband's arm.

'Shh, shhh, shhh,' whispered their daughter, 'you must not disturb his soul with your weeping.'

'Where's the water? I must wash his body,' the old woman asked removing his sandals and wiping his feet with her sarong.

'His soul is clean. A good man needs no more,' murmured their daughter lifting her mother.

Idris and Osman helped the son to carry his body as far away from the track they were following as they could and Osman started to dig. The sand fell in and he dug harder and faster but the sand filled the hole. Perspiration ran down his face. He dug and dug; a shallow indentation was made. Idris took the spade, leapt in and dug furiously hurling sand aside. Osman and Mariam knelt at the sides trying to hold back the sand.

Finally, Solomon was laid on his side at the bottom of a shallow grave and the sand was allowed to flow over and around him in a comforting cradle.

'Go in peace, Father. Go to Allah,' said the son.

'Allah be with you,' sobbed his wife. 'May I join you soon.'

'Allah's will be done,' said his daughter.

His daughter in law was crouching by the shallow dome that covered Solomon's corpse. She stared from it to anonymous sandhills, paths and stones and murmured, 'There is no sign he is here...'

'No,' sobbed the old woman, 'he can't be lost. We can't leave him without a sign.'

She was still clutching the sandals she had removed to clean his feet.

'The sandals that brought him here. They'll show he's here, show how far he came.' She dug their worn heels into the sand where his feet lay.

'Hurry, hurry,' called the driver from the rise by the road.

Everyone was subdued climbing back onto the truck, aware of the gap, sobered by the reminder of their own mortality and the risks they were taking, sad for the family. They avoided looking at the corner behind the cab where Solomon had sat. His wife looked back to see the two little feet protruding from the sand. He was there, all alone in that vast emptiness, swept under sand. Her heart ached.

'Lost,' she sobbed.

Her daughter put her arm round her mother. 'Not lost, mama, forever in our hearts.'

Torpor set in as the truck droned on hour after hour and darkness descended. Finally, they stopped and crawled across the cold sand to sleep in tight groups. Again, they were wakened by torches strobing their eyes. They rose, stiff with the cold and prepared themselves for another long haul. After a while, the little boy they met in Khartoum started to whimper. His mother cuddled him but he wriggled free and rocked himself to and fro.

'What is the matter?' she asked.

'Tummy hurts.'

She gave him a morsel of dry bread. He chewed mechanically but could not swallow. She gave him water. He choked and started to cry, on and on.

'What is wrong?'

'My head.'

He held his head and pulled it from side to side trying to get rid of the pain inside.

The tedium of another day's incarceration in the lorry along with the crying agitated the children. Their parents struggled to contain them. Just after dawn they stopped, and everyone measured out their meagre rations, drank and ate solely to survive. When they were loaded back the little boy was no better. Mariam sat him between her and his mother. She played finger games and rhymes. He followed her lethargically. She looked through her bag for something to amuse him and pulled out a ribbon. She threaded it round her fingers into a cradle, pulled lower loops through and changed its shape then she wound it over his hot flaccid fingers and helped him to do it. His eyes were glassy, she felt his brow, it was a furnace. He relaxed under her cool hands and she settled his head on her lap. His mother watched him give way to sleep and slept herself in relief. At some point sleep slipped into death and his hot, soft body cooled and grew heavier. Mariam watched over him resigned to the end and let his mother sleep as long as she could.

When the driver was notified, he thrust the shovel at the shocked mother with the same instruction.

'Bury him.' Osman took the boy tenderly in his arms and Idris dug the grave while Mariam and the silently weeping mother knelt to hold back the sand as best they could.

'My life, my love. I should not have brought you here, I should not have done this,' she repeated. On her knees she stared across the desert. 'There is nothing for me now. I should not be here.'

'We're here because we have to. All this will end, the living must live. He will always be a part of you,' said Mariam.

The woman struggled to her feet and looked at the pitiless landscape, then at the shallow trench in the sand. 'No one will know he was here. He made so little stamp on life. He had no time to make his mark.'

'He made his impression on you. We can leave a sign here; you must have something of his?'

His mother pulled a bamboo whistle from her belt and stuck it at the head of the grave. Mariam tied her bright red ribbon to it. As they left his mother watched the little pipe, with its fluttering red ribbon proudly waving, gradually disappear behind the sandhills.

They stopped just before sunset and were told to sleep. Their bodies were so wracked by the jolting of the truck and their cramped spaces, they were glad for any relief and settled down pulling whatever they could over their eyes. At midnight they were woken and climbed back on board like automatons for another six hours.

The old woman allowed herself to be led on and off the truck and out to relieve herself. Her eldest granddaughter talked and talked to distract her. She told her how she would be going to school in a new country, how they'd make a home for her and when her grandmother said she was too old, the girl told her doctors there would make her better and she would have ice-cream and cakes nicer than she had ever had before.

When everyone left the confines of the truck they clung together more. Their faces familiar, their belief in each other growing as they suffered for each other. They knew they were leaving Sudan, on to the last leg of their journey but they also knew that they were not even halfway through the desert.

After five hours they were met by a four by four loaded with washing powder. Three Somalis formed a line to pass the packets to the drivers. They were told to line the sides of the truck with them and get back in, squeezed tighter together. They were ordered to lie flat and be silent as they crossed the border. The truck moved slowly on for a while and when it stopped even the children understood. Babies were suckled and they held their breath as they heard.

'Papers?'

A rustle of paper.

'Cargo?'

'Washing powder.'

A corner of the canvas was lifted to reveal bright yellow and blue packets of Cleace. The canvas dropped and the back was banged a couple of times.

'Move on.'

Not much further on, the lorry pulled off the road and parked behind a building. They heard voices, different voices; hard, clipped, business like. One by one they sat up, took down packets and peeped under the canvas. Their drivers were talking to armed guards. They ducked down afraid it was another check point. The back was dropped, and they were called out. Three men with rifles were waiting. Osman, Mariam and Idris were last from their back seat with the bereaved mother and the Sudanese family.

The three men moved around the group eyeing them up; cold, calculating; pushing the young men to one side with their rifle buts, separating them from the families with old people and children. The men were herded into trucks and set off. Osman, Idris and Mariam became part of their adopted family. They were led to an abandoned warehouse and locked in. They looked at each other in shock and clung together in little groups. Idris looked up at the high cracked windows, laced with wire. He checked the interior – a dusty metal shelving unit and a battered grey metal filing cabinet – no table, no water, no food, no loo. The same questions were in everyone's mind. 'Who? How long? What next?' They waited by the door then spread across the room as fatigue and torpor overcame excitement and fear. They settled on the floor to eke out crumbs and wet their lips with their last drops of water. Hours passed, darkness blocked the windows. Someone tried the light switch but the fluorescent tubes had long since expired. They shared empty food boxes to relieve themselves in, men as well as the women but there was nowhere to tip it. Idris dragged the filing cabinet to a window and stood on it to open a window.

'We could escape,' said a woman.

'We're only halfway across the desert,' replied her husband.

There was no one to complain to, no one to ask. They waited, watched over their children and finally slept. When they woke, they listened for voices, the turn of a key but the sun had been warming the room for a couple of hours before the door was opened and a drum of water was delivered with a stack of paper cups.

'When will we leave?' asked one man.

'When the trucks arrive.'

'We're hungry, where's the food?'

'Not part of the deal.'

'How long?'

The man shrugged and left. They rationed the water, half a cup each and only a dribble remained. Families fed what they had to the children. Osman broke Alia's last two biscuits and they each had a half. He tucked the last half into his pocket.

'This is not what I was told,' said Idris. 'I'm sorry.'

'How can we know who's genuine and who's not?' said Osman.

'They're not charities,' said Mariam. 'No, like everyone here, we've just got to go with the flow.'

Their mouths were so dry it was difficult to swallow. By midday restlessness had given way to lassitude and darkness was a relief. Hunger and dehydration kept them inert through the next day, too weak to care.

They heard trucks arriving and scrambled up to listen. The door was opened and a big man in heavy gear barred the threshold.

'You're in Libya now, you pay us,' he announced.

'We've paid all the way to the coast,' Idris shouted.

'You pay us or you stay here.' He nodded outside. 'Nearly a thousand kilometres of desert and another eight hundred kilometres to the coast; you're not there yet.'

'We haven't got the money,' said Idris.

'But your families have, phone!' He thrust a phone at Idris.

'I've got a phone, but no family or money.'

The man grabbed Idris by the scruff of the neck and stared into his eyes.

'You'll have to work it off then, won't you?'

He shoved him through the door. Mariam cried, 'Idris!' And turned, wild eyed to Osman as he tried to follow but the man pushed the phone at him.

'Your turn.'

The only person he could phone was Uncle Birhane, there, in Libya. There was little he could say. His uncle quickly understood the situation. Osman said that his father would pay him back. His uncle agreed to pay and promised to arrange safe transport for the two of them from the edge of the desert to Benghazi. The phone was passed to the man and their uncle made a Hawala transfer. The man addressed the room.

'No water, no food, no transport 'til you've paid.'

'You'll pay for this,' shouted a Somalian accountant.

'Oh, yes? Who're you going to complain to – the police? You'll be deported or imprisoned – you're a criminal, an illegal immigrant.'

'A refugee.'

'Same thing, nobody wants you. Papers? You got papers?'

'And if we have…?'

'Papers or no papers, we're the only people who can get you where you want to go, take it or leave it.' He gestured the endless desert around.

The bereaved mother started to cry.

'There's no one I can ask. His father tried to stop me from going, he beat us. There was no school for Magan.'

The Sudanese family and Osman gathered what extra cash they had to help the bereaved mother. They didn't care about money anymore; it couldn't satisfy hunger or thirst.

There were three open trucks. One after another they were told to get in more and more, everyone moving up, squashing together to get the next one in until they filled every space. Mariam and Osman followed instructions automatically. Their rudder had gone. Without Idris they bobbed on the waters of escape. They felt feeble.

'Where will they take him?' asked Mariam.

Osman looked down. 'Heaven knows…' Mariam frowned, he took her hand. 'Don't worry, he's a survivor. There's not much he can't do.'

'I hope he escapes,' she said.

Osman smiled. 'Be good to see him on the boat.'

'It seems so far away. The closer we get the further it seems.'

'I know what you mean but at least we've still got each other.'

'Losing Idris is like losing part of us,' said Mariam.

Osman nodded and put his arm round her shoulder.

The three trucks set off fast, one after another, bouncing and bumping over sand drifts. Their mouths were too dry to talk. People who had shared and cared now guarded their last drops of water afraid to see the end. A little Syrian girl lay inert in her mother's lap as she fanned her. Her father stroked her hair, called her name but she was losing consciousness, rambling. Her tongue was swollen. The doctor crawled to her.

'She needs water,' he said.

They pounded on the back of the cab and the truck slammed to a stop. The other two caught them up. The driver came round the side furious.

'What's wrong?'

'She needs water.'

'Give her some.' He looked defiantly at the faces lining the truck. Everyone looked down. Osman and Mariam regretted wetting their lip before they left but a drop would not help. Her body relaxed, her mother stroked her face, down her arms and body believing she was resting to get better. Her husband wept. The doctor took a lifeless arm and held her wrist.

'I'm sorry,' he said.

The mother wailed, an animal howl from deep within, mindless, timeless.

'Nooooo…' She cried wrapping herself round the body rocking backwards and forwards crooning a lullaby dirge.

'Let me take her,' the father said. 'You'll tire yourself.'

But the mother could not part.

At the next stop shovels came out, no one had the strength. The doctor, the father and two other Syrian men dug a shallow grave and the sand, like the sea, swallowed her up.

They moved on quickly for another five hours in the heat of the sun without canvas to stop the glare. At the next stop they jumped down grateful to stretch their cramped bodies and stand upright, baking between sand and sun. No one spoke. This was something to be endured, to survive, in order to be free.

When the second truck caught up their surly driver went to meet his mate. Osman watched his transformation into a grinning, friendly man. The two swiped hands than bent over the bonnet for the second driver to unroll paper and foil and sprinkle white powder in a line. They snorted and pumped their noses then leant against the truck watching their cargo. Their driver pulled a flask from his pocket, took a swig, and passed it to his friend. They patrolled the different groups – families in circles close to their lorries. Lines of bodies stretched out on the sand with young men joking and laughing. One of whom mimicked the second driver as he passed, and without warning, a rifle butt struck the side of his face. The driver casually carried on walking. The first driver turned to watch the reaction and raised his fist to a man looking after them in disgust.

'What you starin' at?'

The man waved his hands placatingly. 'Nothing, nothing.'

A fist hit his chin.

The bereaved mother was sitting in the shade with her back against the wheel waiting for her husband. Rubbing his knuckles their driver stopped and looked down at her. He swayed and said, 'What do you think you're doing?'

She looked up squinting into the light. 'It's hot,' she said fanning her face with her hand.

'You don't know what hot is…' He grabbed her hand, then her arm pulling her up and grabbed the other hand.

'What are you doing?' she cried.

He dragged her to the front of the truck.

'Let me go.'

'Get this.'

He unzipped his trousers and pushed up her sarong crushing her against the hot metal of the radiator. Her husband heard her scream and ran. He grabbed the man's shoulders trying to wrench him off and the driver swung round in fury. His punch lifted the man's head up and flung him backwards into the sand inert. His wife screamed and pounded the driver's chest to get to her husband but he held her harder even more determined to show his contempt.

'Nooooo…' she screamed and struggled. Everyone ran to the front of the truck and a shot echoed behind them. The second driver had followed. They froze.

'Help! Help!'

The man enjoyed the fight, slapping her cheeks, twisting her arms and opening her legs with the strength of his, shunt, shunt, shunt and the rape was complete. She collapsed onto the sand shamed by the audience.

'Let's go,' he said, zipping himself up.

They were too appalled to speak. Mariam and a couple of women lifted the victim up and straightened her clothes. Three men lifted her husband up and held him upright. He regained consciousness and twisted and turned trying to free his imprisoned arms.

'Let go, let me go,' he shouted.

'Nah, nah, don't go there, there's nothing you can do, leave it, leave it,' said the third man looking into his unseeing eyes.

'They've got guns,' said the one on the left.

The husband bent and kicked but they held on.

'You don't want to be left here, do you?' Said the other.

'She needs you man,' said the first.

The man sobbed and crumpled. The two men put their hands on his shoulders and led him back to the truck and his trembling, cowed wife. They clung to each other weeping. Everyone hung their head in shame as she passed. It was battle; one man against thirty-seven but he had the power. They only had belief in each other and hope in something else, somewhere else.

They drove on into the night, inhuman hours to sit, starve and de-hydrate. Inhuman hours to drive.

They stopped at midday, desperate for water and space, afraid to be near the driver. He opened his passenger door and showed them a water container.

'That's it.' He smiled and walked away. Those by the door looked at the white plastic tank, no bigger than a suitcase, without moving.

'There's hardly enough for now, never mind the rest of the way.'

'How long before we get there?'

It was a question no one could answer. A question they preferred to avoid. The second and third trucks arrived and opened their passenger doors to show the same containers. There weren't many women in the third truck. Thirsty men clustered round the door jostling.

'Wait, wait!' called an older man standing on the truck step.

'This is all we've got,' explained another lifting the neck of the container and unscrewing it carefully. They pushed closer and knocked his arm. The water in the container sloshed up and down.

'Get back! Get Back! You'll waste it!'

'Everyone can have a drop,' said the other. 'Pass the cups, we'll have to share.'

Hungry eyes watched each sip as they waited their turn.

'Stop!'

'That's enough!'

'Thanks.'

Awareness of each other like they had never known before spiced the moment. An edginess born of grudge and gratitude. A realisation that they depended on each other to survive – share or die.

Led by the Syrian doctor and his family the people of Osman's truck queued along the side and the two manning the supply called women and children first.

The three drivers swapped drinks and one rolled reefers. They smoked sitting on the sand in the shade of the second truck. Its passengers backed away. The third driver unpacked dried tomatoes in oil, dry bread, camel cheese and a box of raisins. More alcohol, another joint and they were ready for a couple of hours sleep.

The first two rose, unsteady and aloof muttering, 'See ya.'

'Thanks,' they said.

'S'all good…' he replied.

When Osman saw their driver on his way back, he threw his jacket over Mariam's head and she shuffled back understanding why. The man scanned the sea of heads around him, relaxed, detached. He waded in and picked out a teenage girl. Her parents pulled her back and pleaded but he kicked down the father's arms and wrenched her up crying. She would not walk so he dragged her through the sand even more determined. Her screams of terror scorched the air. Prickles of sweat stood out from everyone's head and ran down their backs. The other two drivers appeared with their guns at the sound of the screams. The third driver picked out a Syrian woman, her husband stood to defend her. The driver swung his rifle round, the woman struggled free but the other driver cocked his rifle. The husband reached for his wife and threw himself on the man's back as he dragged her away. A shot rang out and the man collapsed with a splintered leg.

The woman crawled back to her husband and the doctor tried to dress the man's wound while the three drivers slept locked in their cabs. Little more than a couple of miserable hours later, they were ordered back and they drove on from dusk to dark and through the night. Dry mouths were filled with swollen tongues. Hunger was suffocated by thirst. There was little need to stop to relieve themselves.

For days the same routine; a midday halt, drop of water, no food, followed by driving through the night.

Osman and Mariam had shared the last quarter of Alia's biscuit on the first day. The husband whose leg was shot trying to save his wife became feverish; the wound was red and swollen and he was sweating with pain. The doctor shook his head and mumbled the word no one wanted to hear, 'Gangrene.'

The smell was sickening even in the open. He was losing consciousness, he rambled and called out, whispered and cried while his wife held his head and stroked his chest helpless. He struggled to get free, pushed her away and threw himself over the back. They beat on the back of the cab. The driver stopped came round, looked back at the body and as they watched the second truck sped towards them over the body. The driver shrugged, got back into his cab and drove on until endless sand gave way to towers, trees, lorries and buildings.

'Al Kufrah?' whispered Mariam.

Osman nodded. 'Must be.'

'Allah be praised.'

The cry passed around the truck muted by wonder and weakness. Again, they headed off road to the rear of an isolated bombed building. They were herded out and down into a basement at gun point and locked in.

They were getting closer and closer to the Mediterranean, but Libya was volatile, the power struggle relentless and, always, they were nameless fugitives, unwanted, expendable.

Their flight to freedom was as unpredictable as Snakes and

Ladders. Their arrival at Al Kufra was a ladder climbed, but the snake of capture could send them right back to the beginning. Only their prison guards could prevent that or keep them from refugee camps to die in. They were prepared to do as they were told.

The children were too weak to cry. The grown-ups picked their way over the dirt floor in the dark and sat on jutting foundations of walls. Osman crossed to a chink of light high on the opposing wall. He stacked bricks and stood on them to feel around the brick, it was loose. He pulled it free and another and another. The cement crumbled to dust under his probing fingers. He replaced them carefully watched by Mariam and several others.

'You're not going through?' asked an elderly man.

'Why not?' asked Osman.

'Police,' murmured a woman.

'We've another eight hundred kilometres to the sea. You'll never get there,' said a middle-aged man.

'We've got help in Libya,' said Osman.

'Our uncle,' explained Mariam.

'It's all over for you then,' said the man wearily.

'With this lot, yes,' said Osman indicating the locked door.

When it was dark, Osman passed Mariam brick after brick and pushed himself through. Two men held Mariam high enough to get herself up and out then replaced the bricks.

They ran, Osman veered off the road into anonymous darkness. They walked in silence crossing wasteland and fields, following tracks then side roads past simple houses and sheds. Goats bleated and camels snorted as they passed.

The half-hearted cheep of a bird and a rustling of leaves signalled dawn before they saw the sun. It was followed by the muffled bang of a pot on a stove and soft voices. Light spread like mist over roof tops, streamed between houses and spread over fields. They were astonished to see grapevines.

'Wine?' Osman asked.

'Could be,' said Mariam.

A chorus of bleating increased in volume as a herd of goats trotted down the lane urged on by a lad eating a stuffed flat bread. He looked surprised, stopped and smiled. Osman and Mariam were afraid to speak and reveal their nationality. A silent Muslim salute might pass but they didn't know if their religion drew them together or split them apart. They smiled awkwardly and he stared, confused by their loose, crumpled clothes, sunken eyes and the beatific expression on their faces. The goats milled around the island of people.

'Shoo, shoo,' he crooned and clicked his tongue prodding them on with his stick.

Osman and Mariam waved him 'goodbye' and carried on. The boy looked over his shoulder several times as the gap between them increased.

The lane they followed was split by a curving road. They turned right and the road ended in a dense belt of bushes and trees beside a canal. Without a word they ran and stumbled to throw themselves down on its bank and scoop water into their mouths again and again, then over their faces and the back of their necks and heads. Mariam threw herself in, Osman followed. They grinned in joy.

When they dragged themselves out, Osman beat the undergrowth with his bag, and they watched a scorpion scutter away tail raised. They heard rattling like a millipede, so they stamped and shouted before collapsing onto the cool undergrowth and slept hidden from view. They were weak and confused when they woke. They filled their hollow stomachs with water and followed the canal. It irrigated a field of potatoes. They dug up a root, ate some little tubers and put the rest in Osman's bag. The fields were getting narrower, radiating from a hidden centre; cereals gave way to vegetables and fruits. They helped themselves to peas, pouring little streams of sweetness into their mouths.

'Are we in the desert?' asked Mariam.

'The middle of the Sahara.' Nodded Osman equally nonplussed.

'I've heard of oases, but this is surreal.' She surveyed a perfect circle of green wedges.

'It's like a massive farm,' said Osman.

'Do we have to go into town?'

'We need money and a phone.'

'There must be work here,' said Mariam looking around.

'We have to let Uncle Bihane know we're here.'

'I know, but we need to rest,' said Mariam. 'It's almost another thousand kilometres to the coast. I don't know if I can take it.'

'We've got to; there's nothing for us here and home isn't home anymore but maybe you're right, not yet.'

The thought of meeting people, explaining themselves, hoping to be accepted instead of impounded made each step towards civilisation more difficult. They braced themselves, glad to have been able to wash away the desert dust. They tidied each other up and walked with feigned confidence along the side of a shed. Two men were lifting crates of beans up to a third on the back of a truck. The three stopped in surprise at the sight of the couple.

Osman said to the Libyan on the truck, 'We're looking for work and somewhere to stay.'

The man on the truck looked at the other two, none spoke Tigrinya.

Mariam translated into Arabic.

'Tell your husband he'll have to see the manager.'

He stacked his crate.

'He's not my husband, he's my brother.'

He straightened up and looked at Mariam's upturned face. The other two were suddenly interested in the conversation.

The Libyan said to Osman in Arabic, 'We'll take you to Hassan when we've finished.'

Osman understood and replied in less perfect Arabic, 'I'll help.' He leapt on to the truck and took crates from one of the men who looked African. The Libyan's wariness melted as Osman fitted himself into his rhythm. The two below worked quicker watched by Mariam who stood in the shade of the shed.

When all was loaded, the Libyan leapt down and gave the keys to one of the other two.

'Al Jawf, before 15.00.'

He told Osman and Mariam to follow him.

They rang a bell outside a little garden and a slip of a girl appeared to show them in. Hassan sat beside his wife in a small room with cushions around.

'Ismael, what have we here?' he asked their guide.

'A brother and sister looking for work, Hassan.'

'Selam Aleykum,' murmured Osman and Mariam together, smiling uncertainly.

'Selam Aleykum.'

The man indicated they should sit.

'Some tea?'

His wife nodded to the girl who stood by the door.

Their courtesy seemed strange, to Osman and Mariam but it restored their humanity. They thanked the couple. Hassan reminded Osman of Sebhat.

'Have you come far?' asked his wife, handing Mariam a cup. Mariam looked at Osman. He remembered the African loading the truck.

'Eritrea.'

'What does your father do?' asked Hassan.

'He is personnel manager at the Bisha Mine, a Canadian company.'

'And your mother?' his wife asked Mariam.

'She grows vegetables and sells them at the market and makes clothes for a local shop.'

'What training have you got?' Hassan asked Osman.

Osman shook his head. 'Basket weaving,' he said sadly. 'But I helped mother with her vegetable plot all year round.'

'Well, we do need help with the potatoes in a week's time.'

'Nothing sooner?' asked Osman. He looked at Mariam.

'Not for you but your sister can help with the canteen and the washing if she covers her hair.'

'I am happy to do that,' she said bowing her head.

'And wears appropriate clothing,' he added addressing Osman.

Mariam tried to pull her arms back into her kaftan and looked at her bare ankles, embarrassed.

'Of course,' she said wondering where she was going to find the clothes.

'I can find things for you,' said his wife. 'You will stay with Laila.' The girl at the door examined Mariam.

'You report to Faisal a week on Monday at 6.30am,' Hassan said to Osman.

Ismael rose and the two men left together.

Mariam only had a chance to look over her shoulder at Osman briefly, enough for him to give her a reassuring smile before Laila led Mariam through the house.

Outside, Osama said, 'See you a week on Monday,' and set off down the track back to the shed. Osman did not want to stray far from the house and Mariam but he was curious about the whole venture. Hassan was only a manager, who owned the farm? How big was it? How could they grow these crops in the desert? It seemed strange beyond reckoning. He explored sheds, barns and a hangar with big farm machinery; this was no small concern. He crept into the heart of the complex, a garage and workshop with a bench. Hammers, saws, pliers and screw drivers hung on a board above a heavy vice. A couple of old tractor tyres were propped against the bench by a battery. There was an air compressor and jump leads hung from a peg on the wall. Osman walked up a ramp and looked round.

*Daniel would love this, I wish he'd come with us.* He longed for Daniel's matter of fact voice, his friendly face.

Overcome by loneliness he needed to see Mariam so he made his way to the back of the house past a barracks with bunk beds and straw mattresses with different brightly patterned covers. Beside that was an open shed with a stack of prayer mats in a corner and enamel wash bowls. The canteen was at the far end with rows of benches and low tables.

He circled round the back of the house past rabbit hutches and found the kitchen. He heard a pestle grinding in a mortar and peered into the gloomy interior through a narrow window but he could only see the slender girl who led them in. Then he heard Hassan's wife.

'Chillies, you'll need lots of chillies and garlic – let the new girl pod the peas, she won't be long.'

She opened a sack of rice and ladled it into a large pan and left the kitchen. Mariam appeared, transformed. Black cotton was draped over her head and shoulders and her body was covered in a loose full length grey robe. Osman was shocked. From behind she looked like any other Arab woman. She turned and he saw her bright eyes and eyebrows, her soft mouth and longed to be with her, to share. It reassured him to see her but on the other side of the garden he was aware of people going about their business, the work of the farm, the men who served it. He had no place there yet and he must not compromise Mariam's.

It was Tuesday. He had a whole week to fill, to survive. He had to eat, find somewhere to stay and try to contact their uncle as well as tap into networks for escape to the coast. He had to brave the centre but he didn't want to go alone. It was hard to drag himself away from Mariam. He wanted to protect her and be protected by her but he had to find out how strangers were treated, how safe they would be and he needed food and somewhere to stay. He emptied his pockets and counted Zair's money, would they accept it? Dare he expose himself? He had no choice. He was weak with hunger. He walked down the dirt track to a road and turned right. He followed the distant roar of motor bikes, screeching of brakes, rumble and clatter of people and machinery toward the centre; a wide street lined with shops of all sizes and intermittent ranks of motorbikes interspersed with parked cars. The town was not bustling with people or activity. Hanging outside the shops was everything from leather to paper, rugs and materials to sweets and candles dangling in twos by their wicks or tied with string. Street vendors had taken to the roadside selling orange juice, couscous and kebabs. Osman was drawn by the smell of pastries to a bicycle stall manned by a boy who was running eagerly to and fro tagging passers-by, pestering them to buy his mother's pastries.

'Spenatove satecky,'[24] he called at their backs. 'Best you've tasted!'

He ran back to his stall then trotted alongside two women.

'Fresh sfinz – date syrup, honey and cheese!'

Osman stared at the plate of crisp golden triangles – salmon and spinach – how he longed for that and the platter of doughnuts; fluffy clouds of dough to fill his stomach. He felt sick with hunger. Suddenly, the noise, the crowds made his palms clammy. He felt dizzy, frightened of collapsing and being taken. He drew hot air through tight lips and stepped back into the shade. The boy had returned to his stall undaunted. He watched Osman duck under the awning and lean his back against the wall then slowly sink down it. Osman was staring blindly ahead fighting some internal battle. The boy came over.

'You all right, mister?'

Osman looked up surprised and smiled weakly at the worried face, the boy wasn't much older than Wani.

'Think so,' he said.

'Can I get you anything?'

'Water?'

---

24 Salmon and spinach pasties.

'Got plenty of that.' He ran back to his stall and came back with a bottle. Osman drank but his legs felt like jelly. He couldn't stand and if he did, he was afraid he would fall.

People gave them a wide berth, some ostentatiously, to show their irritation, others stared back in curiosity making Osman nervous.

'How much are your sfinz?' he asked.

'150 Dirhams.'

'Where can I change money?'

'What you got?'

'Sudanese pounds.'

'You a refugee?'

Osman nodded, defeated by the curiosity of a boy. He leant his head against the wall in surrender.

'Plenty round here, there's work if you want it.'

'Got a job.'

'You're okay for a sfinz then?' asked the boy cheerfully.

'No dinars.'

The boy spat in disgust, 'Sudanese pounds – wastepaper.'

'You take them?'

The boy looked over his shoulder like a professional spy. 'We know people who can change it.'

'How much for a sfinz?'

He clucked his teeth calculating. Osman smiled, he imagined a cash register rolling up his eyes like in the cartoons and smiled then the boy looked at Osman; legs stretched across the sidewalk, back against the wall, his gaunt cheeks and glassy eyes.

'Hundred Sudanese,' he said.

Osman pulled a handful of Zaid's notes from his pocket and counted a hundred. The boy went to the stall and picked out the biggest sfinz.

'What do you want with it – date syrup or honey and cheese?'

'Honey and cheese.'

The boy put it on a square of paper and handed it to him.

'Thank you.'

Osman's mouth was dry, it was difficult to swallow.

'How much for the water?' he asked.

'You can have that, keep the bottle.'

'Thanks.'

After the first couple of mouthfuls, he enjoyed the soft light dough and sweet, creamy filling. The pain in his stomach diminished but his legs were still weak. He wondered how Mariam was coping then pulled his knees to his chest and struggled up. The boy was selling spenatove to a mother accompanied by a boy his own age.

When he stood up his focus had changed – the road and sidewalks looked wider, less crowded, he breathed freer. Men in white jalabiyas with their heads protected from the sun processed gracefully along the roadside. Osman wished he could swap his black T-shirt and jeans for their loose, elegant clothes. It would also make him less conspicuous. On either side of the road there were dark yawning entrances, with no sign of what was hidden in their interiors. Some buildings were abandoned, some damaged by war. He felt too alien and alone to saunter casually inside any shop or bazaar. He wouldn't know what to say, didn't know what he wanted in this town other than a way through, to Uncle Birhane, out to the coast.

There were no African faces here, no foreign clothes. There was no place for him here, no one to turn to. He wanted to crawl back into his shell, go home to Mariam and the farm where Africans were accepted. He turned into the shade of a deserted side street. He heard sounds of machines or voices behind different walls then shouts of abuse accompanied by the patter of feet and rumble of wheels on the road ahead. A man was beating a donkey urging it to go faster. Osman saw that its hooves were curled under its legs. He felt the stretch and pull of the tortured tendons, its crippling agony and longed to shout 'stop!' but dared not expose himself. Anger quickened his pace, running from guilt and shame he vowed to stop this kind of cruelty when the free world freed his voice.

He walked back to the farm and hid in the shadows behind the buildings hoping for a glimpse of Mariam. The sun went down. Lights came on in the barracks and a torch shone in the canteen where a few men were playing cards and drinking. The kitchen at Hassan's house was lit. He crept to the window. Mariam was rinsing dishes. Laila inspected them and dropped some back in the water before drying them and putting them away. When the sink was clear, Laila took a shawl and torch and waited by the door for Mariam while she wiped the table. Laila studied the ceiling while Mariam rinsed the cloth and draped it over the sink to dry. They emerged, Mariam carrying her bag and clothes. She followed Laila to a cabin at the end of the garden with two beds and a little chest of drawers.

'That's yours,' said Laila pointing to a bed in the far corner.

Osman heard Mariam murmur, 'Thank you.' She put down her things and sat on the bed.

'Do you have family here?' Mariam asked.

'No.'

'Where are you from?'

'Stop asking questions and go to sleep.'

'I must go to the toilet and wash.'

Mariam picked up her bag and left. Osman took the opportunity.

'How's it going?' he asked as she crossed the garden.

Mariam jumped. 'Where have you been?' she asked. 'I was worried.'

'I told you I was going into town.'

'Did you speak to Uncle Birhane?'

'No chance. No cafés, not for people like us, no one hanging out.'

He was trying to be brave and Mariam knew it. She stroked

his forehead and ran her fingers through his hair, smoothing away his loneliness and anxiety.

'Have you eaten?' she asked.

'A doughnut,' he replied.

'That's not enough, come with me.'

On the veranda outside the kitchen there was a big old-fashioned fridge. She gave him a glass of milk and dipped a scrap of boiled dough in date syrup.

'Where are you going to sleep?'

'Side of a field?' he suggested.

'Too dangerous. I've been looking. There's a loft over the other end of the barn with straw. It's closer to the centre of things so you'll have to be careful but you'll be safe up there,it doesn't look used. I'll show you.'

'No, I'll find it. You'd better get back to Laila. What's she like?'

Mariam shook her head. 'Not sure. I thought she'd be glad to have help but she's a bit prickly.'

'Sleep well,' he said.

'Nye, night.'

There was a tap in the courtyard and no one around. He had the luxury of a wash followed by a straw bed and an eyrie all to himself knowing that Mariam was not far away. The noise of trucks, tractors and machinery being dragged out woke him. Peeping out from above, he watched the morning routine as men assembled and departed for the day's work leaving the place deserted then he went to find Mariam.

They were clearing breakfast from the canteen. Mariam surreptitiously loaded a pan lid with vegetable couscous, bread and a banana and hid it between the enamel bowls by the entrance. When she saw Osman, she pointed in its direction while Laila was occupied. He collected it and took it out towards the fields to sit behind a row of bushes and eat while listening to birds and distant machines.

During the day Osman toured the outskirts of the city. There was little vegetation around. Some of the older houses rose from the earth as if they were still part of it; red clay walls like vertical chequer boards were punctuated by dark gaps. There were fewer camels in the centre and not so many goats as home. There were sheep in one field, but no cattle and he didn't see any horses. It seemed to him that the people led simple lives without question. He saw no evidence of rebellion here. The Arab Spring had not reached Al-Kufra or swept around it.

Familiarity gave Osman confidence to brave the centre, to go between its mosques and water towers, schools and clinics in search of people he and Mariam could connect with. But everyone was simply getting on with their own life, minding their own business. No eyes met his with interest or warmth. The cafés and restaurants he passed were small family places or for business meetings not groups of young men. The comfortable, middle-class shops along the main street were of no interest to him. He turned to the back streets and found two or three possible places where they served meals and soft drinks to those with pockets less deep who wanted to share food away from home.

After his week's wandering, Osman was glad to bend his back and get his hands dirty. It was a relief to come out of hiding and take his place in the barracks and not to worry about Mariam smuggling food to him. Red and yellow plastic net bags were dotted along lines of uprooted potatoes. They had to fill the bags and load them onto the trucks. A man, similar in age to Osman, smiled at him as they swung their bags on board.

'What you called?' he asked.

'Osman – you?'

'Khaled.'

They grinned at each other before turning back to their rows.

Khaled's smile and the general competitive banter in the trucks to and fro made Osman as happy as the old days in the café with Robel, Jamil, and the others. Khaled sat beside him on the truck going back.

'How many bags did you pick?' a big, muscular man asked a local.

'Hundred,' answered the worker in a satisfied tone.

'Slacker,' said the first, 'hundred and forty.' He tensed his biceps to show their shiny black, knotted bulges. The man beside him pushed his chest and he overbalanced on to the floor of the van. They all laughed, and he joined in.

Sleeping under the same roof, doing the same work for proper pay and sharing adequate food round the same platter, mouthful by mouthful sauced with relaxed talk, brought them all together. No one was allowed to ruffle the surface of their calm – the surly were left to themselves. The argumentative or selfish were laughed out of order.

After supper a few days later, when Osman was leaning against the wall outside looking at the stars, Khaled joined him.

'Why don't you tell anyone about your wife?' he asked.

'Wife?'

'You have the most beautiful wife in the world. If it were me, I would be parading her for all to see and be the envy of everyone.'

'I don't have a wife.'

'I don't know what you're hiding man, I've seen you together. The girl with thick wavy hair and bright eyes, tall and slender – the profile of my idol.'

Osman looked sympathetically at Khaled and curbed his smile.

'Who is your idol?' he asked.

'Nefertiti.'

Osman laughed, 'Oh, I must tell Mariam.'

'Mariam? Her name is Mariam? It is written in my soul. You are blessed with your treasure Osman, guard her well.'

'You must meet her.'

'No, dear friend, I could not profane our friendship or her perfection with my attentions.'

'When have you seen us together?'

'In the evenings outside the canteen and walking out to the fields star gazing as you are now. It is sad that work must separate you.'

'We are not separate.'

'No, it's true. Love is never separate.' He faced Osman. 'But you have not answered my question.'

'Why I keep her hidden?' Khaled nodded and Osman replied, 'To protect her from lustful eyes maybe or because we are immigrants without papers passing through to a better life. I don't know, probably because it didn't occur to me to talk about her to our work mates.'

'Where are you heading?'

'Italy.'

Khaled whistled quietly. 'Italy, that's a long way. A big dream and dangerous; be careful.'

'Our parents are not poor. They wanted something better for us than conscription in Eritrea.'

'Subjection and poverty there, war here, nowhere is safe. But I am concerned for you my friend. If you're found they'll put you in detention centres, Mariam will be targeted for sex and you'll be beaten and starved. We are a lawless country since the loss of Muamar, money is hard to come by, gangs sell refugees as slaves, kidnap them for ransom and get away with it. Leave Al-Kufra as soon as you can.'

'Detention centres?'

'The West pays Libya to stop immigrants so they are crowded into makeshift camps, tortured and starved. No one cares.'

'But the West is free.'

'And rich enough to pay others to carry their burdens.'

'It's not worth getting there?'

'Oh yes, if you can. It's getting there that is the problem.'

'We'll get there.'

'Good luck.'

'Look, there's a shooting star.' Osman craned his neck to follow its brilliant path across the blackness.

'Khaled.'

'Yes.'

'She's not my wife, she's my sister.'

Khaled's eyes widened ever so slightly and a look of wonder suffused his face just as it had when he followed the shooting star. 'Your, your…' He looked at Osman in disbelief.

Osman nodded. 'Sister.'

The smile that softened Khaled's mouth suddenly faded and he bowed his head.

'But we are camels in the desert,' said Khaled finally.

'Passing in the night,' said Osman.

'No chance she'd stay here with me?'

'No repressive regimes, for a woman it's more important.'

'True, she has courage.'

'You can join us.'

He shook his head sadly. 'Family here need me and my wage. The war flares, Isis threatens, I must protect my own.'

'Osman laid a hand on Khaled's shoulder. 'You are a good man, Khaled.'

He bowed his head. 'Thank you and a good friend I hope.'

'Indeed.'

They turned into the barracks just as the lights cut out all over the farm. Candles came out from cupboards, bags and under beds. The water pumps stopped. Osman understood the importance of the reservoirs and water towers. Everyone shrugged it off and lit their candles.

'Every couple of weeks, Allah knows when it will end,' his partner on the lower bunk told him.

Khaled whittled and carved wood from the stack by the bread oven into an elephant with a howdah to hold a candle and asked Osman to give it to Mariam.

'You can give it yourself. She knows you are my friend.'

The three met the next night after supper. Khaled wore his best head dress and jalabiya and smelt of fresh mint and cologne. He was a good-looking man. They walked out to the field and sat around a fat steady flame admiring the perfect proportions of the elephant; its long trunk curled almost to the floor, its tasselled blanket and head covering. From ears to tail it was finely detailed.

'It's beautiful, thank you, Khaled.' Mariam's smile was enough for Khaled, his breast brimmed with joy.

'Like you,' he replied. Mariam lowered her eyes. He took her hand. 'May I call you Mariam?'

She nodded and withdrew her hand.

'I want you to listen to me, both of you.' He looked at Osman.

'You have to go. Every day you stay is dangerous. You don't know who is a spy here and there's a bounty on your heads.'

'We must contact Uncle Birhane in Tripoli but we don't have a phone,' said Mariam.

'That's not important. If you had one it probably wouldn't work; phone, computer, electricity; you can't rely on them since the war and it's getting worse.'

'The farm couldn't survive without a phone; Hassan must have a reliable connection,' said Mariam.

'Maybe but how can we use it?' asked Osman.

'I'll ask him.'

'Then he'll know you're illegal immigrants,' said Khaled.

'He didn't ask for papers,' said Osman.

'There's a difference if he doesn't know. If he knows and is seen to help, he could be fined or fired.'

'You'll have to do it behind his back,' suggested Osman looking worried.

'Or say it's a mercy call because our aunt is ill,' said Mariam.

'Perfect,' said Khaled. 'Hassan's decent.'

'Thanks, Khaled,' said Osman.

'Don't delay.' Khaled searched Mariam's face and saw the strength behind her smile. She nodded. 'That's good,' he said, getting up. 'Good night.'

'Good night and thank you,' said Osman and Mariam together.

Moths silently swept the flame with their soft wings. Mariam extinguished the candle and held the holder up.

'It's lovely, Khaled's a good man.'

'We were lucky.'

'Night.'

'Night.'

It had not taken long for Hassan's wife, Atifah, to get the measure of Mariam and appreciate her cooking skills. Mariam fitted herself easily into Atifah's way of doing things. She even managed to demonstrate some of her mother's recipes. They relaxed into a routine that excluded precise, uncommunicative Laila.

It pleased Hassan to see his wife happy so when Mariam explained her concern about her aunt, Hassan offered the phone without question. But Birhane was away on business, she had to make excuses and ask to repeat the call in two days time. Atifah and Mariam returned to the kitchen like family and Laila bent over the dish she was stirring.

'Let me help,' said Mariam feeling guilty.

'You can chop the onions,' said Laila.

The next evening was Friday and Hassan and his wife were invited out. Laila and Mariam only had to cook for the men.

The couscous was prepared and lamb stew bubbled happily in spices. Mariam started to grate cucumber for the yoghurt when she heard Atifah shouting and crying. She went to the door and listened.

'Hassan, Hassan, I can't find my bracelet!'

'I'll look.'

'Not there. It's not in my box, not in the drawer. I wore it last Sunday; it should be back in its box...'

Laila looked at Mariam.

'There's nothing we can do, it sounds as if Atifah's lost a bracelet,' said Mariam.

'Her gold bracelet?' asked Laila. 'She won't like that. It was her fiftieth birthday present from Hassan.'

'No wonder she's frantic, I hope she finds it,' said Mariam.

Laila spooned couscous into large serving bowls while Mariam ladled out the lamb stew.

Atifah's anxious cries were punctuated by the patter of their feet overhead. Sounds of furniture being moved and Hassan's attempts to calm his wife until finally he yelled, 'We're late, forget the wretched bracelet, we've got to go.' Not long after they heard the slam of the door and the car starting up.

Saturday morning when they were clearing away the breakfast dishes Ismael came into the canteen looking for Mariam.

'Hassan would like to see you in the office.'

'Now?'

'Yes.'

She had never been in the office; it was a small reception hut near the entrance. She wondered if he were going to let her use the office phone to make her call. When she stood before him, Hassan picked up a bundle of thin gold bracelets from his desk and dangled it in front of her.

'My wife lost this bracelet. It caused us a lot of grief.'

'I know. Last night we heard, I'm sorry.'

He stood.

'Sorry? It was found in your bag under your bed.'

Mariam's mouth opened in shock; her breath stopped. Like a goldfish her mouth opened and closed but no sound came out. She knew denial was useless, the evidence was in his hands. She knew where it came from and the futility of protestations but she made them, nevertheless.

'I did not take it. I would not harm Atifah, she is like a

mother to me. I am grateful to you. I would not do a thing like this.'

Hassan was unmoved. 'I know what you are, where you're going – how much that takes.'

'Laila gave it to you. I know she did. She's jealous, she wants me gone.'

'Who found it is irrelevant. I've been a trusting fool. You will return your clothes and leave immediately and no further action will be taken.'

The weariness of the desert returned. She knew that strangers have no chance in foreign lands, refugees even less, there was nothing to do but leave.

Mariam saw Laila in the kitchen comforting Atifah as she passed on her way to their cabin. Osman was out in the field. Would he be stopped too? All she could do was hide in the shadows until she could see him.

She heard the trucks return, the men talking quietly, banging in the dormitory, the tap running outside and prayers from mats spread for sunset. She hoped Osman would enjoy his meal and look for her in the field afterwards.

When he came and he heard her explanation he wrapped his arms round her and held her tight to his chest.

'We were paid today. Tomorrow we'll go into town,' he said.

'How can we speak to Uncle Birhane? I can't be seen anywhere near the house.'

'The farm phone is our only chance.'

'There has to be one in the office.'

'Yes.'

'I'll break in when no one's around,' he said.

Osman slipped down off his bunk in the middle of the night and crept to the little hut by the gates. It was locked and the windows were wired. He circled it in desperation, finally looking at the corrugated tin roof. He dragged a petrol drum over and stood on it to inspect a bit of bent roof metal. A couple of nails were loose. He tried to use his torch to prise it up but had to go back to the workshop for a claw hammer. With it, he pulled up enough to wriggle through.

Inside was dark. He shone his torch to find the phone keeping the beam as low as possible. He sat on the floor with the phone in his hands and dialled his uncle's mobile.

'Hello?'

It was a huge relief to hear Birhane's warm voice.

'Who's that?'

'Osman, uncle.'

'At last, where are you?'

'Al Kufra. We've been working on a farm.'

'That's good, that's good. But you need to get out of there. I've spoken to Amin, he can take you to Ajdabiya.'

'How soon?'

'I'll speak to him tonight and let you know.'

'It's difficult, we haven't a phone and we've got to leave the farm.'

'Stay for a few days so we can speak.'

'Not possible, I'll explain another day.'

'If you say so. How can I tell you?'

'We'll go into the centre. Try to find someone who can help us. Maybe there's a public phone?'

'None of those will be working if there are any left. You be careful in the centre. Libya's lawless and refugees are targeted. Be careful who you speak to.'

'We will, thanks uncle.'

'Wish I could do more. Take care, love to Mariam.'

'Bye.'

The phone went dead. In the dark silence Osman felt very alone. He looked at the hole in the roof he had made and stood on the desk to pull himself up through it. He replaced the section as best he could and jumped down. He hoped that Mariam was sleeping somewhere safe.

In the morning at breakfast with the men, Osman slipped food into a T-shirt on his lap when he could and wrapped it up for Mariam. He filled a couple of water bottles.

They met where they had sat around the candle with Khaled. Osman had not told him that he was leaving. Sister and brother did not speak. They held hands as they walked along the lane away from the farm towards the centre. After half an hour they stopped and Mariam ate a little breakfast.

When they set off again, she said, 'Osman.'

'Yes?'

'I want a hijab and head dress.'

'We'll get you one.'

'I have my first two weeks' pay.'

'I know and I have mine.'

'Uncle will help us, won't he?'

'He can get us to the coast but it's dangerous, Mariam. Since Gaddafi fell it's a pot of snakes – all fighting each other. Not one or two but different groups all over. No one knows who is friend or who is foe.'

'Atifah hates it, she says they're all bad – out for what they can get, intoxicated by the power their weapons give them. They can rape, kill, steal and get away with it. Everything they see belongs to them,' said Mariam.

'And they're destroying it.'

'Will we be able to keep clear of it?'

'The men who'll take us run a business and security is part of it. The rest we don't know. Birhane is packing up.'

'Going back home?'

'Eritrea's better than a war zone. Tripoli's closed for oil. Crowded with people like us and the boats to take us.

'So many countries in ruins.'

'Libya is destroying itself. Thank goodness we don't have to stay.'

'Here we are.' Mariam looked down the main street; people

carrying on as if nothing were happening. There were one or two gaps in the frontages filled with rubble.

'Let's kit you out,' said Osman.

'You should do the same. We'll be less conspicuous and it's more comfortable.'

They browsed the first clothes emporium they saw but they felt too exposed on the main street with people passing by and their hijabs were too expensive and looked too formal. They turned the corner to get behind the shop and found a whole street of tailor's shops. They watched a woman sewing a blue silk hijab on a machine like their mother's.

The woman finished her line of sewing, pulled the material free and bit through the threads. She got up and folded the garment onto the top of a rainbow stack. She beckoned Mariam and Osman into the back of her workshop where folded garments were stacked on shelves.

'We'd like to buy a hijab,' Osman said proudly.

'Cotton?' she asked. Mariam nodded.

'Here.' She banged a long shelf with piles of different coloured and patterned hijabs. Mariam chose green with a tiny pattern of white leaves and a white head dress. Osman chose the standard white with a blue chequered head dress. They changed in a corner behind the shelves and felt like completely different people when they emerged to pay. The woman smiled and stood waving to them until they turned into the main road.

Mariam looked at the robed figures walking on either side of the road and then at her hijab and said, 'That's better.' Their bodies straightened as they stepped out, their heads came up and their steps were longer as they glided past boutiques and garages, parking lots and cafés.

'I'm tired,' said Mariam.

'I'm thirsty, let's have a drink.'

At the end of a line of motor bikes there was a café with a freshly painted green door, tables and chairs.

'Looks as if a big pot of green paint fell off a lorry,' said Mariam.

'They knew you were coming,' said Osman.

They sat at the first table and ordered mint tea. The waiter burnt charcoal and lit a shisha. He set it by Osman. Mariam raised her eyebrows then smiled impishly.

'Go on,' she said, daring him.

'Don't know what's in it.'

Mariam looked around. 'It's not going to kill you.'

Osman sucked but nothing happened.

'Quicker, quicker,' said a voice from just inside the door. A round faced, bearded man was sitting back comfortably with his pipe at his side. Osman pulled and pulled and smoke puffed out. He spluttered then returned, watched by the man and Mariam. Tea was set before them and Osman smiled his thanks – more for the pipe than the drink, it was relaxing; quite different, not hot, and dry, just steamy and pleasant.

'Try it,' he said to Mariam.

'Oh no, I couldn't,' she said looking round.

'Don't be daft, just once.' He passed the mouthpiece. She sucked tentatively and puffed, just a little.

'That was nothing, go on.'

'It's not unpleasant, doesn't make you choke,' she said. 'Hmm, interesting.' She sucked steam softly in one long draught.

'Pleasant,' she said, 'very pleasant.' She passed it to Osman and sat back. He puffed, sipped his tea and watched the purposeful progress of passers-by; women in groups, wings flapping like crows, men like yachts out at sea. A couple of young men in white jalabiyas with red chequered head dresses came and sat at the next table. Their black beards made them look important, not old, not wise, but glossy, healthy, in control. They were bosses but not like Sebhat. They sat behind desks in glass offices and studied computers.

The tea was delicious, Osman felt he could stay there all day. Mariam watched him drift. She didn't want to spoil it so she tucked her bag under the table, arranged her head dress, smoothed her new hijab and sat back, bright eyes studying the neighbourhood, wondering how far they were from the hotels, empty hotels. The trickle of tourists had dried up; no one wanted to holiday where tanks and machine guns reigned. Their welcome in the café made more sense with the lack of others. For the first time she saw the resignation and wariness of people's faces. They weren't relaxed, they were too focused on survival, grimly going through the motions of their everyday lives, not knowing when it would explode around. She finished her tea.

'Would you like anything more?' asked the waiter.

Mariam's face lifting to answer the man caught the eye of one of the newcomers. He was fascinated. Osman shook his head. 'Later perhaps, maybe mahgroudhi.'[25]

The waiter removed the cups and pipe.

'May we provide the cake?' asked their neighbour. Osman looked at Mariam whose eyes widened with surprise. The man smiled at her, the other sat back and studied Osman and Mariam. They looked respectable. She lifted her hands and shrugged her shoulders to Osman. 'Why not?'

'Thank you,' said Osman. 'Would you like to join us?'

Everyone was a friend. The two men smiled at each other and rose.

'Selam Aleykum,' said the lean-faced younger man to Mariam. 'I am Omar.'

'Mariam.' She indicated her smiling brother. 'And Osman.'

She turned to his companion.

'Selam Aleykum.' He inclined his head slightly before taking a chair. 'Masud.'

The waiter returned.

'Basbousa, please,' said Hassan authoritatively.

---

25 date filled with pastries.

'Are you staying in Al Kufra?' asked Omar.

'No, we're passing through,' said Osman.

'Good, good; not the place to stay. Libya is full of brigands fighting for they know not what. Bombs, tanks, guns, destruction everywhere. Oil's gone down, all that's left are hungry homeless people.'

'Libya's not the only place like that.'

'I know,' said Masud nodding.

'We fought for independence and gained tyranny.' Osman thought of Idris.

The waiter distributed four small metal bowls containing glossy pastries with dark hearts. Mariam tasted a corner, sweet and moist, she closed her eyes wishing her mother could taste it. When she opened her eyes, Omar was staring at her, his cake suspended in his fingers. He dropped his eyes and took a quick bite, embarrassed. Mariam laughed and he did too.

'It's fresh, isn't it?' she said.

'Simple things are good when they are shared,' he said seriously.

'True, true,' said Osman happily, still on his steamy cloud.

'Where are you going?' Masud asked Mariam.

'To Europe.'

Omar and Masud stiffened, frowning. 'No, no, it is too dangerous.' Masud turned to Osman. 'You cannot take your wife to the coast. Smugglers take your money but they don't guarantee your safety. They'll crowd you into unsafe vehicles and starve you. They hold people for ransom or sell them as slaves and there's no one to stop it; law and order has broken down. Police are as bad as the rest.'

'She cannot go back to Eritrea and she's not my wife.'

The two men sat back looking at them in questioning disapproval.

'Osman is my brother, my protector,' said Mariam and the two men softened.

‘Our parents wanted us to have a chance in life,’ explained Osman.

‘The smugglers will make them pay again and again. They will hold you for ransom,’ said Hassan.

‘We have an uncle in Tripoli. He is organising our transport to the coast,’ said Osman.

‘We only have to make a phone call,’ said Mariam.

‘Come back to Egypt with us. We’ll find you work, you can have a good life there,’ said Omar.

Osman shook his head. ‘From the Mediterranean to the Red Sea and beyond, there’s nothing but tyrants fighting rebellion and rebels fighting each other.’

‘With all the poverty and suffering that brings,’ said Mariam.

‘Mainly on women,’ said Omar sadly.

‘And children,’ added Mariam.

‘What can you find there that you can’t in your own country?’ Masud asked Mariam.

‘A University education. A career. Children free to choose their lives.’

‘We have to cross the Med to find peace and freedom,’ said Osman.

‘Another pipe?’ asked the waiter.

‘Why not?’ Masud looked at his guests.

‘What do you do?’ asked Mariam.

Masud replied, ‘We are traders; Egypt has transported food over the border for centuries. Fruit and vegetables from Israel, rice, canned food, spices. Now, four years after the fall of Gaddafi people are hungry and missing the things they had. It’s time to rebuild.’

‘And expand into construction,’ said Masud.

‘Knock it down, build it up,’ said Omar.

‘You make it sound like a children’s game,’ said Mariam. ‘Lives are lost, history destroyed, ugliness swapped for beauty.’

‘True, true, sister,’ he puffed. ‘Human nature.’

'Men's nature,' said Mariam.

'But not all are like that,' said Omar urgently searching Mariam's face for reprieve.

Osman smiled, sucking at steam; let the cloud continue. War slipped away bathed in mist.

Masud's phone chimed. He excused himself. They nodded contentedly. Mariam drew on the pipe then asked Omar if he had a phone. When he nodded, she asked if they could pay for a call to their uncle. He gave her his phone and would not hear of payment. She tapped in her uncle's number and waited. The dialling tone carried on and on. She looked at Omar's concerned face. Finally, Birhane's voice; sharp, tense.

'Yes, who is it?'

'Uncle Birhane?'

'Mariam! How are you?'

'We're well thank you, still in Al Kufrah. How are you?'

'The company's folding. The pipeline was bombed and there's nothing in Tripoli apart from offshore. Giana is packing.'

'Going back to Eritrea? What about Pranith and Tanvi?'

'Pranith has another year in Cairo and Tanvi will come with us. Your Transport is arranged for Tuesday morning.'

'Where?'

'There's a sports complex beside a school near the aerodrome. Be in the school playground at 5.00am.'

'Thank you, uncle.'

'It's a jeep. There'll be twenty of you.'

'Thank you, good luck for your move. Give my love to aunty and Tanvi.'

'You take care, look after each other. Libya's not safe for anyone anymore.'

The phone went dead. Mariam held the phone, disturbed by her uncle's agitation. Osman was staring at her; she forced a smile and returned the phone to Omar.

'Thank you.'

'Not bad news I hope,' said Omar.

She shook her head. 'No, not really.'

Masud returned to the table.

Omar turned to him. 'Anything important?'

'Chain store, appointment tomorrow.'

'Well?' asked Osman urgently.

Mariam looked apologetically at Masud and Omar. 'We leave Tuesday morning.'

'One step closer to your dream,' said Omar rising from his seat.

'It's nearly a thousand kilometres to Ajdibaya and half of it is desert. How can you do it?' asked Masud.

'We have no choice; there's no life behind us but there's hope ahead. We crossed the other half to get here; it was grim but we survived,' said Osman sobering up.

Masud rose. 'May Allah be with you.'

Omar studied Mariam's face and said quietly, 'Our prayers go with you.'

'Thank you for a happy memory of Al Kufra and Egypt,' said Mariam looking into Omar's deep, dark eyes. His face was lean and aristocratic and he seemed earnest and caring. She stood, to give him her hand. He was tall. She felt a twinge of longing, a pang of regret. He bent over her hand and touched it with his forehead, her chest constricted. She felt an urge to run her fingers under his head dress, through his wavy hair. She took a deep breath, regained equilibrium and smiled bravely at them both.

Osman stood a little unsteadily and said, 'Thank you for the cake.'

The two sailed away disappearing into the evening rush leaving the brother and sister desolate.

'What shall we do?' asked Osman.

'Find the school so we know our way on Tuesday.'

'Good idea.'

They followed the road out of town. A group of mainly African men were clearing rubble from a bombed warehouse. Osman stopped to watch, one of them looked Ethiopian or Eritrean. He saw Osman watching him and asked if he was looking for work.

Osman shook his head, 'Nah, just passing through.'

The man stopped work and looked around. 'You got papers?'

Osman shook his head.

'Be careful, without papers you might as well be dead.'

'We'll be out in a couple of days.'

'Not out of Libya, you won't. They've got detention centres everywhere and they're looking for you.' He looked at Mariam. 'And she's bait.'

'We've got travel to the coast,' explained Osman confidently.

'Make sure you do what they say. Soldiers, police, criminal gangs; they're all the same. Only the smugglers know how to avoid them if you've got good ones.'

'We have. What're you doing?'

'Earning enough to get a good one.'

'You plan to cross the Med?'

'Sure do but not any time soon.'

'Why's that?'

'It costs, my funds ran out. I'm not taking my parent's money anymore.'

'You've got papers?' asked Mariam.

He shook his head. 'I just keep my head down.'

'Where's the airport?' asked Osman.

He leant on his spade looking impressed. 'Straight on, turn right. Thought you didn't have passports.'

'No, we don't. You don't need passports in Eritrea.' Osman shrugged. Where are you from?'

'Ethiopia, thirty years at war with you and look at us. What was it all about?'

'Swapping a foreign tyrant for a local one,' said Mariam.

The three of them went quiet for a moment and Osman said, 'We just have to get on with our lives.'

The man shook his head looking at the hole he'd made in the rubble. 'Yep, as best we can,' he said resignedly.

'Good luck,' said Osman turning back to the road.

'See you in Italy,' said Mariam over her shoulder.

The Ethiopian laughed and put his finger to his lips. 'Sshh…'

'There must be signs for the airport,' said Mariam.

'We can look but we can't go too far. We've got to sort ourselves out for the night.'

A plane rumbled overhead, coming into land.

'Can't be far,' said Mariam and their pace quickened.

They followed a bend hand in hand and there was the sign, 'Aeroport' and below it another with a picture of school children.

'That's it!' shouted Mariam. Osman squeezed her hand.

'Where to now?' said Osman.

'We need to eat and find somewhere to stay,' she replied.

'Where? Osman stopped. 'I don't trust anyone here. Khaled said to be careful, we don't want to ruin things now.'

'Sleeping rough may be more dangerous than renting a room,' said Mariam doubtfully.

Osman's face suddenly lit up. 'I know what to do.' He hitched his bag higher up his back and set off.

'Follow me.'

Mariam was pleased to see Osman striding out purposefully and followed mystified.

As they returned to the edge of town, just before parking lots and rubble gave way to shops, there was a roadside kiosk on wheels.

'Sfinz, spenatove – secret recipe; super tasty, you try.'

A gangly twelve-year-old was chasing after a group of teenagers.

'Ya Gazma,'[26] one shouted back.

'Chelb,'[27] shouted Osman after them.

The boy recognised Osman and ran to him, shook his hand

---

26 Sole of a shoe.

27 Dog.

and whistled. 'Look at you, very smart.' He looked questioning at Mariam.

'My sister, Mariam.'

'Selam Alaykom,' said the boy and turned to Osman. 'Beautiful,' he said grinning. He proudly punched his chest. 'Mustafa.'

Mariam laughed in surprise and delight. 'Selam Aleykum, Mustafa.'

'You want more sfinz?' he asked Osman.

'Not now, Mustafa. We have to stay here tonight and tomorrow night, do you know anywhere safe?'

Mustafa checked along the sidewalk then the road, came close and said in a conspiratorial voice.

'We have a room. My mother is good cook, you get dinner too; hundred dinars a night.'

Mariam's eyes widened in disbelief. 'Won't your mother mind?'

Mustafa shook his head. 'No, no, happy family. She good mother. Not far, we live not far.'

'How long before you finish?'

Mustafa looked at the almost empty plate of spenatove and half a dozen sfinzes.

'Give me half an hour; people finish work hungry.'

'We'll have a couple of spenatove,' said Mariam delving into her bag.

'We'll be back in half an hour,' said Osman and they wandered away burying their teeth in golden pastry, creamy spinach and salmon.

'If his mother can cook like this, dinner will be a dream,' said Mariam.

'I wouldn't count on it; she doesn't know we're coming.'

They passed through throngs of people leaving work, stopping at cafés, climbing onto all kinds of transport or talking quietly as they purposefully made their way home. It wasn't long before Mustafa caught them up.

‘Come back,’ he said, ‘and follow me.’

He pedalled his kiosk ushering Osman and Mariam down side streets away from the centre to a narrow two storey house in the middle of a row of cream, pink and blue buildings with different heights and styles of rooves. Some with pots of plants outside, some with mosaic murals. He parked his mobile canteen in front of a red mud wall around a small courtyard.

‘Stay here,’ he said and sped inside like an arrow. Inside the courtyard they heard a ball being batted against the wall, a parrot squawk, a toddler laugh, someone clap their hands and over it all, Mustafa’s voice followed by explosive female protestations and imprecations.

‘We’ d better go,’ said Mariam.

‘Doesn’t sound promising,’ laughed Osman nervously.

They turned back the way they had come. A minute later Mustafa was running after them.

‘Come back, come back,’ Mustafa cried.

Osman swung round, and Mariam looked back. A tall, stately woman in a purple hijab with gold embroidery and a black head dress was standing in the pathway by their back door watching them. She shook her head and smiled, stood with her back against the door to hold it open and beckoned them inside.

They turned. Mustafa’s mother smiled and nodded.

‘Selam Aleykum,’ she said.

‘My friends, Osman and Mariam, Mother,’ said Mustafa proudly.

‘Farah Musrata,’ she replied studying their faces.

‘We do not want to trouble you,’ said Mariam.

‘Our table is sad when there are no friends to sit around it, come.’

She led them into a courtyard where an oven sat in a corner beside a hob. A table in the centre was shaded by a home-made pergola covered with palm leaves. She turned to Mustafa.

‘Go prepare their room.’

A baby sat; legs straddled, on the dirt floor guarded by his brother. A young girl was talking to a parrot on a stand. The children watched the newcomers.

'You will want to refresh yourselves. Rashid, show our guests the tap.' Rashid passed the baby to his sister and led them through a narrow corridor to a yard with a tap. One corner was screened by a curtain hanging from a cane and behind it there was a shower with a palette floor. They pulled off their head dresses and washed their hands and faces. Mariam combed her hair. Mustafa passed them on their way up the narrow winding staircase. Rashid ushered them into a room with two thin mattresses covered in bright cotton covers.

'Thank you,' said Osman.

Rashid smiled and left.

The room was hot and dark. There was only a narrow slit high up for a window, but it was quiet. The calm and sense of security was enhanced by familiar sounds of family chattering below. Normality seeped into their tense, aching bodies. They lay on the beds and relaxed, relieved to be together safe in a home.

'Bless you Mustafa,' muttered Osman.

'Bless Mustafa and his family,' mumbled Mariam.

'We don't need to go anywhere, do anything…'

They almost fell asleep.

'Mister, miss!' Mustafa's voice called up the stairs.

They rose and made their way downstairs feeling quite feeble.

The table was a feast for the eyes as well as the soul; decorated with nasturtium flowers and mint. There was a carton of pineapple juice and a jug of water, six coloured plastic beakers and, in the middle, a platter with aubergine and tomato sauce, balls of minced lamb, tabouleh and mint yoghurt beside a basket of flatbread.

The baby was in a highchair next to his sister. Mustafa and

Rashid stood on either side of their mother.

'Please be seated,' she said indicating chairs in the shady corner by the parrot, away from the hot oven.

'This is beautiful,' said Mariam.

'What did I tell you?' said Mustafa beaming.

His mother stood at the head of the table and the children bowed their heads.

'Worship the lord who feeds us and keeps us safe.'

No one moved or spoke.

'You may begin,' said their mother.

Still, no one moved. Osman smiled and loaded a flat bread with tabouleh, sauce and lamb. Mariam followed suite and the meal began. The baby was fed, the little girl refused the meat but enjoyed the tabouleh and yoghurt while the rest of them moved from one tasty mouthful to the next waiting while each took their turn.

Mustafa related his day, Rashid boasted of being top in arithmetic and his sister said her picture of daddy at the swings was put up on the wall. They all fell silent and the boys looked nervously at their mother. Her face tightened just a little. She praised them for doing well and occupied herself by tempting everyone to eat more.

'But we've got orange semolina,' said the little girl.

'With lots of honey,' said Rashid.

Osman and Mariam's hearts were filled as much as their stomachs and when the children had been packed off to sleep, they sat companionably with their hostess drinking thick, dark coffee.

'Thank you for a very special night, a reminder of home,' said Mariam wistfully.

'You're a long way from home,' Farah replied.

'It must seem mad to leave family we love,' said Osman.

'No, no. Wars and dictatorships can't destroy family but they can destroy life. I understand, you need a future.'

'Do you mind me asking what happened to your husband?' asked Mariam.

Farah sighed wearily and slumped back in the chair.

'No, nothing can change it, it's what we have to live with. They put a gun in his hands; he wasn't a soldier, he wasn't one of them but they wanted him to be. They pointed to a child playing in the road and said, 'shoot him.' He wouldn't, he couldn't, so they shot him.'

'He was killed because he was a good man,' said Osman quietly.

Mariam rose silently and put her arms round Farah's shoulders. 'I am so sorry,' she said.

She kept her head in her hands for a while, then lifted it slowly and caught hold of Mariam's hand. 'Thank you,' she said.

'So, you have to cook and Mustafa has to sell it,' said Osman.

She sighed, 'He was such a bright boy at school. Heaven knows what will happen to the others when they're his age.'

'Pray Allah the fighting will have stopped,' said Osman, 'and you will have enough to let them carry on at school.'

She nodded solemnly.

'You're doing such a good job, they're lovely children,' said Mariam.

'On a good day.' She smiled and pushed back her chair. 'Time for bed.'

They slept in soft inky darkness, safe and almost happy. When they stumbled down to wash in the morning, Mustafa and his brother were sleeping on a nest of straw in the courtyard. They showered as quietly as possible.

Breakfast was a sleepy but organised affair seeing Rashid packed and off to school, helping to load Mustafa's canteen, then waving 'goodbye' to Zara when she left for school holding her mummy's hand.

In the suddenly quiet courtyard, Osman asked, 'What now?'

'Prepare for tomorrow morning,' said Mariam.

Osman groaned, 'Still over a thousand kilometres before we smell the sea.'

'And board the boat to freedom. No more hiding; we'll find work and get back our dignity, it'll be worth it.'

They bought two big bottles of water, a couple of oranges, dried bananas, dates and biscuits, tins of beans and flatbread. Mariam chose a necklace of golden beads for Farah as well as their two hundred dinars and Osman gave Mustafa his pen knife.

A second happy meal and they left the sleeping house at four in the morning with a package of 'breakfast' left by Farah.

The streets were eerily quiet. In the distance they heard muffled explosions and shots. A fan of flames silhouetted buildings. Osman's torch lit their way but he did not want to run down the batteries or attract attention so they passed between houses in darkness where they could.

Following the airport signs, they saw tiny lights in the distance and then, at the end of a side road, a big, dark, empty space.

'The school playground?' whispered Mariam looking at her brother.

Suddenly nervous, Osman turned off the torch and whispered, 'Sshh…'

They crept around the entrance gates and, eyes accustomed to the dark, they saw a pregnant woman sitting on the step of a temporary classroom with a man at her side. Six young men were sitting on the ground, some resting their backs against the wall, one or two smoking. Their dark arms and legs almost indistinguishable against the tarmac. Their skin glowed in the red light from their cigarettes and the whites of their eyes shrank and grew with each puff. Mariam and Osman skirted around them and passed the couple on the steps, nodding acknowledgements. They did not want to break the silence or disturb the order, so they sheltered by the wall on the other side. A couple of Libyan men arrived looking furtive and anxious. They kept their heads down and crept out of view around the corner of the classroom. Four men crossed the dark road quickly and purposefully. Osman and Mariam looked at each other. They felt sure these men were Eritrean. Before long, another couple appeared, Osman thought probably Syrian. Each newcomer was greeted with a nod of the head in silence. As time passed, the tension rose, people didn't fidget, the only movement had been from the smokers and they had long since extinguished their cigarettes. The taut silence was broken by the sound of feet running louder and louder, closer and closer, accompanied by panting. A mother and daughter, hand in hand, ran to them. Their distress unblocked the assembly's paralysis; the woman on the step stood and the Syrian couple put their arms round the mother.

'It's all right, you're safe now.'

Her pants gave way to sobs. Her daughter clung to her. 'We're okay, mama.'

'Sit here,' said the pregnant woman leading them to the steps.

Everyone stood and surrounded the newcomers; they became a group. Once the mother's sobbing subsided, the torpor of waiting returned. Resigned to their impotence, they waited but not for long. At 5.30am, a land rover parked in front of the school and they assembled around it. The driver stood at the rear with a list calling names to board. There was general relief at the sight of their transport and the orderly loading. It was reassuring to hear their names. They were all anxious to get away from the fighting and felt confident that this part of the journey was reliable, so excitement rose as they passed out of the city and wound out and away from traffic and lights. The sound of exploding shells and gunfire diminished. Daylight was no longer a threat outside the city and what it revealed filled them with wonder and confusion. Circles of vivid green, lush, high crops with rotating water sprays bathing them – alfalfa, wheat, barley, millet and maize, potatoes, beetroot, fruit trees and grape vines – were all growing in the desert.

There were gasps and cries of, 'Look there!'

'Can you believe it?'

'There's even maize,' said one astounded man.

'That water is as old as the oil. There's a lake of it under there. Gaddafi masterminded it, quite something isn't it?' said the Syrian woman.

'It can be seen from space. One of the wonders of the modern world,' said the Syrian man.

'Fossil water makes the desert bloom and fossil fuel makes the planet a desert,' said the doctor.

'And too many countries into war zones,' added a Libyan.

'Libya's the richest country on earth,' said another.

'We haven't seen it,' said an Eritrean youth wearing a red baseball cap.

'It's hidden underground,' said the other Libyan.

'Sold off to line Gadaffi's pockets.'

'No more,' sighed a Syrian shaking his head at the fickleness of fortune.

'No, now everyone's fighting for it. That's why we're getting out,' said the first Libyan. His wife's big eyes never left his face. They seldom spoke. Rocks, stones and cacti replaced crops and pipes, fences and tractors. A low horizon crenelated by dunes encompassed them; nothing behind, ahead or on either side but sand with an occasional rocky outcrop.

The monotony and heat wilted them into silence. Their midday stop for water, food and relief was a desperate and futile search for respite, shade and air. Some pushed themselves under the four by four but the heat of the sand and the engine cancelled the benefit of shade. They did not waste their energy on words. They knew the tedium ahead of them and were glad to get back and get it over and done with.

Mariam wished for their mother's market parasol. Osman thought of his father cool and neat in his shirt and shorts, setting off for work in the moist cool mornings. He remembered the bird song and the trickle of water from the hose pipe over his mother's plot. The sound as it splattered on the leaves, the smell of tomato plants and, in the distance, the misty mountains, studded with trees and shrubs and flowers starting to bloom.

They expected to stop at the setting of the sun but the jeep carried on. Unease spread and people became restless. One of the Africans joined Osman and Mariam at the back. He looked earnestly at Osman indicating his need to pee over the side. Osman nudged Mariam and they moved aside so he could lean over the side. Others followed. The little girl whispered to her mother, who answered, 'Hold it' and the girl began to whimper, then sob. Mariam caught the mother's eye and crawled over to her. She said a few words, the mother nodded. Mariam took the girl's hand and led her to the back where Osman cleared a space and held Mariam's shawl as a curtain so she could hold her over the side to relieve herself. After a couple of hours counting stars dimmed by the dusty air, they stopped.

'Now it's cool enough to sleep,' said the driver setting them free, 'but not for long.'

Unease exploded into laughter and gratitude. There were several, 'Thank yous' as people descended onto the rapidly cooling sand with their meagre provisions.

They watched the others unpack plastic boxes of couscous, cheese, eggs and fruit. Some of the African boys ate camel burgers and cheese. After they had eaten and taken shovels for a walk, families chose their places to sleep. The African boys leant along the side of the truck smoking and chatting. The four Eritreans carefully packed the remains of their meal and washed their hands before settling at the rear of the truck.

Osman and Mariam climbed a sand dune and stood, absorbing the extent of the darkness that stretched around them; the silence and stillness now everyone had settled. The moon was dim, stars muted to a hazy yellow and red. The desert brooded under them. It had begun. They were on their way, in safe hands. They sank into the curve of the dune and slept.

'Hola! Hola! Wake up!' Metal rang on metal, loud and persistent. The driver passed from group to group.

'Get up! Get up!'

People rolled onto their sides and stared vacantly into darkness. The driver nudged the sleeping African boys with his foot.

'We're off!' he shouted and went back to the jeep and hauled plastic jerry cans of water from behind his seat and half a dozen paper cups.

'Water!' he called and covered the bottom of a cup and passed it out again and again. 'Not much but we travel light.'

'Better than nothing,' said the husband of the pregnant woman handing his cup to his wife who drank and insisted he drank his mouthful too. When the empty bottles and cups had been stowed away, the driver saw them into the back and secured it. He then sat in his cab and watched them settle through his mirror drinking coca tea and eating biltong.

A comfortable silence filled the jeep. The coast, the Mediterranean, was getting closer. Light appeared, the headlights of another truck behind them. They looked at each other, their bodies tense, afraid of capture and imprisonment or refoulement.[28] They prayed for their driver to speed up as it came closer and closer. As it overtook, the driver concentrated on the road ahead like a man possessed, taking no notice of them. Inside, refugees were thrown tightly together, some clinging to the sides. They heard groans and it was gone.

After a brief break mid-morning, they carried on until a heat haze shimmered over the sand and their heads pounded. The jeep slowed to a crawl but carried on. They sipped water, tried to cover their heads, fan themselves but it was no use. Their limbs were too heavy to move.

---

28 Return to their country.

They noticed a couple of dark objects by the side of the road ahead. Osman tried to make out what they were.

'Dead bodies,' said a Somalian man.

'Are you sure they're dead?' asked one of the women.

'Course they are.'

A little further on, the truck they had seen in the night had broken down in the road and was surrounded by men, women, and children. Their skin drawn tight over faces, eyes sunken. Some stood, some squatted some were prostrate; silent, waiting for the inevitable. At the sight of their truck their faces lit up and they looked at each other in profound relief.

Their jeep accelerated and, as they passed, Mariam rose as if to help, then sank back. The look of horror on their faces as they passed hurt. Everyone on board their jeep felt guilty and grateful.

That night they slept on cooler sand for a while then drove on through the dark. Their headlights lit distant rocks, cacti holding fists up to the sky and a dry channel of stones and dead bushes. When the sun climbed the mountain, it glowed furry red in a sky, lowering grey and gold. Wind caught their clothes and flapped the canvas. A cloud of dust rose above the sand, whirled and billowed, taller and wider hurtling towards them faster and faster. The driver tried to outrun it but within minutes its stinging, cutting edge of fine glass scoured their faces and bent everyone double. The jeep jolted to a stop. The sand stripped its paint, whipped their bodies, forced itself into every crevice, corner, fold and hair. Sand was forced into their lungs, ears, eyes and stomachs. There was no escaping its fury. Until it ended leaving profound stillness and silence and the desert re-shaped, with every dint or crease smoothed into flawless curves; an infinite horizon of sculpted sand. Osman realised how puny they were. Nothing in time or space. Tiny specks looking for a fairer world.

The truck was three quarters buried. So, they disturbed the peace, dusted themselves off, manned the shovels and carried on until night's cool let them sleep and wake to the prospect of Adjabiya.

As they bumped over dunes or rocks in the night, the pregnant woman bent down and groaned. Her husband held her hand and watched her face. She grimaced and held her womb low down. Their row of passengers swayed; shoulder pushing shoulder. She tried to stand.

'Aah,' she cried as water trickled down her leg.

She bent over holding her husband's forearms. She stood and wobbled. People shuffled aside. Someone on either side supported his legs to steady him. His wife groaned, lowered her back and buried her head in his stomach. A Syrian woman crawled to her as she groaned desperately.

'I can help,' she said, 'it's what I do,' looking up into the woman's face from the floor of the land rover. She lifted the woman's skirt and disappeared. The woman moaned. The Syrian woman said, 'Not long, soon be over.'

Two boys close to her edged anxiously away. On the other side the mother tried to inch away pulling her daughter along with her. Mariam passed her shawl down the truck. The Syrian woman folded it beneath the wife and helped her down onto it. The father pounded on the cab window.

'Stop! In the name of Allah, stop!' he cried.

The land rover ground to a halt. When the driver saw the situation, he walked along the road smoking a cigarette, checking his watch and looking nervously around.

A baby boy was wrapped in his father's T-shirt and everyone sighed with relief.

'It's not over yet,' said the midwife. 'If the after birth's not intact…'

She pressed the mother's stomach. The mother searched her face anxiously. The joy of delivery was stifled by concern. They waited; the father looked apprehensively at their helper. Another contraction and a small bed of red sponge slipped between the new mother's legs.

The driver returned and looked impatiently over the side.

'Okay?' he asked.

'Okay,' said the new father and added with resignation, 'you can carry on.'

The driver kept a steady speed, not too fast or bumpy and everyone shuffled back into routine and the monotony of the desert. They were touched to see the little bundle in his mother's arms.

The sound of distant thunder and muted explosions crossed the dunes from the right followed by louder bangs and repeated shots in front accompanied by the thud and boom of grenades. They scanned the desert. Red and yellow arcs surrounded by smoke rose above the horizon on the right. They couldn't see ahead. The truck accelerated. The stutter of bullets, thump of grenades and whizz of rockets grew louder, more clearly defined. The new mother folded over her baby, her husband put his arm round her.

Mother and daughter clung to each other wide-eyed and the old widow touched her forehead and muttered, 'Soloman was spared, better a story than a bullet.' Osman leant over the side and saw tanks and jeeps, men in jeans and head dresses blocking the road aiming at a uniformed contingent emerging from behind a bank of rocks on the left of the road – two tanks and three trucks with rocket launchers all trained on the road. Their driver veered right into the sand.

'Allah save us!'

'Allah be with us!'

Two of the older men counted their prayer beads.

'The sand will suck us in,' whispered an African boy. But the truck carried on at a steady pace. The sounds of battle intensified. Rockets ripped through the sky, some spreading fans of debris and some clouds of sand as they landed. Bullets pounded metal, ricocheted off the road or thumped bodies backwards. A rocket seared the air over them and exploded in a dune. The land rover stopped.

'Out, out!' shouted the driver.

'We'll be shot,' said an Eritrean boy.

'This is our only way out.' The driver banged the side of the truck. 'It's stuck.' He threw a spade at the man.

'Dig us out!' Another couple of spades were added. 'You and you.' They hurled sand frantically back into the desert until the wheels were free.

'Now walk behind or we'll sink,' he said before climbing back into the cab.

They hid on the right side of the land rover pacing themselves to its speed flinching with every explosion, every new burst of fire. The truck crawled past the battle ground just out of sight. The fighting grew more sporadic, shouts replaced bullets and there was a lull followed by the sound of vehicles rumbling down the road. The truck stopped.

'Wait!' urged the driver as a few men leapt down to run to a high dune to get a view.

For half an hour they hid in silence then followed the truck back to the road and climbed in. Behind them the shell of a tank burnt, a jeep lay on its side and the driver of another sat lifeless behind its window. Along the road, sheltered by vehicles or exposed to the sun, lay over a dozen bodies.

It had all burst on them so quickly and ended so abruptly that it didn't seem real to Osman. Those dead bodies: he wanted to wake them up, stop the fight like a playground squabble.

'They may not all be dead,' said Mariam.

'Nothing we can do about it,' said the Syrian man.

Another man nodded. 'It's not our war.'

'It never is,' said the Syrian's wife.

Once they were a safe distance from the battle ground, the driver stopped.

'We'll break now. We don't want to catch up with the army.'

Osman and Mariam walked away from the road in search of the peace and quiet of the desert to calm the trauma. They ate standing up watching the inscrutable Sahara and its infinite sky without birds, trees or plants.

'It's like creation stopped at the fourth day, isn't it?' Said Mariam.

'Yeh; peaceful before man came along.'

Mariam squeezed his hand. 'Think of Mum and Dad, Davina and Wani,' she said.

'They're good,' he said. 'But not the man who prevented us from staying with them.'

'We'll go back and make their lives better.'

Osman looked at his wise sister. 'Yes, we will. It'll be worth it for that.'

He touched the sand in his pocket. They watched a scorpion march towards a date stone they had dropped. Osman spat out a little biltong. It was devoured in an instant. Mariam dropped some bread which it examined with curiosity before returning to its kingdom under the sand.

Back in the truck, relief to be alive and the proximity of Ajdabiya overcame the shock of battle. They approached the shell of a town; deserted houses, remains of buildings amid rubble, walls pockmarked by bullets. The gate where British tornados defeated Gaddafi was free. It was reduced to its essence: High struts supporting nothing straddling a barren waste; hardly a triumphal entrance to the town. Inside the city they passed a petrol station without fuel, empty warehouses, closed shops and shells of offices, shops, and houses. They looked around in wide eyed silence. The truck crept further into town.

A hand grenade exploded on the roadside; a rifle barrel slid from a corner to fire at a soldier crouched behind a parked car. They played cat and mouse, popping out to shoot at each other. The street battle escalated into concerted shelling and indiscriminate firing as others advanced to join the pair. Women in burkas fled screaming from buildings holding children's hands.

A bullet hit the land rover's bonnet. They all ducked down and braced themselves. Another hit the roof of the cab. Osman spotted the sniper on the roof of a house, gun at his shoulder. For the first time in his life, he wished he had a gun. Their driver swerved into a side road and careered at full speed through narrow streets and screeched to a halt.

'Ajdabiya! You're on your own,' the driver shouted as he lowered the back and helped them jump down before speeding away. Everyone ran, scattering into alleyways, buildings, anywhere, to hide from the fighting.

Mariam and Osman walked quickly on down the street listening to the stuttering gunfire a few blocks behind. It died down and their street led to a main road.

'Which way?' asked Mariam looking left and right.

'The coast,' said Osman equally nonplussed.

A list of destinations was attached to a post by traffic lights. They studied it uncomprehending.

'I think left,' said Osman.

'So do I.'

Left was their direction but not via any main road. They threaded their way through back streets and down alleyways. A woman's head, covered in black with a tan-coloured abaya backed from a doorway in front of them. She lowered the rear wheels of a push chair onto the street. A bag dangled from the handle and a little boy stepped down after her. He held his mother's hand. As she walked, her head turned like a bird at a drinker looking nervously all around. A car retort made her jump. Her son kept quiet, walking dutifully, head down, beside his mother. She carried on determined. Osman and Mariam followed. The mother took no interest in them. There was a market stall of fruit and vegetables at the side of the road a little further on. A large, elderly woman enveloped in dark blue and white printed cotton sat on a stool beside it. Her head and the side of her face were hidden by a white shawl. She was too busy shooing children away to notice Osman and Mariam and when she did, she quickly dismissed them as unlikely customers but not dangerous. The second she was distracted, the oldest street urchin filched a slice of watermelon before joining the others running down the street. The mother had disappeared inside a shop beside a café where two middle-aged men were playing chequers at a table. The men raised their eyes and coolly assessed Osman and Mariam before continuing their game. There was no spark of interest or humanity in their gaze. There were none of the usual greetings.

Osman and Mariam peered into the dark interior of the tiny bar, it was silent and empty. They carried on past pockets of destruction and oases of normality getting more and more weary.

'I'm thirsty,' said Mariam.

'I'm hungry.'

They found a corner café supervised by a middle-aged man, whose sleek hair, shiny face, and rounded figure exuded well-being. Someone untouched by the war or profiting from it. Osman and Mariam straightened their backs and raised their chins before confidently ordering their fruit juices. He was not the man to question. They listened to conversations lamenting the war, complaining of the collapse of law and order, the stopping of the oil fields and the growing black market. One man declared that the coalition was putting things right. Mariam raised her eyebrows to Osman over her straw. Osman shook his head in agreement; there was little evidence of that after what they had seen. To expose themselves in this volatile situation was asking for trouble. They drank in silent accord, resigned and lost. They paid their bill and left.

At the corner of the street, they studied both directions. On either side, channels of buildings flowed into yet more meaningless streets.

Osman swept his cap left and right. 'Which way?'

‘It’s a labyrinth,’ protested Mariam.

‘No one to ask.’

They followed distant sounds of traffic, the bang and clatter of activity, voices and found their way onto Al-Askri Street, a minor road with a couple of parked cars, a grocer’s, toy shop and newsagents, a bar and a café. Cars, lorries and buses rumbled past one end.

‘That way,’ said Mariam pointing to the mainstream traffic.

The sun was sinking when they reached the main road and a tracery of little lights twinkled in patches along its straight sides as far as the eye could see. Left or right was impossible to choose. Opposite there was a sign with an arrow ‘Central Hospital.’ For some unknown reason they followed it.

It was an old, square, cream coloured building of only three storeys with small windows and a dark framed glass entrance. There was a car park and an area enclosed by low hedging with concrete benches for people to sit on. They were overtaken by an ambulance as they walked up the drive and round the side. They watched a stretcher carrying a young man covered in blood being transferred to a trolley and wheeled through rubber flaps into the bowels of the hospital. They toured the building hoping to see someone approachable. There was no one on the benches or in the car park. Under the bright lights of reception, the woman looked officious.

‘Don’t want to try her, do you?’

Mariam shook her head. ‘The place is like a goldfish bowl in a cat sanctuary…’

The adrenalin of battle and excitement of arrival were waning and taking their toll. They were exhausted. They had to move on and find somewhere to rest, not here in full eye’s view of the road, its busy traffic, noise and people. They looked for greenery, peace but the only trees were surrounded by paving slabs or gravel in busy public places. Neon signs outside hotels invited people to stay in luxury. There were no quiet corners; everywhere was concrete, metal, walls, or parking lots. Osman longed for the tranquillity of home, the date palms, rivers, and hills.

A harsh, mechanical voice called the faithful through several loudspeakers set around a minaret that stabbed the sky not far away. They scurried in its direction hoping to shelter in its precincts. The entrance was hidden behind a veranda with three wide arches. The door to the courtyard was locked. They looked at each other, confused and desperate.

'We can't sleep here,' said Osman, 'it's too close to the road, anyone could come…'

'The back?'

There was rubble and rubbish at the back, more car parks, shops and offices. The mosque did not sit in its own grounds. There was not much space but it was quieter and darker off the main road. Their ignorance of city life made them cautious; so many different strangers plying the streets and car parks; nowhere seemed safe.

'Look Osman,' Mariam was holding the sides of a narrow metal ladder looking up to the roof.

'Go on up, worth a try…'

They stepped out onto the roof of the mosque itself with its dome and the minaret at one side. They hid in a corner away from the minaret and the road and slept.

Loudspeakers broadcasting the monotonous recorded voice of a muezzin's call to morning prayer woke them to a blazing sun. They stumbled down to wash and find a café to relieve themselves, caution thrown to the winds. Across the road, there was a café almost full of middle-aged men sipping syrupy black coffee, talking and smoking. Red laminate tables with metal frames and metal chairs with red plastic seats gave it a jaunty air but the screech of metal on the cracked marble floor jarred Mariam' s nerves. They ordered mint tea and flat bread with yoghurt and honey and devoured it quickly in silence relishing its fresh flavour and smell.

'Hello, been here long?' said a friendly voice in Arabic.

They looked up at a man in a clean white T-shirt and dark blue jeans with a red plaited leather belt and white trainers.

'Not very,' replied Osman warily.

The man whipped out a chair, spun it round, straddled it and leant over its back to smile at them.

'Welcome to Ajdabiya!' He extended his hand and grabbed Osman's, squeezing it confidentially. 'Hamza.' He turned to Mariam. 'And this is?' he asked Osman.

'My sister, Mariam.'

The man's eyes sparkled; his smile widened as he examined Mariam.

'Pleased to meet you lady.' He reached for her hand but she kept both hands folded in her lap and simply nodded acknowledgement.

'So, where you from?' he asked Osman.

Osman's mind went blank; what to say? He examined the ingenuous looking face of his interlocuter.

'Eritrea.'

'Ah, tch, tch; sympathies. I've met some of your friends…'

He shook his head sadly. 'You're not staying here? Libya is not safe anymore.'

'No, we know, we saw…' Osman floundered.

'Do you live here?' asked Mariam.

He looked at the beautiful young woman with the straight back, the proud chin and challenging voice and lowered his head, softened his tone. He looked sad and serious.

'My family live here. I cannot leave, they need my protection. My father was killed by a bomb, my brother shot. I am the only man with five sisters to look after.'

'I'm sorry,' said Mariam.

'Never mind me, what about you? Where are you heading?'

'To Europe,' Osman replied.

'You need a port, Benghazi's blown. For boats across the Med, it's a harbour near Tripoli.'

'That's a long way,' said Mariam.

'No, not that far; eight hundred kilometres. Two, three days, coast road, sea view all the way!' The man exclaimed.

'How?' asked Osman.

'You found the right man,' he smiled. 'You want transport?'

'Yes.'

'You have money?'

'Yes.'

'I can arrange it, don't worry.'

'How will we know?' asked Mariam.

'You have mobile?'

'No.'

'Tch, tch…'

'Meet you here?' suggested Osman.

'Never the same place twice, spies etc.' He took a pen from his pocket and scribbled on the back of their breakfast receipt.

'27 Tripoli Street,' he looked at their empty bowls. 'It's not far.' He checked his watch. 'An hour?'

He swung his leg free and screeched the chair back under the table and touched the peak of his white cap with his fingertips.

'See you.'

His back disappeared through the café's door into a stream of people. The clamour of cars, motor bikes and muezzin calls rose as the door opened. Osman and Mariam sat dazed not knowing what to think.

'We don't have to,' said Osman.

'We haven't much choice.'

As they walked the streets, Ajdabiya seemed sterile. It was not just the war, it was as if it had been stagnant for a long time before. It was not a productive place, people seemed furtive, cautious, stealthy. There was no sense of purpose, not even of a fight for survival. It was just resignation and endurance; they were closed within themselves. The war was over for most, only rats and vultures were left to pick the remains. Everyone had their own agenda. No one was going to call them to account. Mariam felt that being Libyan was no glue for these people.

27 Tripoli Street was a travel agent, an impossible dream. They had no passports and no hope of visas. They were beggars at the door of freedom. Inside the tiny office of the luxury holiday business was a cover for the real trade in passports, papers and transport on the wings of hope to ports for freedom. Osman and Mariam had to unload every note they had onto Hamza's desk.

'Umm, okay, that'll get you to the port.' He swept it into a drawer and locked it then pushed the key into his pocket.

'But not the boat?' asked Mariam.

Hamza stood and looked through the window.

'No, it's a dangerous business, costs keep rising. You understand?'

'We have to take what we can get.' Osman looked at his sister. 'The port's a start.'

Hamza relaxed. 'Where are you staying?'

Mariam looked nervously at Osman.

'Nowhere permanent,' he said.

'Okay.' He came round his desk and put his arm round Osman's shoulder leading him to the door.

'I can take you to a safe place. My bike's outside.'

He mounted a Honda Shadow, turned and patted the seat behind him to Mariam. 'Here,' he urged. 'You behind,' he told Osman.

They roared down the road, turned and wove their way into dark city back waters, past ruins and finally stopped outside a deserted warehouse. Mariam's heart sank. He led them down concrete steps to a basement door, unlocked it and ushered them down three steps to a wasteland of rubble and dirt lit by a single slit of a window high up.

'We can't stay here,' said Osman.

'There's no water, nothing,' said Mariam.

'It won't be long, just 'til we have a truck full. It's dangerous out there; police, detention centres, rebels, soldiers.' He looked at Mariam. 'I wouldn't risk the streets. You can't trust anyone, spies everywhere.'

'We didn't pay for this,' protested Osman.

Hamza swung on him. 'You paid for the impossible and I'm doing it for you,' he snapped.

'It needn't be this bad,' said Mariam.

'You don't know,' he replied and left, locking them in.

The next morning the door opened. Two couples, one young, one old, were ushered in.

'We need a toilet,' shouted Osman. Hamza disappeared and reappeared with a dinted bucket. Osman recoiled. Hamza threw it down the steps. The new arrivals looked at Osman and Mariam as if they were aliens. It made them feel like specimens in a zoo or forgotten prisoners found too late. When they heard the key turn in the lock, the family looked at each other and turned to Osman.

'How did you meet this man?' asked the husband of the older couple.

'In a café, he promised us protection,' said Osman looking bitterly at the locked door.

'Anything else?' asked the man cautiously.

Osman eyed him up; a crumpled suit and worn leather shoes. His wavy hair was grey at the temples. 'Transport,' he replied.

'Far?'

Osman nodded. 'Far enough.'

'We're together for the long haul then.'

'You're heading for the coast?' asked Osman. He looked at the two women and young man who were listening to their conversation.

'Yes, no other option, our house was bombed.'

'Syria?'

The man nodded. 'We lost everything.'

‘And the boys. And the boys.’ His wife started to sob. The girl put an arm round her shoulder.

‘Allah preserve them. They’re better off out of it. Crying won’t bring them back mama.’ Mariam came forward and the girl told her, over her mother’s head, ‘The school was hit.’

Her husband brushed the tears from her cheek with the back of his hand.

‘We aren’t the only ones, habibti.[29] We have to be brave for Raaha’s sake and the little ones who will come.’

The girl looked up. ‘Shh papa, that seems a long way away.’

He spread his arms and shrugged. ‘You’ll be surprised how things can change and all this will be forgotten.’

‘Never!’ Swore his wife vehemently. She looked at him in disbelief. ‘And our boys? Our beautiful boys?’

He held her shoulders and looked into her wide eyes. ‘Not our boys, habibti, never the boys. Allah grant them bliss. Here we have only each other and Raaha and Parwaz to hold on to.’

His wife descended into sobs and he held her against his chest. Raaha and Mariam looked at each other sadly.

The girl asked, ‘Have you come far?’

Mariam nodded, ‘Eritrea.’

The girl took in a deep breath. ‘That’s a long way.’

‘And difficult going,’ said her husband visibly impressed.

‘To end up here,’ said Mariam looking at the bucket in disgust.

They looked around the stony floor, to the tiny window and back to the door.

‘We paid him well for this,’ said Parwaz.

‘We gave him all we had,’ said Mariam.

‘We’re in their hands,’ said Osman.

‘We don’t know how long we’ll be here; my name is Mariam and this is my brother, Osman.’

‘Selam aleykum,’ said Raaha smiling, relieved to have Mariam with them. ‘I am Raaha and this is my husband, Parwaz and my

---

29 My love.

mother Aisha,' her mother looked up from her handkerchief and turned her deep brown eyes on Mariam. Her lips trembled into a smile, she had a lovely face, untrammelled by lines, she has led a contented life, thought Mariam. Aisha turned to Osman and took a deep breath. This straight and handsome young man, so quiet and attentive, was how she wanted her sons to grow.

'Salem aleykum,' she said. Her voice was gravelly with grief. 'Meet my husband, Gafur, our rock.'

They shook hands. 'Well done young man, no easy journey. It's almost over now.'

'Only another eight hundred or so,' wailed Mariam and they all laughed.

Their travels had taught them all patience. They didn't talk much of people lost along the way or people left behind; not even of dreams for the future. It was too painful. They were too exhausted for any of it. All they wanted was to get it all over and done with and save only those bits of the past that would enrich their futures.

They cleared a spot in a corner and Aisha sat beside her husband. Osman and Mariam sat under the window slit. At some point they ate what morsels they had with them and dozed. The slit of light was extinguished without hope of a star. They slept or lay on their sides and backs, trying to get comfortable. The hours passed and light filtered through the slit enough to see each other's faces again.

'Good morning.'

'Sabah al-khair.'

They clambered up, dusted themselves off, sipped their water and chewed dried fruit.

They heard Hamza's voice and excited chatter; lots of voices. Suddenly, Hamza shouted, 'Shut up! Shut up the lot of you, listen. You'll wait here until I've got the vehicles ready. You'll be collected from here.'

The key turned in the lock and to the amazement of the six

inside, a tide of anoraks; red, green, black and blue, jeans, thongs and trainers pushed past Hamza down into the basement. Amid this sea was a big woman, in her twenties, wearing a black wrap with patterned panels of vivid yellow. Last to come through the door was a young girl in pale blue jeans with frayed holes and a dark blue sweatshirt that drowned her tiny frame. Osman wondered what her story was. Her Nike trainers had seen better days, too much walking to get here?

The basement was crowded. Mariam felt claustrophobic and horrified at the prospect of needing the communal bucket. The newcomers split into groups. The woman in yellow was part of a group of five. 'Brothers? Work pals? Travel acquaintances?' Wondered Mariam. They were at ease with her. She pretended to punch one in the chest and they grabbed her hands and wrestled, laughing. The other girl was in a far corner leaning against the wall with a knee braced against it. She looked bored. The men settled on the floor and talked quietly or played cards. No money changed hands.

A young man in a bright blue nylon anorak and a pink collared T-shirt stretched tight over his stomach, joined Osman under the window. He kept his head down, studying the floor and didn't speak. Finally, he stuck little black plugs into his ears and took out a mobile phone. Osman wished he could listen with him; music; he'd forgotten the joy of it. The boy's eyes were far away, well out of the heat and grime, the uncertainty. When he pulled them out and looked around Osman asked, 'what were you listening to?'

The boy came out of his reverie and looked nervously at Osman, 'Kizz Daniel.'

'Where's your family?'

'Juba.'

'South Sudan. Civil war?'

The boy nodded miserably. 'Started two years ago.' He shrugged trying to be brave. 'No winners, lots of losers.'

'Your family?'

'The women in our village were raped and shot. The men recruited to fight or tortured. One side, the other side, it was all the same; rape, plunder, destroy.'

'That's worse than Eritrea.'

'Yeh, Sudan's top of the league in cruelty.'

'How did you get out?'

'I wasn't there, they recruited me as a boy soldier early on and beginning of that year, Yau Yau opened the barracks and set us free. Free to find nothing.' He closed his eyes and shook his head from side to side.

Osman put his hands on the boy's shoulder. 'Sorry, so sorry.' He hugged him.

'It was my uncle who gave me the money to get away. My cousins died fighting. He didn't care for what. He told me to save myself, so here I am.'

Osman patted his back. 'Nothing to lose, everything to gain, eh?'

The boy nodded bravely, tears in his eyes. 'Want to have a listen?' He offered his phone and ear plugs.

'Thanks man, that's cool.'

Osman and Mariam sat tight together so they could share the ear plugs and listen together. They found Jovi's, 'Zélé' and lost themselves trawling pop for half an hour before returning it. The boy sat beside them hugging his knees and looking warily about.

After a while people shared what food they had. Mariam and Osman pulled out their morsel of bread and a few raisins. The boy delved into his bag and brought out boiled eggs, cheese sandwiches and peanut cookies. He saw their amazement.

'My aunt likes to cook. She misses her big family so she cooks and cooks and Uncle spreads it round. She feeds all the war strays, me too.' He tapped his belly. 'Too much. I had to get away or she'd have killed me with kindness!' They laughed. 'Help me out,' he said and handed them each an egg and a sandwich.

He tore into his bread and cracked his egg against the wall. 'It's so much better with company,' he grinned.

'What's your name?' asked Mariam and sank her teeth into soft bread and cheese.

'Peter.'

'What did your father do?' asked Osman.

'He was a scientist, working on seed development.'

'And your mother?'

He stopped chewing and stared into the distance. 'She was a musician,' he said quietly. They finished their meal in silence.

Before long the bucket was in demand. The boys passed it with a laugh and a joke. Aisha, Raafa and Mariam held Mariam's shawl across the corner for privacy. The bucket filled, heavy and slopping, as it passed from one person to another.

When dark fell the door opened. The bucket was taken and replaced by two.

'We need food and water!' shouted one of the men.

It wasn't Hamza who stood at the top of the steps, it was a small, thin man, bent almost double, with little eyes that darted suspiciously to and fro. He took the bucket in silence and slid two more to the top of the steps without looking anyone in the face. One of the new arrivals ran up the steps.

'You can't keep us here without food and water!'

A large man stepped from behind the shrunken man with the buckets.

'Transport, that's what you paid for, the coast, nothing about a hotel. We're keeping you safe, be grateful,' he shouted.

'Grateful? We paid, you're making a fortune out of us.' The young man was at the door, close to the man's face. The man pushed him back down the steps.

'Get back and shut up.'

'Robbers!'

The man took the full bucket and threw its contents over the youth then slammed the door shut and locked them in. People edged away from the stench. He stood appalled for a moment then started to strip off his clothes and push them into a heap by the door. He whimpered in horror and tried to rub his body down. He took his last T-shirt from his bag and underpants. Someone gave him a pair of green trousers, a little too short but clean and warm. He mumbled thanks and sank onto the floor to bury his head in his knees.

Water and bananas were delivered the next morning as well as empty buckets. The stinking clothes were removed. By the end of the day the air was stifling and people were gasping for oxygen; listless, sick. The turning of the key in the lock filled Osman with a mixture of relief and fury.

'Time to go.' Hamza stood on the top step in the doorway tapping the key on his palm. 'Keep quiet if you don't want to be caught. Land rovers outside, one by one, I'll load.' He gestured to Gafur to bring the family and Osman and Mariam followed.

Two battered four by fours waited outside with their drivers, dressed in black with revolvers in their belts. Gafur helped Aisha on board. Raaha and Parwaz joined them along one side followed by Osman and Mariam.

They could hear Hamza hissing instructions, 'Slide along, move down, get in!' The other side filled quickly, more were packed in. Every space was filled with a body, twenty-five in the first vehicle. Osman was glad to see Peter and the man in short green trousers.

They sped through the dark for six hours cramped but getting increasingly excited by the knowledge that they were following the sea, heading for harbour. Suddenly the vehicle swerved off road bumping over clumps of grass, scratching through bushes. They could see lights ahead, a dimly lit abandoned petrol station.

'Out! Out!' he yelled.

They jumped down and were herded into what had been the garage shop. A light bulb hung from wires looped across the ceiling.

'It's a long way to Tripoli; dangerous. You pay.'

'We've paid,' said a Syrian man.

'A lot,' added the woman in yellow.

'Not enough,' snapped the driver.

'We haven't got any more,' muttered an older Somalian man.

'You've had all we've got,' said a young Sudanese boy.

'We were told Tripoli,' said a Syrian.

Hearing the general dissent strengthened the group and gave them courage. They surged forward.

An ominous click behind stopped them. Two men guarded the door with rifles pointed at them. Another two, heads and mouths covered, joined the driver from an adjoining room.

'You pay,' said one.

'What if we can't?'

'Your families pay.'

'We can't speak to anyone at home. How do we contact them?'

There was a line of cheap mobiles on the dusty counter.

'You phone, we give details.'

'My family have paid enough,' said a young Somalian despairingly. One of the guards slapped his face; hard, deft, cold.

'They'll pay,' he said.

The boy dialled, 'Hello?' His voice was thick.

'Yasir?'

His eyes filled with tears.

'Where are you Yasir? Did you make it?'

He shook his head silently, tears rolling down his cheeks. A gun barrel poked his back.

'I need more money…'

'You said it was enough… It's difficult, Yasir, you know that.'

'I know,' the boy sobbed.

A fist punched him in the kidney, another hit the back of his head. The boy screamed.

'Yasir, Yasir, what is happening?'

The guard grabbed the phone. 'We need money.'

The boy's back was beaten by his accomplice until he howled.

'We'll pay, we'll pay. Leave him alone.'

The transfer was made in minutes. The rest of them paid or called with grim resignation, anger burning in their hearts. Mariam spoke to their uncle. He was afraid for their safety, told them to be careful and paid.

The three men stood together by the door. One of the guards said, 'You stay here tonight; the truck will collect you in the morning.'

Mariam edged around the counter, could she take one of the phones? The other guard saw her and swept them all into a bag. There were toilets outside and they were allowed out one by one when they needed. The guards were smug, they knew no one ran when they were so close to the boat. Everyone there knew they would not survive in the lawlessness of Libya with its lucrative migrant trade.

The next morning, they filed onto a bigger truck indifferent to place, comfort, or sun. It was nearly over. None had felt so 'in transit' as then, without country, family, work or friends. They were naked, reaching out for the protective dome of democracy – people looking after people. Another truck load arrived to follow them.

They drove all day avoiding the coastal road and ambush by renegades but the heat of the sun was tempered by the sea air. After a long day's progress, they stopped the next night closer to the coast.

Their bodies were stiff, legs numb as they groped their way through sand dunes to settle and sleep. Mariam and Osman were anaesthetised to the misery of the journey. Detached from everything but the end, their goal; a place where they would be able to make a good life and work hard so that they could help their family. They were almost there. The worst was over. Mariam could smell the sea, it reminded her of childhood holidays by the Red Sea. The same sense of excitement.

When the dunes hid their occupants and the last desultory conversation had ended; humanity extinguished for the night. Mariam fell asleep to the shushing of the sea. Osman too let the waves lull him into a deep sleep.

'Almost there, almost there.' Months of tension and agony dissolved and he sank into a deep sleep.

Sunlight, murmurs and people moving, made him open his eyes and reach across the sand for Mariam but her shawl and bag were abandoned. He sat up to wait, the others were sharing their breakfasts in their tight knit groups. Mariam was taking a long time; he was reluctant to abandon their nest but he had to go too. He expected to see her eager face when he skirted the sand dune back to their bags but she wasn't there. Some of the others were standing, shaking out their 'bedding' packing away their breakfasts. Osman thought he'd better set out their breakfast. He raided Mariam's bag, split the food and set it out on the back of his bag ready for her. Time was passing and Osman was getting anxious. it wasn't like Mariam to hold them up. Perhaps there was something wrong, she needed him. He heard the driver calling and set off across the sand. There was no track to follow near the camp because so many had beaten the same retreat.

He ploughed inland and wandered around the sand hills, without any sign of her. He called, 'Mariam!' No reply. He ran to the side. 'Mariam!' And listened; silence. He stumbled on until he saw the truck's shovel and near it, a gash in the sand, lots of little pits, then channels like railway lines, through the sand up a dune. Osman's heart pounded; his breath stopped. Fear built to explosion point.

'Mariam!' he called stumbling on, peering ahead. 'Mariam!' The footprints were not so deep. The twin lines stopped. He looked around; searched stillness for movement, sand dunes for heads, a body. His ears stretched for sound; nothing.

Uncomprehending, he climbed a high dune and searched the horizon; nothing. His heart hammered his chest. He stood confused then turned full circle searching, searching, unable to believe the barrenness, the suffocating void that stretched around him.

'Mariam!' One last desperate howl still staring and his mother's words, 'You cannot find what is not there.'

The emptiness was filled with her absence.

'Nooo! Mariam! Mariam! M A R I A M!' he screamed. She was there, she was there, she was always there…

He waded through sand around the dunes, searching, searching until he found the tracks of a vehicle. Its direction – back in land. Behind him the group were assembling around the truck. He could hear their voices, low, tired, intense, ready to sail to freedom.

'Osman! Mariam!' their fellow travellers were calling them.

He turned back and staggered towards them, confused, lost.

'Help!' He did not know how or what or why. Just that he needed Mariam. He had to have her back. He cried, 'Help! Help!'

They came running. Gafur and Peter first, followed by the driver.

'There, there.' He flung his arm desperately in the direction of the tracks.

'Mariam!' he howled and at her name, he cried, loud and desperate, running through sand, in tears, to the tyre tracks. The driver ran on ahead found the shovel, the gash and foot holes in the sand. Then the twin lines dragging between the hills to the high dune and down to trenches made by a four by four. He turned back to the panting, anxious people around Osman.

'Traffickers! Slavers: too late; these tracks are old.'

He tracked the tyre marks back to a high, pointed ridge.

Dents and slits in the sand showed where they had knelt watching. He stirred cigarette butts around with his boot.

'They got her in the middle of the night. She'll have been passed on by now. On the way to Egypt or inland.'

'Noooo,' Osman screamed. 'They can't do that, Mariam! I've got to get her.'

'We've got to go.' The driver looked around nervously.

'Call the police, get help,' begged Osman.

The driver looked at him as if he were mad.

'Police?' he asked. 'What police? Rebel police? Gaddafi police? You'd end up in detention centres.' He looked at the group. 'The lot of you. Don't want that do you? Come on.'

Osman sank to his knees. 'Follow them, follow them. We've got to follow them.' He grabbed the driver's knees.

'They're hours ahead, in a good four by four not overloaded. We'd never catch them, accept it, there's nothing you can do.'

'I can't abandon her.'

'You're not abandoning her. She's not here, she's gone. You'll never find her.'

Osman sobbed, 'I did, I did. I abandoned her, I went to sleep…'

'There was no way to know they were lying in wait. It's not your fault. Give me your hand,' said Gafur and he pulled Osman to his feet.

'There's nothing you can do,' said Yasir.

'Save yourself,' Peter mumbled sadly. 'it's what she would have wanted.'

'We've got to go…' The driver looked desperately at them.

'T'll fetch her, just give me a day.'

'We don't have a day,' said the driver.

'I'm not leaving her!'

Osman ran back away from their transport.

'We can't leave him here, he'll blow us up,' said the driver.

Two young Sudanese ran after him and tackled him then

dragged him back to the vehicle struggling with in human strength. A Libyan came to help, and they carried him back sobbing.

The engine fired into life. All the stricken onlookers stiffened, fear quickening their pulses. They looked from Osman to the back of the truck.

'I can't go on...

Gafur put his hand on Osman's back, 'you can't stay here, there's nothing you can do. We have to go, if we're caught there's no chance of finding her,'

Osman stared at Gafur in a trance. His words and Osman's silence broke the spell that kept the watchers waiting and they clambered into the four by four. Peter put his hand on Osman's arm, 'on is your only chance Osman, and hers too once you get there. They'll help you find her.'

Gafur said, 'he's right, she's not dead, she will save herself and find you. No good staying here.

'No o 0... Osman stared back to their sleeping place; Mariam next to him on the sand. The engine revved. Peter and Gafur pushed him backwards into the jeep and pushed his legs up.

He curled into a ball on the floor and one by one the rest jumped aboard shuffling around him. The jeep lurched forward. The uneasy silence with Osman curled like an animal at their feet continued until the girl in frayed jeans made her way over to him and knelt by his side. She stroked his hair, then his forehead. He did not move or make a sound. She prised his hand from under his stomach and held it. His body relaxed a little. She ran her hand up his arm to the back of his neck and gently massaged it. His head relaxed and he gasped in air as if he had been holding his breath. He went limp.

'Don't underestimate us. We women are fighters too. I watched your sister, she's no fool, believe me. It's not the end of her. She'll get away and you better be ready to welcome her.'

He looked up beseechingly. She nodded. 'You'll see. Do you

want a drink of water?' She handed him a flask of cool water. He turned and struggled to sit up. His body was weak. He took it and drank.

'Thank you.' It felt like the first words he had ever spoken.

She squeezed his hand. 'You can do it. You've got to do it.' She helped him up and a place was made for him to sit. He was trembling. The older Sudanese man said, 'She's right you know. She's got a chance. If it's kidnappers, they'll demand money and if your family pay, they'll let her go.'

'Where? Where can she go without funds?'

'That will be sorted, at least we know she's alive.'

The world had changed, the desert was no longer behind, it lay ahead, dragging out an existence without Mariam, his family, friends.

'I can't go on.'

'What else is there to do? I bet you planned this together. Your family dreamt of your freedom. You can't let them down or your sister, you owe it to her to carry on. Remember, she's still alive. Your family's still there. Their dreams haven't changed.'

'I can't do it.'

'Yes, you can. You've got this far, you must.'

Numbness would have been kinder than the suspended agony that was Osman.

After only a couple of hours, they passed prefabricated offices sitting on rocks, then hangars and sheds, piles of plastic tanks, pipes, and metal cages. They were entering a harbour with empty container ships – long rusting palettes and a motley array of fishing boats and oil field machinery. The high pink walls of a fort guarded the sweep of the bay. There was very little activity. At the end of the dock a couple of soldiers chatted with their guns slung over their shoulders. Two of the smaller boats had men in ragged jalabiyas and black headdresses stacking equipment. There was a workshop with engines of all sizes spread on tarpaulin.

They turned down into a container terminal and crawled slowly past stacked metal containers and wooden crates to park at the end between two aisles of containers leaving room for the second truck to park hidden from view.

The driver came round the back and hissed, 'Who wants Italy?'

Everyone nodded or murmured, 'We do.'

'Get out, quickly, quiet!'

Gafur helped his wife down and looked at Peter. He was already at Osman's side, hand on his arm, guiding him down and out.

As each person dropped down, he indicated the end of the aisle on his left.

'Behind there, run, head down!'

Peter held Osman's hand as they ran to the end and crouched behind the bank of old red, blue and grey containers in front of a long, faded green one. Two men in jeans and sweatshirts with guns over their shoulders herded them inside followed by the second truckload of hopefuls and two more men with pistols strapped to their waists.

'Not a sound,' said one of the men at the door.

'Move back, get back,' hissed another as the first arrivals crowded round the door. They shuffled back hardly taking their eyes off their captors/saviours, no one knew which. When the final refugee had passed through the door, it clanged shut and the four men lined up in front of it.

'Boat $750,' announced a tall, heavy shouldered man in black, standing in front of the door.

'We paid,' said a Sudanese man with a wife and child.

'Not for the crossing.'

'We did, we can't do any more, we haven't got $750.'

The man's foot swung up behind him and kicked open the door. He grabbed the top of the man's arm and swung him out. His wife shouted after her husband from the entrance. He pushed her after him. The child skidded on the grit and dirt to land by his parents.

'Run,' the bandit yelled after them, 'or you'll be shot!'

He closed the door and looked challengingly at his cowed captives. Locked in their metal prison with the sea of freedom lapping at their feet no one protested. Those who had them fumbled for their phones. Osman watched their desperation; detached, numb. He did not care about phones. When he was confronted, he muttered, 'no phone.' The smuggler thrust one into his hand and glared at him. Osman hesitated; he couldn't face his family, break their hearts. He had let them down; he hadn't looked after Mariam. Ask them for money?

'I don't have a number,' he said.

'You playing funny games? How you get here without family?'

'No more,' whispered Osman wearily shaking his head.

The man slapped his face hard.

'Speak! You're wasting time.'

He pushed Osman's hand with the phone up into his face. Shocked, Osman stepped back and looked around: tension and excitement filled the container. The last leg of the journey had begun, the sea would take them away from indifference and exploitation to a life of hope; strangers, crowded together talking into phones, clinging to each other. He was alone, no one knew him, no one cared. A child's need for comfort overwhelmed him; a familiar voice, a reminder of normal times suddenly became the reassurance he needed – he was alive, he mattered to someone.

Birhane's phone cut to answer phone. Osman looked helplessly at the man.

'You get someone quick.' He was looking around, checking the others. Ariam's father was the only other person whose number he knew; clever, ambitious. Mr. Adami was a good father like his own, a good man. He dialled.

'Hello.'

'Mr. Adami?'

'Yes?' He was trying to fit a face to the voice.

'It's Osman.'

'Osman!' His voice burst into a smile. 'How are you? More important, where are you?'

'Ziltan near Tripoli.'

'By the sea, well done.'

The smuggler hissed, 'Get on with it.'

'I can't talk. Mr. Adami, can you tell my father I need money for the boat?'

'I will Osman, when?'

Osman hesitated. The smuggler was indicating to another, a man holding his phone in the air.

'As soon as possible.'

'How can he get it to you?'

'By phone, they have a special network, Hamza transfer. It's immediate, from family they know the money's there.'

'You have a phone?'

'No, it's the agent's.'

The smuggler was pushing his way through the crowd to a woman pleading and crying over a phone.

'He wants the money now,' said Mr. Adami resignedly.

Osman nodded and murmured, 'Yes.'

'How much?'

'$750.'

'For both of you?'

Osman's mind went blank. He floundered.

'Just me.'

'Mariam?'

A tide of grief drowned Osman in tears. His breath became staggering sobs.

'Osman, what happened?'

'She's gone, I couldn't find her. Kidnapped, passed on, I don't know.'

'She's not the only one, Osman. Ariam was taken.'

'You lost him?'

'Kidnapped, I bought him back. It may be the same for Mariam.'

Osman's crying eased.

*'Has anyone heard from her?'*

Osman shook his head. 'No, nothing...' And started to sob again.

'When did it happen?'

'Last night.'

'Too soon.'

'I should look for her,' said Osman.

'You're a refugee in Libya. You'll be put in detention, then refoulement – that means sent back to be tortured and killed.'

'I don't care.'

'No, you owe it to your family to carry on. You've got to the port, get the boat, Mariam will join you later. We are all waiting to hear about your life on the other side of the sea. Your parents want you there making the most of it. You're their only hope, you've got to do it.'

The smuggler returned and held out his hand for the phone looking questioningly at Osman.

'I'll try,' he promised.

'$750, I can do that.'

'No, no, Mr. Adami.'

'Good people your parents, Osman. Ariam would want me to do it.'

'Where is he?'

'Egypt.'

'The university? I'm glad.'

'Put the smuggler on.'

He passed the phone into the smuggler's palm and it was done.

Osman felt weak but real again after re-connecting with Eritrea and his loved ones there. Ariam had survived kidnap.

The pilgrimage was hard but worth it. He would re-pay the money once he had a job and help Delina and Wani. They would be proud of him. He and Mariam would be together again in Italy and who knows where after that?

The bustle in the container subsided. The smugglers waded through the tide of people to the door; payments made, heads counted.

'No bags, no phones, onboard.'

They departed after reminding everyone to keep quiet. The heat in the container became unbearable. The only light and air came from rough holes cut through the top. They sipped what little water they had. Time passed, exhaustion and heat reduced many to apathy, others to anger, voices were raised.

'How long are they going to keep us here?'

'What are we waiting for?'

'A boat?'

'More people?'

'How do we know they'll come back?'

'I didn't see any boat.'

'They going to leave us for dead?'

Faces dimmed with the fading light and became ghost like shadows before being blacked out. A couple of torches spotlighted figures squatting on the floor, hugging their knees. There was not enough room to lie flat. Others stood, some swaying. A woman leant against her husband's side. A mother knelt combing her little boy's hair. The silence was surreal, so profound that they all heard the footsteps; two, three, four more people. The door was unlocked and they poured out to breath and hide to relieve themselves. They joined a dense line of people to follow the smugglers to a quay stretching its gritty concrete arm out to sea; the Mediterranean, sparkling in the moonlight.

Beside it, moving gently with the swell, a big metal fishing boat was waiting for them. They were relieved. Its blue prow with a white band rode high and proud. A couple of young men ran towards it.

'Stop!' A guard cut them off.

'We load the boat,' said another lifting a gun to his shoulder.

Everyone froze and the two escapees slunk back into line. One of the smugglers escorted an elderly Libyan in torn jeans, shirt and jacket to the engine room. He looked nervous. He was carrying a compass and a piece of paper. Two guards climbed aboard, the others passed among the crowd sending young men forward first, Osman among them. He and Peter were separated in the rush. He saw no more of Gafur and his family or the girl. Onboard, they were sent down into the hull, an empty shell with metal struts like the ribs of a corpse. Its curve made it difficult to sit or stand. Osman crouched on one side. More and more joined him. He saw Peter's pink stomach carefully descending the stair.

'Come on, come on,' the boy behind him complained. Osman wanted to wave Peter over but his section was already full. He wouldn't be able to get across the bodies. They squatted, haunch to haunch; quiet, tense. There were no women in the hold. He and Mariam would have been separated. She would have had the air up on deck, cold too. She felt the cold, he remembered the train, her hands were frozen when they jumped down. Where is she? How are they treating her? Is she with other women? He didn't want her to be alone but he wanted her to be important to her captors. He wanted them to see how special she was, not just any girl. He prayed that they were kidnappers, not sex traders – just what she was running from. He had to find a place where women were protected. He steeled his soul, he was the last family envoy, he had to do it for them.

In the crowded bowels of the boat, he came to terms with being alone and the responsibility it thrust upon him. He had learnt more on the journey than animal survival or geography. He had found his strengths and weaknesses, his core values, and the variety of human nature. He learnt that those who shared his views outnumbered those who sought to exploit them. He thought Peter was probably as clever as his parents and would go far in the new world. He wished him luck. Osman's horizons expanded. He knew he would find a place to do worthwhile things, make a new life, new friends, and help those in need as well as Delina and Wani.

Whatever happened Mariam was alive, she would survive, she would escape, she had the courage and the strength and he would find her through the family network. Everything had changed, there was no going back. His beloved Eritrea was captive, even that could change and who knows? He touched the sand in his pocket – one day.

He watched more and more keen, quiet, hopeful young men descend into the hold, 'nearly there' ringing in each one's head. They stepped over bodies to fill imaginary spaces. Those on the ground moved over where they could. Overhead Osman heard feet and scuffling as more people piled into the boat.

'Move over! Move over!' a smuggler called down. Over a hundred faces turned up to the stair well.

'We can't go down there,' cried a frightened boy.

'Shut your face! Get down!'

A figure in a blue hoodie and dark blue jeans fell through the hole onto the people below.

Osman heard people complaining overhead.

'It's too crowded, it'll sink.'

'It's a boat, it floats. Get moving.'

'There's no room.'

'Where you think you're going? Luxury cruise? You want to get to Italy? Close up, move, get in there.'

'We'll die.'

'You'll die here too. Get down.'

'We can't move.'

'There's no water, food.'

'You'll be across before you know it.'

'Where are the life jackets?'

The smuggler swung round as if hit in the face.

'You want hookah and cushions? You don't need life jackets; it's not going to sink.'

Osman was too agitated to talk. The boat was big. It was metal like boats should be, not an inflatable like he'd heard about. He was safe in its belly like the man in the big fish. He smiled, not knowing how that popped into his mind. Perhaps because he could feel the slight rise and fall of the boat, hear the gentle slap of water at its side as if it were beckoning it out. All was fluid. He didn't know what he'd find when he got out the other side, kindness he believed, freedom and an end to fear. A life like that was hard to imagine but he was going to find out. If only Mariam were with him, backing him up, making a new life together.

Memories of their outings to the foothills and river made him home sick. He had missed the sight of camels waiting beside donkeys to carry dates and oranges to market and the colours of home – vivid blues and greens of parrots and cockatoos, the red and purple of gerberas. The birds were his friends, coming close, keeping him company, even in the mountain. It wasn't just the birds at home he tempted with coconut and corn around the house. He remembered his mother complaining about the parrots breakfasting on her figs because of him.

No land could be as fertile or full of life as Eritrea – zebra, gazelles, leopards, elephants and monkeys. He had seen them all and so many more at the foot of the mountains, among the trees by the rivers. He pressed his palm against the sand in his pocket, he would find Mariam, return triumphant and have a family of his own at home so his mum and dad could share it. That's how it should be; things could change, would change. They'd all be free. The riches of Eritrea in his pocket, would he return and make it bloom, or would he tip it onto a garden somewhere unknown to bless it with fertility? He kept his hand over his left shirt pocket like a talisman.

There would be rivers and mountains, trees, crops and gardens in Europe too, just like his mother's, growing lots of different vegetables. Perhaps he could grow things, work with seeds and soil. He'd like that. He hugged his knees and tried to picture Europe. He'd seen bits in films and on television at Ariam's. It looked busy but organised, purposeful, regulated, predictable and behind it all; respect for human life – the poor, the weak – they had voices too. That was what Jesus and Mohammed said wasn't it? They do it there. He hugged that knowledge tight to keep himself afloat.

The engine sputtered into life and growled. Voices shouted from the wharf.

'Catch this!'

There were cries of surprise as a rope landed across heads and laps.

'Grab it!'

'Here's another!'

A great commotion of voices, feet and bodies shuffling along the deck started up. Osman listened.

'Where has it gone?'

'Ow!'

'You're in the way.'

'I can't help it.'

'Got it.'

'Pass it here.'

'That's my leg!'

'Where does it go?'

'There's a post here.'

'I'll wind it on,' a woman's voice; steady and clear.

The boat shuddered, slipped and slopped free.

'We're off!'

It wobbled then headed steadily forward as it gained speed,

suddenly it lurched to one side; bodies swung one into another. The boat was turning. Osman was kept upright by the pressure of bodies at his sides. People cried out, more in surprise than fear. It was dark in the hold. They didn't talk, what was happening was too momentous. They all felt it. There was nothing to say.

An hour or so later they started to bob up and down. The slap of the waves against the hull was louder. The water was choppy. They were out in the open sea. Osman sensed the vastness of the Mediterranean around their tiny vessel, felt it bravely ploughing into unknown waters but a small boat heading out to sea meant only one thing – refugees escaping Libya. If it were spotted by a patrol boat, they were finished. Around him, Osman felt the tension. They could not breath safely yet. How long? How far before patrol boats became rescue boats? It took more than a day to cross, he knew that. He had no watch to count the hours and would not have been able to see its face in the dark.

The boat rose and fell rolling from side to side, wallowing through the waves, while the engine droned on and on. The hull filled with hot breath and diesel fumes. All Osman could see were the whites of eyes straining to see, darting to and fro in fear or still and trancelike, staring ahead. Eventually the silence was broken by the squelching, pumping sound of sick rising from stomach to mouth followed by retching, heaving and the inevitable rush of liquid into hands from anonymous bodies along the sides. There was no room on the floor. Osman's stomach felt queasy at the sound. He wished he were on deck, he loved the sea. The Red Sea; going out in Yusef's motorboat. Bumping over waves with the wind in his face, beside Hanna, her hair flying free. Her exultant laugh as they topped a wave and how they stopped almost out of sight of land and fished. He caught a big red bream and Yusef took a photo of him holding it with Hanna. He wondered if Hanna still had the photo. He smiled wistfully. That was the past, there would be time for girls when he had a job and had made his mark in the free world.

Down in the bottom of the boat, Osman was part of a wall of warm flesh breathing fear, excitement and patience. The heat, the smell of vomit and fumes of diesel were suffocating but this long tunnel led to the promised land. All these people around him, would they become friends? Or would they all disperse and spread out over the continent? He thought of the desert, the people he'd met, kind and cruel. The paths they forged, not always chosen. How much choice did anyone have? Circumstances, means, birth, dictated so much. He was lucky his father had a secure job and his mother had land. Lucky with Sebhat and the baskets too. He was just unlucky to be part of a slave economy with no hope of a life of his own. The packet of sand crackled against his chest, Eritrea. A wave of yearning swept over him; the sight of the mountains from his back yard, date palms by the river, Lemlem and Genet nudging his hand, gentle and persistent.

The outline of the hatch at the top of the ladder glowed grey and light filtered through to reveal faces, jackets, trousers. The mass of bodies became a crowd of people. No longer were they casting about inside themselves for comfort and reassurance. They found it in each other, they were together. On the other side, a red track suit with white stripes down the sleeves was the first to emerge from the gloom. It hung loosely from the bony shoulders of a tall, thin boy about the same age as Osman. He did not look like a sportsman; Osman didn't think he had ever run or jumped. He had a light fuzz on his cheeks trying to look older than he was. The boy stared Osman down, stiffened his back and checked his pockets as if something precious there might be stolen. He hunched his shoulders away from the people pressing against him and stared at the floor to avoid eye contact as the shadowy light crept down to them. Osman was shocked to see how many others were packed in with him but the boat had got them this far, all the more for freedom alley.

The shadowy light and the freshness of morning in their minds, made them believe the air was fresher. They flexed cramped limbs, bent their knees to their chests and looked around. The lucky ones pulled water bottles from their pockets and sipped. Osman's stomach was a cavern hollowed out of his flesh. He was numb, too exhausted to connect with anyone. The sick tried to clean themselves. There was nowhere to relieve themselves. They squatted in the bilges. Osman was too dehydrated to need to pee. He wished Mariam was above feeling the same excitement. That would have made the tedium of water sluicing over metal and the throb of the engine more bearable. On and on they droned. Small groups of friends made the odd comment to each other but the boat was eerily quiet. An attentive silence. They were in limbo waiting for redemption.

The regular rhythm of the boat beneath the steady hum of the motor lulled him into dreams of the end of the journey. He tried to imagine his promised future – to grow things would be good, everyone needs to eat – a garden, a big garden. It would be different, different soil, different climate. He'd have to learn how to nurture foreign soil, like he had his mother's. Where would he get seeds from? Could he forage for plants? No, land was the most difficult part. He'd have to work a long time for that but he'd be learning at the same time.

Suddenly the engine coughed and spluttered, stuttered to a halt and died. The silence was interrupted by the slap of waves against the hull, the creak of the boat as it surfed the swell. Voices on deck shouted:

'What's going on?'

'What's wrong?'

'Fuel, it's empty.'

'There must be a can…'

'Look!'

The boat lurched dangerously to one side.

'To the other side!'

Feet pounded overhead. The boat righted itself like a drunken man reaching for a wall.

'Nothing!'

The boat dropped down a trough of water, a wave crashed over the deck sweeping people into the sea. Their screams penetrated the dark interior of the hull. Water sprayed down through the gap around the hatch.

'Nooo!'

'Help!'

'Aahh!'

Feet pounded to the side in answer to the calls and the boat tipped again, more acutely. There was a hollow banging of waves against metal followed by a creaking, wrenching as if the boat were being twisted and hammered. Someone scrambled over Osman's legs. At his side men struggled to get up. Osman was pinned for a moment by a red track suit tumbling onto his chest. Those who rushed for the ladder were pushed back by a cascade of water flooding through the hatch, a powerful torrent without end, on and on. The sea, an uninvited guest, coming to their party.

On the other side of the ladder Osman saw Peter's wide eyes and his wet anorak. He was floating. The bilges filled. Osman hardly registered the rush of water, bodies hurled on bodies, the sea taking possession; mighty, monstrous, shaking them up, rolling them round. Green trousers and bare ankles floated on the surface of the rising water. Osman felt its cold slop rise up his chest, under his armpits, over his shoulders. The weight of it pushed him back against the hull. Remorseless, it rose up his neck to his chin. He turned his head from side to side and breathed deep, desperate breaths possessed by terror. He closed his eyes and drew his legs tight under his chin, back to his mother's womb all alone, with home in his pocket and a head full of memories – Mariam stepping out from behind the shelves in her green hijab, her radiant face over the flame of

Khaled's candle. Delina plaiting her hair for the first time. His mother shaking out a dress by her sewing machine, watching him, always watching over them.

The Mediterranean; he had made it to the middle of the sea of freedom. Now all he had to breathe was its cold salt water. The sand in his pocket, imprisoned with him, going down, carrying loss, the good he sought, the good he had to give, down beneath the waves to a seabed littered with dreams. Mariam's bag of surprises – what happened to that?

***

Le Barcone sank on April 18*th*, 2015. It is thought that between eight hundred to one thousand people were on board. It was a fishing boat meant for a crew of thirty. Osman is corpse PM 3900013 found locked in the foetal position; 180cms tall, thin, in a black jacket, a black pull over with ITAOIL written on the front, a black T-shirt, jeans, pale blue underpants and white tennis shoes; in his shirt pocket there was a cellophane packet of Eritrean sand.

And the flower? Osman and 528 others from the boat were given the dignity of burial because a pathologist dedicated herself to recording as many of their identities as possible to give bereaved families a chance to trace their lost loved ones. The field where her initiative began in marquees by the sea, is now covered with pink flowers. Cristina Cattaneo keeps one of those flowers in her diary. It is through her determination that this work began and continues with the support of the Italian government.

# Author Bio

Clare Roberts lives in Charente Maritime, Southwest France. She was born in Manchester and studied Drama and Art at Cheshire College before emigrating to Western Australia where she studied English, Classics, Psychology and French. This led to a First-Class Honours Degree in English Literature, and a place as a postgraduate student at Oxford University for her Master of Philosophy in Shakespeare and his Contemporaries.

She has taught at schools in Warrington, Chipping Norton, Taunton, and Gloucester. Her passion for Literature led her to Warwick University where she gained the Master of Arts in Writing which included three months in Milan working with Tim Parks on *'Betrayal,'* a novel set in Italy.

With her husband, she created a trout farm in the Cotswolds and helped at a shelter for the homeless in Bristol at Christmastime, eventually accommodating young people in transit through the system.

Her belief in ordinary people inspired her collection of short stories, *'The Menagerie.'* Her care for the underprivileged and refugees led to *'The Boy, the Sand and the Flower.'*

# Acknowledgements

Thank you to Dick Hansen, in Holland, for his careful reading of the manuscript and encouragement to expand it, and also to Josief Abraham, in Asmara, for meticulously checking its authenticity.

Thank you to my friends around the world for their appreciation and support.